UNDECEIVED

PRIDE & PREJUDICE IN THE SPY GAME

KAREN M COX

Adalia Street Press

UNDECEIVED

(Second Edition)

Copyright © 2019 by Karen M Cox

Adalia Street Press

978-0-9991000-6-6

978-0-9991000-7-3

First edition published 2016 by Meryton Press

ALSO BY KAREN M COX

Son of a Preacher Man

I Could Write a Book

The Journey Home

1932

Find Wonder in All Things

ANTHOLOGIES

Rational Creatures : "A Nominal Mistress"

Dangerous to Know : "An Honest Man"

The Darcy Monologues : "I, Darcy"

Sunkissed : "Northanger Revisited 2015"

DEDICATION

For my son, whose existence started the most exciting and rewarding adventure of my life.

And for my granddaughter, whose appearance reminded me the adventure never really ends.

PROLOGUE

East Berlin, GDR
October 1982

HIS VISION BEGAN TO DARKEN. He heard shouts again, a man's, no... there was a female voice in the mix, but he lacked the brainpower to muster a care for who it was. Was it English he heard? Or was his mind, so inured to translating, automatically interpreting the German? He was tired, so tired, but if he could only rest a while, he could recruit some strength and get...where? *Ah yes, West Berlin.*

The voices grew even as his consciousness faded. His mouth tried to form words like "over here" or "help me." But nothing came out except more blood—from his side, from his shoulder, from his hand. There were pinpricks behind his eyelids again, moving faster like a giant kaleidoscope, and the world continued to melt away. He felt movement when he slumped out of the pantry door and cursed when someone pushed him back up to a sitting position.

"Come on. Wake up, old chap! We're getting you out of here. Stay with me. My car is right outside."

"USBER. Hurry." His speech slurred as if he'd been on a three-day drunk.

"Yes, straight across the border."

His lips twitched. "Fitz?"

"I'm here. You're going to be fine. Hang on."

William Darcy forced his eyes open, but it wasn't Fitz he saw in front of him.

"You arrogant bastard," *she* said in a clipped tone. "What don't you understand about 'stay put'? We've been looking for you for flipping ever! You're damn lucky Fitz remembered the location of this safe house."

"Hi, little cutie. What are you doing here?" His head lolled about on his shoulders.

"I'm saving your overconfident, egotistical hide."

"Aww, honey, don't nag. Hey, how you gonna get us out of this one? How good is your German?" He grinned, inwardly laughing at the asinine situation in which he'd found himself.

"You know it's damn good, *danke*. And I'm going to get us out of here 'cause, unlike you, I've got my ducks in a row," she quipped then gasped as she drew back her hand, covered in his blood. "Holy shit!" She stared at her blood-soaked fingers. Apparently, he'd bled through his last attempt at a bandage. She heaved him toward her and ran her hands over his torso, assessing the damage as he groaned again.

"Fitz"—she spoke with a forced calm—"find something to check this. We've got to get him out of here. And there had better be a medical team waiting as soon as we get across the border."

Fitz disappeared and returned with a couple of musty towels, one of which she slipped under Darcy's armpit and tied firmly.

"Good god, woman!" he said through gritted teeth.

"I have to stop the bleeding."

"If you put a tourniquet on there, I'm liable to lose my damn arm!"

"Stop being such a baby. It's not that tight."

"Is...too." He was losing the burst of alertness fostered by the hope of rescue and the pain in his shoulder.

She tried to pull his shirt up to see, but it was stuck to the side wound. Looking at it, she sat back, horrified.

"Bad?" he whispered.

"Not so bad."

"Liar," he murmured.

Over her shoulder, she spoke in a low voice. "We have to go —now."

"Chief said they're sending an ambulance from a hospital near Zehlendorf. No sirens. Should be there when we arrive."

"But first we have to get him into West Berlin."

Darcy clutched at her arm. "Set up..." He gasped.

"What?"

"Sniper at the drop. Shooter at my flat"—Darcy indicated his side wound—"traitor...they're gone now. Took them out. Both of 'em. Natalia...she played me. Damn it, she played me!"

"Traitor? Who is Natalia?"

"Wilhelm," he said, becoming agitated.

"That's your name, Darcy."

"No! Said...Wickham...no! Wilhelm."

"Okay, okay, shh now. We're loading you into the car. Try not to draw attention to yourself."

They hustled him to the curb as if carting him home from a night full of booze and debauchery. He felt weightless—like a baby might, being carried in its mama's arms.

Once in the car, there was only silence as she worked to stave off disaster. There was the occasional unintelligible mumble from Fitz behind the wheel and a low response from the woman tending Darcy's wounds with quiet, efficient desperation. He clung to the sounds; hearing was the only sense left to him, the only thing that told him he was still in the land of the living. He no longer felt anything, no longer could see.

"It's the end," he whispered, still incredulous that this could happen to him, of all people.

"You're too full of yourself to die," she said in his ear, grasping his uninjured hand, now cold and clammy.

The car rumbled quietly through the calm Sunday morning traffic of East Berlin.

She looked away. "Can't you go any faster?"

"Going as fast as I can." Fitz met her gaze in the rear view mirror. "They have good medical facilities on the other side, probably better than anyplace he's been assigned in the last five years. Don't worry about our friend."

"I'm not worried," she snapped. "And he's my colleague, not my friend."

Fitz gave her a kind smile. "Of course he is, love."

Darcy's last thought before he lost consciousness wasn't fear but an overwhelming sorrow. His life really was over, a done deal; he was going to punch his ticket at last. He was down for the count, slipping under for the third time. All the euphemisms in the world couldn't soften the cold, hard fact.

William Darcy, aka Liam Reynolds, aka Darby Kent, aka the London Fog, veteran of the CIA, recipient of the Distinguished Intelligence Cross, was dying.

PART I

1

Charleston, West Virginia
October 1980

IT IS A TRUTH, universally acknowledged that, when a young woman decides to follow her late father's career path—especially when her father died in pursuit of said career—her mother will be vehemently opposed to that plan of action.

"Lizzy, I don't understand your thinking. You were at the top of your high school class. You left for college to be a UN interpreter. I thought you'd move to New York City, meet some dashing diplomat with a ton of money. You'd get married, quit your job, and give me a passel of smart, dashing grandchildren. Not be some kind of...*career girl!*"

"Mama." Elizabeth Bennet rolled her eyes and gritted her teeth with the effort of being patient. "This is 1980. Women aren't just entering the work force; they're changing it. There was a Women's Liberation Movement a few years back. Maybe you read about it. There was a song, 'I Am Woman.' It was on the radio, remember?"

"Pfft. That agency is a man's world."

"There is nothing mannish about the CIA. Lots of women work there."

"If you have to be a career woman then, why can't you work somewhere else? Anywhere else! That agency sent your father away, and I never saw him again. I was left all alone—with a baby girl to raise by myself."

"Jim helped you a lot with that."

"Your stepfather isn't the issue here! The CIA robbed me of my husband. Now they want to take my baby too."

"They didn't rob you of him. My father was a hero. He died in the line of duty."

"And you want to do the same?"

"Don't be ridiculous. Of course, I don't want to die in the line of duty. I just...well, I *would* want him to be proud of me, but that isn't all there is to it. I've wanted to join the CIA since I was fourteen and toured the headquarters building—since I saw the stars on the Memorial Wall and knew one of them stood for my father."

Not for the first time, Elizabeth wished for her father—her real father. As a CIA man, she knew Tom Bennet would have supported her need to pursue this path. At least, she assumed he would have. She was only three years old when he died, and she remembered almost nothing of him. Until her mother married the affable, perpetual newspaper-reading Jim, the word "father" meant a handsome photograph in a frame—one that was put away in a drawer after Jim arrived on the scene.

"Besides," Elizabeth went on, "I'm not working in clandestine operations. I'm applying for a linguistics position. It's not the same thing as my father's job. Not at all."

"You've always idolized him, but he wasn't that larger than life man you've constructed in your imagination. He was a real man with real faults like any other."

"And real principles and a real need to find the truth. Serving my country by working at the CIA is an honor. It's a family tradition, Mama. I'm proud to continue it and proud to be my father's daughter."

"I brought you back here to Charleston to keep you away from that nonsense. It's all politics—the crazy assignments, the weird, hushed phone calls in the middle of the night—and not worth the pittance they pay you. I wanted a better life for my daughter, something normal. When you got that scholarship, I let you go to Duke to learn all those languages. I thought you were learning Hungarian to please your great-grandma!"

"Yes, that was a big part of it. Dédi taught me so much, and she was proud when I wanted to learn more of her native tongue."

"But instead of studying to be a secretary or learning to do hair or something else you could do until it was time to raise a family, you go and do this crazy thing!"

"I don't want to be a secretary or do hair! There's nothing wrong with doing those things, but it's not what I want."

"But then you could go back to work later if you felt like you had to."

"The first step to having a family is finding a man to make one with. That's certainly not happening here in West Virginia. And a family isn't high on my priority list right now. The decision's made, Mom. I've applied for the job, been accepted into the training program, and I start right after New Year's."

Francine Bennet Langdon shook her head. "I will never understand you."

Truer words were never spoken.

The Farm, CIA training facility
January 1982

"THREE WEEKS, three blasted weeks, and I'm finally through with this place."

"I know exactly what you mean." Elizabeth's classmate, Kitty, inspected her fingernails. "The only good parts of these last few weeks are all the yummy veterans doing the lectures."

Elizabeth shook her head, smiling. "Is that all you think about?"

"Well, duh. That guy who was here last Thursday was totally hot."

"The inks expert? George?"

"Girl, I'd blot his ink any time."

Elizabeth laughed. "Yeah, he was cute."

"Speaking of totally hot. Check out the guy standing in the doorway. If George was a looker, this guy's off the charts."

"Mmm." Elizabeth looked up, and she was compelled to stare as if drawn by a magnet. Kitty's observation was right on the money.

He was tall and handsome with a noble profile. Dark wavy hair. Broad shoulders. Elizabeth could barely see his hazel eyes from her seat in the front row. Too bad. She had a thing for blue eyes. He was good-looking even without the baby blues. But it wasn't only the outer trimmings that captured her notice. It was the intensity in the eyes. The intelligence. The hint of ruthless cynicism around his mouth. Yes, he was definitely a damned fine man to look at.

"Hey, wait a minute. I know who that is." Elizabeth noticed the unsettled titter that swept the classroom as he stood arguing with their instructor in urgent whispers. "It's Darcy." The murmur in the crowd confirmed the name.

"Who?"

"William Darcy. He's a big shot in clandestine operations—a well-known field officer. He has this ridiculous nickname, the London Fog, but he's supposedly the real deal—received the Distinguished Intelligence Cross and everything. I thought he was overseas somewhere. There's a rumor he's after the COS position in Moscow."

"He's going to be the chief of station in the USSR?" Kitty breathed out. "Wow."

"That's the rumor."

He glanced her way at that moment and caught the two women gaping at him, but instead of winking at them like George—the inks expert from last Thursday—he narrowed his eyes and motioned for the instructor to join him in the hall.

Intrigued, Elizabeth stepped out of the classroom and over to the water fountain. The two men had their backs to her several feet away, giving her free rein to eavesdrop. Darcy's voice proceeded to get louder until she could hear him over the splash of water.

"What the hell is this?"

"Guest lecture, Darcy. Interrogation techniques."

"Like I've got nothing better to do than babysit a bunch of snot-nosed trainees."

"You agreed to do the lecture."

"I was *told* to do the lecture."

"It won't hurt you, and it's good motivation for the newcomers to have a seasoned officer talk about his experiences."

Darcy snorted and jerked his thumb toward the classroom door. "Like those two girls in the front row? If they're the best the CIA can recruit these days, no wonder everything's going to hell."

Elizabeth almost choked on her water.

The instructor's annoyance flared. "Quit bellyaching and do your damned job! And stop standing around like you've got a stick rammed up your ass."

Elizabeth scurried back inside to her seat and told Kitty the whole exchange.

"Forget what I said earlier." Kitty leaned over and whispered in Elizabeth's ear. "What an asshole!"

"Too right." Elizabeth was a pretty good judge of character, even at first glance. She liked to think it was a gift she had inherited from her father.

"Kitty, my friend, I have learned that there are some fatal flaws that even extreme hotness can't erase."

"Amen, sister."

Darcy gave a fifteen-minute lecture on basic interrogation techniques used in Eastern Europe, fundamentals that they'd learned months ago. Obviously, he underestimated either the class's level of knowledge or their intelligence. He took exactly three questions from the group and gave them terse, supercilious answers. Then he looked at his watch and abruptly stopped the question and answer session.

They watched him strut out the door, back ramrod straight, without another word or a single glance behind him.

Elizabeth filed the incident under *Officers to Avoid in the Future*. She already had some idea what type of colleague she preferred, and Mr. Darcy had come down on the "no, thanks" side of that equation.

It's odd, the twists and turns that shape one's life. I never set out to be a spy, much less a mole. The dreaded double agent. Part of me regrets it. Part of me knows that I'll never be clean again, pure again, honest again. That life will be simple. It's a burden I carry now, and sometimes it's a heavy load. But other times, the rush is titillating, orgasmic, addicting even if I can't share my successes with the world. It's enough. I walk around, looking at the bland lives of those around me and know in my heart that I carry a secret, a devastating little secret.

2

Northern Virginia, CIA Headquarters
February 1982

ELIZABETH EXITED THE PERSONNEL OFFICE, pushing the door open with her hip while she lovingly eyed her brand new CIA employee badge. "Oof! Excuse me. I'm so sorry! Wasn't looking where I was—" She stopped suddenly, staring up into a familiar face. "Hi!"

He did a double take. "Well, hello there. Please tell me we've met somewhere before."

"At The Farm last month—you gave a lecture."

"Oh yeah, I remember. You were in the new recruit class." He paused, squinting at her while he tapped his lips with an index finger. "Question about homemade inks, I believe."

"Wow, good memory!"

"Good memory is a must in covert operations."

She laughed. He put a hand to her elbow to move her to the side and let the gruff man standing behind her through the door. "It's Elizabeth...Bennet, right?"

"Good memory, again."

"Why are you skulking around human resources on a fine day like this?"

"Got my badge this morning." She smiled and showed him her picture, proud as a new parent. "I'm official." She turned it back toward her, thinking she might seem a bit overeager, like a kindergartener at Show and Tell.

"Oh." He turned his head to look at the badge from her viewpoint. "The photographer did you justice. Nothing like mine."

She glanced at his badge and tossed him a dubious look. His own picture showed off his Hollywood-handsome face to perfection. "Yeah, right."

"Look, I've got about a half hour to kill before I go to a meeting upstairs. Let me buy you a cup of coffee or something. A congratulatory cuppa joe for the new girl."

"Oh, you don't have to do that, Mr. Wickham."

"Please, I insist. And call me George."

She hesitated.

"It would be my pleasure."

"I'm not exactly sure where..."

He jerked his head toward the corridor. "Come on. I'll show you a shortcut to the cafeteria."

He led her past three hallways and made two left turns before they found the elevator. He pressed the down button and turned to smile at her, making her cheeks pink up, a telltale sign of emotion. A failing indeed.

"So have you got an assignment yet?"

"I think I'll be at the State Department."

"Here in DC?"

She nodded and stepped in as the doors opened. "Isn't that where we all start out?"

He grinned. "Not all of us."

"Guess I'm not a hotshot rising star like you and the other guy who spoke to our class that last month."

"Uh-oh, who was that guy? How did I compare?"

"Favorably. He was Uber-CIA Man, William Darcy."

George's smile dimmed. "Don't put me in the same category with 'the London Fog.'"

"Geez, do people really call him that? I thought maybe it was a joke."

The handsome grin returned full force. He leaned in and lowered his voice to a dramatic whisper. "He comes and goes almost before dawn, cloaked in a mysterious shroud of secrecy, protecting the ignorantly blissful citizenry from the machinations of the Evil Empire. If you be a Commie, be afraid, be very afraid."

Elizabeth stifled a snicker.

"Unfortunately, being 'the Fog,' he's also dull and gray." He paused and tossed her a mischievous look. "And cold and clammy, according to the ladies."

Her eyes widened even while she laughed. "You're bad, you are."

"I am. You've discovered my fatal flaw. I'm bad to the bone."

The elevator door opened, and they stepped into the cacophony of the employee cafeteria.

"Go grab us a table, and I'll get the coffee." He turned and pointed at her. "I'm getting a doughnut too. You want?"

"Um..."

"All new personnel need to be baptized with bad coffee and a greasy doughnut."

"You talked me into it."

She sat down at a chipped Formica two-top and turned to look for George. As he approached with a plate balanced on two coffee cups, she stood and reached out. "Here, let me get those before you drop the whole mess."

"Thanks." As he sat, he fished in his shirt pocket and drew out some sealed creamer cups. "Didn't know how you took it, so I brought these."

"Great." She dumped in sugar from the glass canister on the table.

"Oh man, I forgot a spoon. I take mine black, so I don't think about that stuff."

"I'll get it." She stood and felt his eyes on her as she walked away. He was interested, she could tell, but she also knew she'd shut him down pretty quick. It wouldn't do to let him turn her head, but neither would it do to be rude to a colleague, and a possible contact.

"So," she said as she sat across from him. "Big meeting today?"

He waved his hand. "Boring counterintelligence departmental stuff."

"I'll bet it's not boring at all, but it's top secret stuff and several levels above my pay grade. So I understand if you can't say."

"I'd tell you but I'd have to kill you."

"Then for Pete's sake, don't tell me!"

He smiled at her. "What about you? Do you have any idea what you'll be doing at the State Department?"

She stirred her coffee. "Well, I'll be here at Langley for about another month, doing more orientation classes. I'm assuming they'll assign me to one of the foreign embassies, probably as an interpreter."

"An interpreter! That's exciting. What language?"

"My degree is in Slavic languages, so I know Polish, Russian, Ukrainian. But I have sort of an unusual specialty—in Hungarian, which is of Uralic, not Slavic, origin—and I know a smattering of German as well."

"A woman of many talents."

"Guess my nerd is showing."

"Say 'thank you,' Elizabeth. That was a compliment."

"Thanks." She stirred her coffee again, looking down to cover her awkwardness.

"After you finish up your training, you can pretty much write your own ticket."

"I suppose I can as long as the ticket's to Eastern Europe. But I gotta pay my dues first, like everyone else."

"Ah, but see, you're not like the others."

"I bet you say that to all the girls."

"Ha. What I mean is, it's not every day I run into an officer who speaks fluent Hungarian. Let me hear some."

"Absolutely not." She laughed self-consciously.

"Come on. It's a beautiful language."

She relented. *"It's a good morning. I've got my new identification badge, and I'm having coffee with a handsome guy who has a gentleman's manners."*

"See? Beautiful." He took a sip of his coffee and studied her over the rim of his Styrofoam cup. "And I don't understand any Hungarian whatsoever."

He glanced around, and in a hushed voice said, "Tell me, have you ever considered counterintelligence? A specialization like yours might be valuable there."

"I think every officer thinks about CI at one time or another. You know, catch the bad apple who's ruining the whole bushel." She considered telling him her CIA service was a family tradition, but then she decided against it. Elizabeth Bennet wanted to be known for her own accomplishments, and she learned early to keep information about her father confined to a select group of friends. "I heard you need field experience before you're considered for counterintelligence." She took a bite of doughnut.

"You need certain skills, no doubt about that."

"How did you get there?" She winced. "Wait, that didn't come out quite like I meant it."

"I know what you meant." His smile was kind. "What you're saying is, you want to hear the tale."

"Exactly," she answered, relieved he hadn't taken offense.

"It's kind of a long story."

"And one you don't want to share?"

"No, it's not that. It's just...well, let's just say it was a blessing that came out of a curse."

She waited, catching and keeping his gaze.

He sat back and pointed at her. "That. See there? You've got some counterintelligence skills already with your wide-eyed, 'tell-me-your-story' expression. And it almost worked, even on a cynical veteran like me." He winked at her and bit into his doughnut. "The conventional wisdom might dictate that a counterintelligence man—or woman—have experience in the field," he said after a moment, "but sometimes, I think it's better for a CI officer to come in fresh, without preconceived notions or other agency contacts to cloud perceptions."

Definitely glad she hadn't spilled the beans about her father. "Interesting point."

"Officers who've been around a while—they have a history with people in the organization. It makes it harder to be objective, especially in a setting like CI where you might have to investigate a respected colleague, even a friend."

He finished off his coffee and expertly tossed the empty cup in the trashcan across the aisle. "As much as I hate to, I gotta run. It was great seeing you again, Elizabeth."

"You too."

"Maybe we can run into each other again."

"Maybe."

"Maybe I'll make sure we do."

Time to let him down easy. "If you can find me. I plan to be all over the world for the next few years."

"I'm sure you will if that's what you want."

"It's definitely what I want."

"Well, then, since I only have one halfway decent foreign language to my name, I'll just cop out and say *auf Wiedersehen*."

She returned the formal German goodbye. Apparently, he'd gotten her unspoken message; she was on a well thought-out career track with no time for personal entanglements. She watched him go, thinking it was a shame she wasn't ready for a handsome, steady guy. George Wickham would certainly have fit the bill.

3

ELIZABETH ENTERED HER APARTMENT, groceries in hand, and instantly noticed the blinking lights on her answering machine. Pressing the button, she listened to the latest message from her mother.

"Hi, Lizzy dear. I hope you're out on a date and that's why you didn't answer your phone. Give me a call when you get in."

The second message was from her friend Charlotte.

"Let's get together next weekend for some dinner and a round of barhopping. I could use a night out on the town. You tell me the day, and I'll round up the usual suspects."

Elizabeth smiled at Charlotte's enthusiasm and mentally reviewed her calendar for the coming week. She began putting away groceries but paused when she heard the low, smooth voice with an undercurrent of excitement in it.

"Elizabeth? Hi, it's George Wickham. Listen, I've got to talk to you, and I hope you don't mind me calling you at home. I had to cajole your number

out of a little sweetheart in HR, but I think it will be worth it. Hopefully, you haven't gone on to your next assignment yet, but even if you have, I want to bend your ear about something that just came down from the higher-ups."

He paused.

"Something big. There's a meeting tomorrow morning—just come up to my department at 9:00 a.m. Let the secretary know who you are. I'll leave your name at the front desk. Sorry I can't give you more time to think about it or more information, but we're better off discussing this face-to-face. Hope to see you then."

He paused again.

"Please come. I think you're just what we need. And this meeting could change your life."

She played the message again, twice. She thought back to their conversation in the cafeteria. It had seemed so innocuous, like a dozen other pickup conversations she'd participated in over the last year or so, but something in it had led him to issue this mysterious invitation. "I think you're just what we need," he'd said. Could it be a chance to work for the coveted CI department? Even a simple assignment would look good on her track record.

Regardless, she was going to show up and see what was what. It was flattering to be singled out.

Her mother's shrill voice echoed in her head. "*Weird, hushed phone calls in the middle of the night…*"

"You hush, Mama," she muttered. "It's not even the middle of the night."

Elizabeth disappeared into her closet, pulling out every power suit she owned in hopes of finding the one that made her confident enough to say and do all the right things. Tomorrow, she was going to a meeting in CI.

THE DIRECTOR HELD out his hand and shook hers, holding it with his two in a fatherly gesture. "So, you're Miss Elizabeth Bennet, Tom Bennet's girl. It's good to meet you at last, and all grown up too. I worked with your dad, respected him."

"Thank you, sir."

"The day we lost him was a tragedy. It's good to see you honoring his service with your own."

"I'm proud to do it."

"Well, well. Let's get down to business, shall we?"

"Of course, sir."

He ushered her into a conference room where George Wickham was sitting at the long mahogany table.

"I believe you know George Wickham?"

"We've met and talked briefly," Elizabeth replied.

"Nice to see you again, Miss Bennet." George leaned forward and offered his hand.

The director moved around to the head of the table. "Good, good. Elizabeth, we have an opportunity for you. A position we wouldn't typically offer a brand new officer, but your unique talents are an excellent fit for our needs."

"I'm honored."

Elizabeth looked at Wickham for a sign. He smiled at her to show his support. "I gave the director your name after our conversation. You said you'd thought about CI."

"But most importantly," the director interrupted, "you have the languages we need. In particular, you're fluent in Hungarian."

"So the position's in Hungary?"

"You'd be stationed in Budapest."

"Traveling to Hungary has always been a personal ambition of mine. I'm certainly intrigued, but I've already been offered a job at the State Department here."

The director waved that off. "Not a problem. You can do both. The

State Department's a good cover for a CI officer; we'll just transfer you to the Hungarian Embassy."

"What, exactly, would I be doing?"

"On the surface, you'll be translating: reports, documents, that sort of thing. For us, you'll be gathering intelligence. Specifically, we're looking into one of our officers because we've had some recent concerns. Your assignment would include monitoring phone calls, contacts, that sort of thing. You'll feed the information to us, or rather to Wickham here. He'll take care of the analysis and report to me."

She indicated George with a nod in his direction. "Where will he be?"

Wickham sat up and folded his hands in front of him on the table. "West Germany. *Sprechen Sie Deutsch?*"

"Reasonably well," Elizabeth said in German.

He laughed. "I told you, Director. She's perfect."

"Don't you think you should tell me who I'm investigating?"

"Not until you've gotten your additional security clearance. So, not until you say you'll take the assignment. If you do take it, and clearance is granted, Wickham will brief you. I will say that you'll have an advantage. I pulled some strings to get this man posted to Budapest recently. He knows very little of the language, and he's been asking for an interpreter for weeks now. So, he'll be glad to see you. Play your cards right, and getting information on him will be a breeze. Wickham says he has an eye for the ladies, which you might be able to use to your advantage. Think it over, and let us know by the end of the week."

"I don't need to think it over. I'll take it."

"Excellent." Wickham's approval shone on his face.

"Just like that?"

"Yes, sir."

"You're sure?"

"Absolutely."

"I'd like you to take twenty-four hours to think about it."

"I will if you like, but it won't change my mind. If you'll have me, the job's mine."

ELIZABETH SAT in the same room two weeks later, her security clearance approved, her bags packed, and her new colleague across from her at the same long conference table.

Wickham spoke first, rubbing his hands together. "Okay, Busy Lizzy, here we go. You're going to love this. The guy we're investigating? It's Darcy."

She couldn't hide her stunned reaction. "Pardon?"

"We've begun a counterintelligence investigation of William Darcy," he repeated.

"You can understand my shock. I mean, Darcy has a pristine reputation—"

"True enough. He's been a stellar officer in many ways. At one time, the top echelon here at Langley thought he had the potential to go far. But things have happened recently—events that have made them wonder. Anyone can go rogue, and part of our job is to ferret out who does and who doesn't."

She looked at Wickham, gauging his expression. "You had an inkling about this before, didn't you?"

"I never trusted him much. Not really. But a lot of this came to light after we stopped working together—particularly, after Prague." He rested his chin on steepled fingers as if lost in his thoughts. A look of misery passed over his face, and his eyes filled. He wiped them with the back of his hand. "What happened in Prague definitely makes more sense now." He cleared his throat. "There are some things I still can't talk about—things above your security clearance—but I think you deserve to know as much as I can tell you. That's how I prefer to deal with my colleagues."

"Okay then."

"Darcy and I had been working together off and on since London. We were both ex-military: me from the Army, he from the Air Force. So we 'got' each other. We joined the agency at about the same time, attended classes together at The Farm. When he was assigned the station chief position in Prague, I was happy for him, happy to work for him. We made a good team. He was the golden boy, and I the street-smart kid from the other side of the tracks. But a lot of things began to change when I met Jirina."

"Another officer?"

"An asset. She was a walk-in." He shook his head, a touch of sadness under his smile. "She just strolled into the American Embassy one Sunday morning, saying she had information to trade. It so happened I was the one manning the desk that day. She claimed she had an American father and family in the States. Her mother was a Czech actress who had died about three years prior. Jirina was beautiful, but she was also brilliant with scientific research, with technology. Through her mother, she knew several of the intellectuals who had disappeared after the signing of Charter 77, a petition criticizing the Czechoslovakian government's implementation of human rights policies. Finding what happened to those dissidents and publicizing the government's treatment of them throughout Czechoslovakia was a pet project of Darcy's. He pushed me pretty hard to recruit her and then to keep her in place. We're supposed to 'keep them in the field' after all. But Jirina's goal from the beginning was to get to the States and find her father, and Darcy used her potential defection as a carrot to lure her into spying for us."

"What information would a young woman have that would be so valuable? I know she was a scientist, but who did she work for?"

"It wasn't just the type of work she did. Jirina had remained close to her aunt and uncle since her mother's death, often staying with them for long periods of time."

"Makes sense."

"Her uncle was a deputy minister in the Czechoslovakian government—"

"Ah, so in addition to the dissidents, she also had some access to government officials. No wonder Darcy wanted her to stay in Prague."

"You catch on quick, Elizabeth."

"That family connection must have made her especially valuable."

"It did, but Jirina was more than just an asset to me. I was younger then, more idealistic, and I broke a cardinal rule in covert ops. I began to harbor feelings for her. I have no excuse. I just couldn't help it. She was an amazing woman.

"I was her case officer for several months. Many times, she expressed frustration that the CIA wouldn't get her out of Prague. I tried all the old tired lines and platitudes, but she was starting to lose faith until some of the dissidents she knew expressed a desire to meet with the CIA station chief. That was almost unheard of—considered to be too dangerous for the CIA operatives. Nonetheless, Darcy was considering it. Jirina saw that as her chance to convince him to work on her escape to the US. She arranged the meeting between him and some of the dissidents she knew. At the last minute, Darcy backed out and sent me to take her instead. I had no idea why; he made unilateral decisions like that a lot, but Jirina was disappointed. She thought about refusing to report back to us about the meeting, but she was afraid of pissing Darcy off and never getting to the West to find her family. His new plan was for me to escort her to the meeting and pick her up at a nearby cafe afterward. He sent her in alone, because he'd do anything to get the information she had, including risking her safety.

"I'll never forget; she asked me where the station chief had gone. Wanted to meet him afterward to press her case, and I..." George put his head in his hands.

"Are you all right?"

"Yeah." He sat back up, straightened his shoulders, and set his chin firmly in place. "I told her not to worry." He laughed without humor. "Famous last words. As it turned out, the place was crawling with KGB, and before she could make it back to the rendezvous point, she was arrested—almost right in front of me."

"How awful! I'm so sorry, George. Did our guys find her?"

He shook his head. "We assume she was taken behind Soviet borders and interrogated, but no one knows for sure. I'm almost sure she's dead, or lost to us at any rate. I was devastated, and in my grief, I accused Darcy of betraying her to the Soviets. Why else would he have changed plans at the last minute? I must have gotten too close to the truth because, next thing I know, Darcy made sure I went stateside—plunked down in some low-level analyst position. It seemed like my career was over.

"Well, I'll be *damned*"—George pounded his fist on the table—"if I'll just let him get away with treason, so I went to CI with my story. The director thought the circumstances worth investigating, and that was how I got a second chance at a career—in counterintelligence." He gave her a sad smile. "Now you see why I didn't—couldn't —tell you about how I got into this department. The CI division does important but sometimes depressing work. Now, you're part of that. Darcy betrayed me, but even more important, he betrayed his country by discarding a woman who believed we would protect her. And I suspect he continues to betray his country to this day. I don't know if his original motives were money or politics, but he needs to pay for his crimes. I've sworn to make that happen. You'll help me, won't you? Help me get justice for Jirina?"

"No matter what it takes, I'll do everything I can to find the truth."

"Thank you. I know I don't have to tell you how much this case means to me."

She stood. "My flight to Budapest leaves day after tomorrow. I'll grease the line by the tenth to make sure our communication set up is secure."

"Safe journey. And Elizabeth..."

"Yes?"

"Be careful. And above all, for god's sake, don't make Jirina's and my mistake. Don't ever give Darcy your trust."

Elizabeth covered George's hand with hers. "I think I can safely promise you that I will never trust William Darcy."

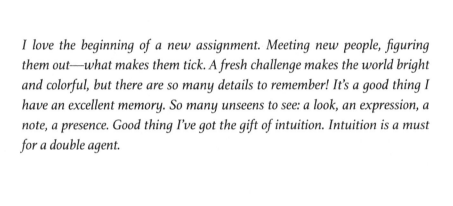

I love the beginning of a new assignment. Meeting new people, figuring them out—what makes them tick. A fresh challenge makes the world bright and colorful, but there are so many details to remember! It's a good thing I have an excellent memory. So many unseens to see: a look, an expression, a note, a presence. Good thing I've got the gift of intuition. Intuition is a must for a double agent.

4

Budapest, Hungary
April 1982

"For Darby Kent?" The young messenger tried to wrap his tongue around the English pronunciation of Darcy's alias as he handed him the envelope.

"Thank you," he replied in Hungarian and put a forint coin in the kid's hand. Still, after four months in this country, Darcy had trouble with the Magyar language and kept his small talk to a minimum. His cover as an American businessman consulting with the Hungarian government wasn't ideal for gathering intelligence, but given his lack of finesse with Hungarian, it was probably a necessity.

The language barrier was one more reason this new assignment made no sense whatsoever.

He slid the letter opener across the flap and retrieved the sealed envelope inside. Lifting the false bottom of his desk drawer, he found his Cardan grille and laid it over a newspaper article planted in the *Baltimore Sun* society page.

"Smart ass," he muttered, referring to the Central European station chief's idea to put the coded message in the society page. The

COS took any opportunity to goad him by testing the famous Darcy photographic memory. Now, Darcy would have to remember the content in the article in case someone referred to it. He was sure state security routinely opened his mail. His pencil scratched across the notepad as he wrote down the letters left visible through the Cardan grille card.

Fine Eyes rendezvous at Pied Piper's gamble. SIP. Dossier to follow.

Finally, they were sending him a translator! Anyone was better than Bill Collins over at the State Department, a bumbling idiot who stuck out like a sore thumb. Everything about that nitwit—his walk, his talk, his manner—screamed American.

Darcy lit the scratch paper with his lighter. He stared into the flame and let the ashes fall into the fireplace until he had to drop them, making sure they burned completely. He washed the soot and pencil lead from his hands and adjusted his tie in the gilded mirror, reminding himself to stay positive. As covers went, this Budapest gig was pretty cushy: a nice flat in the Castle district, access to a phone (wire-tapped but useful for unclassified correspondence), eating establishments and laundry facilities close by, and the best household amenities that Hungary and its "goulash" brand of communism could provide. Even his car—a Zsiguli, a luxury in Budapest—was provided. He certainly had been in worse situations over the years.

He ran a hand over his hair to smooth it and tried on his most devilish grin. Darby Kent was a smooth operator, and Darcy knew how to play the part, almost to perfection.

———

THE US EMBASSY was a festival of lights, the interior converted into a facsimile casino for the evening's party. Darby quickly found a champagne flute and scanned the place for familiar faces. His eyes landed on the ambassador's wife, a svelte and stunning blonde named Cara.

She was hard to miss, mainly because she had planted herself directly in front of him.

"Darby Kent." She sidled up and took his arm, reaching up to brush a drop of rain off his shoulder and kissing his cheek.

He pasted on a smile and returned the kiss. "Mrs. Hurst, how are you this evening?"

"Oh, don't be so formal, darling. Those of us thrown into diplomatic exile in Hungary quickly become a close-knit group." She ran her hand up and down his bicep.

"Like one big, happy family." Her laugh rang out, throaty and seductive.

"Of course."

She leaned over to whisper in his ear. "My husband is upstairs, talking to some boring government official. Why don't you ask me to dance, hmm? Keep me out of trouble?" *Standard Introduction Procedure Number One.* Cara Hurst played the bored trophy wife to perfection, but there was some substance under the shallow veneer. She also dabbled in espionage when it suited her. Keeping her "out of trouble" signaled that she was the means of introducing his newest case officer. Perhaps the new guy would ask to cut in while the dashing Darby Kent danced with her.

He summoned up his most charming smile while he eased her onto the dance floor and assumed a respectable distance between them. "So, who's new at the embassy?"

"All business, darling? Can't you even enjoy yourself first? Or better yet, enjoy me?" She leaned in close to his ear. "God, you look good enough to eat." She leaned back, a wicked smile on her lips.

"Apologies, Cara, but I'm not on the menu tonight."

She sighed dramatically. "Ah well. Can't blame a girl for trying. Buy me a drink, Darby, and I'm yours forever."

"As you wish." Perhaps the new guy was waiting at the bar.

He led her around the edge of the room, taking stock of the guests. State secret police, much nicer than their KGB advisors, littered the doorways. As he approached the bar, a young woman sitting at one end and sipping a glass of red wine caught his eye:

pretty, with long brown curls tumbling across one shoulder. She had a petite, almost delicate, frame with pleasing curves inside her black cocktail dress. She held his gaze with a friendly smile.

"Ah," Cara replied, following his line of sight. "I see my husband's brand-new employee with the fine eyes has caught your attention."

He startled. *Fine Eyes?* This was his linguist? This wet-behind-the-ears, painfully American-looking cheerleader of a girl was his new case officer?

"Shall I introduce you?" Cara asked, a twinkle of amusement in her eye.

"No, let me get the lay of the land, so to speak. How about that drink?"

"*Szilvapálinka*, if you please."

Darby leaned onto the bar. "Excuse me," he said in butchered Hungarian. *Might as well stay in character.*

"Yes, sir?" the bartender said.

"Can you make a martini?"

The bartender narrowed his eyes, insulted.

"Yes, sir."

"One of those for me, dry as you can manage. *Szilvapálinka* for the lady."

Darby glanced at Miss Fine Eyes. She'd pulled a cigarette out of her purse and turned her dubious charms on the barrel-chested bureaucrat two bar stools away. That was the female version of the agreed upon contact signal, asking a stranger for a light, so Darby abandoned his post and swept in behind the man before he could dig a match out of his pocket.

"Allow me," he said, flicking open the stainless steel lighter he carried and watching her gaze travel from the shamrock on the lighter to his face and back again. Signal number three, and they'd identified each other.

She gave him a cool smile. "Thank you."

Her voice was a pleasant alto, deeper than he'd expected, given her youth and diminutive person. There was an innocence about her that intrigued him, even though the undercover intelligence officer in him found the whole ingénue vibe annoying as hell.

With a subtle glance, he gave Cara leave to disappear—which she did on the arm of the French ambassador. He turned to his new officer, noting he had been observed by at least three probable security officers since he'd lit the girl's cigarette. If he was to develop a relationship with this young woman, he might as well start while he had an audience. No way she'd be a buddy of any kind, so he supposed he should try to pick her up.

"And who might you be?"

"Liz Hertford."

"Darby Kent." He sat down beside her on the bar stool so he was facing the room instead of the bar, effectively blocking her portly, would-be suitor from her sight.

"I've heard about you, Mr. Kent."

"Have you now?"

She nodded, and her eyes seemed to twinkle with amusement and a giddy sort of delight. It just made him feel tired.

"What's a pretty girl like you doing in a place like this?"

"That's not a very original pickup line."

Darby stifled a yawn.

The girl noticed, and the light in her eyes dimmed. "If you must know, then, I'm following my boss's instructions."

"And your boss is—?"

"I've just been assigned to Ambassador Hurst's office."

"Well then, you're the new arrival."

She nodded and tapped her cigarette against the ashtray. "It's my first job abroad." She wiggled a little on her barstool as if she couldn't contain her excitement. "And you?"

"Formerly vice-president of foreign marketing for Mackey Glassworks. Currently an economic officer at the State Department."

"Where is—?"

"Mackey? Beautiful downtown Baltimore." He stood, extending a hand. "Would you like to dance, Liz? It's a shame to see a lovely woman sitting here all alone when sad, beautiful Hungarian music is playing."

She stubbed out her smoke and hopped off the barstool. "Hopped like a rabbit or an overeager child," he thought with a grimace. He took her elbow and led her to the dance floor then twirled her under his arm to draw her close.

And that's when the world stopped.

He felt the life in her almost vibrating under his hands—a snap and sparkle that burned, licking at his tired and frayed psyche. Leaning close, he drew in a whiff of her perfume, some kind of clean fruit and flower blend—oranges, gardenia? He couldn't place it—just knew it was lovely. Without thinking, he pressed her body to him, almost as if he were trying to pick her up for real.

Later, he would remember little of what he said to her during that dance. Only when she pulled back, staring at him with a god-awful look on her face, did he come roaring back to reality. She was a new officer, working under him—and wasn't that an interesting double entendre?—and he was having extremely inappropriate thoughts about her. Almost laughing at himself for his foolishness, he grinned.

"Masterful expression of 'shocked, yet intrigued.' You look like I just proposed you do something salaciously scandalous."

As he brushed his palm over the small of her back, he was reminded of the softest, warmest silk. Leaning down, he whispered in her ear, "I think we've given them a good enough show. Let's get out of here. I'll brief you on some of the mission parameters while I drive you back to your flat."

"Whatever you say, sir."

He brushed a finger across her jaw, the barest hint of a grin playing at the corners of his mouth. "Look at me."

She looked up, frowning.

"No, really look at me. Let's make a good impression for our dossier pictures."

She glanced quickly over his shoulder, her eyes widening slightly as she recognized the state security. She looked down at the floor, and he stared at the crown of her head, willing her to play her part for

God and country. He was about to give up when she looked up at him from underneath her lashes, biting her lower lip in a provocative manner. Then her very fine eyes sparked and took on a sultry expression with a dark humor underneath. She laid a delicate-looking hand on his arm and rose up on her tiptoes to murmur in his ear, "Put this in your dossier and smoke it, Mr. Kent."

He pulled back, momentarily taken off guard. Then he laughed and took her hand. "Maybe there's hope for you yet." He led her out into the rainy dark.

DARBY DROVE along the narrow streets, glancing periodically in the rearview mirror.

"So you're the new gal."

"Yes, I'm the new *officer*."

He ignored her correction. "All right then. Let's go over a few standard precautions. You'll need to be careful while you're here. Hungary might look like a cushy post in some ways, especially compared to other East and Central European assignments, but there is some real danger here. Always keep in mind, most of the embassy offices..."

"Are bugged. Yes, I know that. Sensitive information needs to be encrypted using Magpie, and there's a secure room on the second floor of the embassy that directional microphones don't reach. Where are the dead drops located?"

"Well, I guess you aren't a complete greenhorn."

"No, I'm not. I've completed my training at The Farm."

"Baby, that's only the beginning." He merged into evening traffic. "The only drop you need to know is in People's Park; that's the one you'll use. Most of what we're collecting in Budapest is information about economic expansion—plans for factories, shipping routes, etc." He shrugged. "Boring stuff, really. Especially compared to the disappearances in Prague, but I suppose boring is a good thing. As Soviet minions go, the Hungarian government is relatively tame. However, that doesn't mean you can be careless. You're expected to follow protocols and procedures without exception even if you make friends of the locals or start dating some young Hungarian stud."

Elizabeth sniffed. "I know my job. I'm sure the new chief of station will be satisfied with my work." Darby might have been the more experienced officer, but he wasn't her official boss, and she wanted him to know it.

"Then we won't have any problems." He took a corner almost on two wheels, forcing Elizabeth against his side. "What are you doing?"

He glanced in his rear view mirror. "We've got a tail. I'll try to lose him. Where's your flat?"

"Number 4 Molnar Street."

"I have a good sense of direction. I should be able to wind around and come in the back way."

An awkward silence settled over them.

"So, you're fluent in Hungarian."

"*Yes, I am, you arrogant jerk,*" Liz replied in practiced Magyar, ending with a sweet smile.

"You do sound like a local, but that innocent expression tells me I may have just been roundly insulted."

"*Well, aren't you observant! You're a bit of a horse's ass, but you do have lovely eyes.*"

"Hmm."

They rode on through the city, passing old, dilapidated buildings and burned out streetlights, until they came to the stretch of buildings on Molnar.

"It seems the powers that be know you're new here. The secret police are waiting on the other side of the street. Who got your apartment for you?"

"Some officer with cover in the State Department—Collins, I think?"

"No wonder the Hungarian government knows where you are. Collins is an idiot."

"I'm starting to get the impression that everyone's an idiot except you."

He turned to her, flashing what her stepfather would have called a shit-eating grin. "Now you're learning, Ms. Hertford. It will save us a lot of time and consternation if you assume I'm always right."

"How do you know this audience across the street is because of me? How do you know they didn't track your car? Or that it isn't bugged right now?"

"I swept the car for bugs myself this afternoon. And nobody can follow me if I don't allow it." He got out of the car and jogged around to open her door.

"A gentleman. Who would have thought?"

"Gotta complete the suave, dashing diplomat disguise."

When they got to the door, he leaned in close to her ear. "Not to intrude or anything, but I should probably come in for a little while."

"Just how far are you planning on taking this little charade?" A frisson of alarm that felt suspiciously like excitement moved through her.

"Only to your sitting room, so don't get the wrong idea."

He looked around the apartment as Liz flipped on a light and put her evening bag on the counter. "Nice place."

"It'll do. I want to fix it up. You want a drink or something?"

"Sure."

"Beer or wine?"

"Wine, thanks. How about some music?"

"Help yourself—stereo and albums are over there." She pointed and turned toward the kitchen. When she came back with two glasses of wine, he was sitting on her couch, an arm draped lazily over the back of it and an ankle crossed over his knee. "Gimme Shelter" belted out of the stereo, just a tad too loud for mood music. He beckoned her to sit beside him.

"The music will mask our voices—keep the secret police out of our conversation. If we sit close, that adds to the illusion that we're about to become an item."

"Understood."

He spent the next half-hour briefing her on current projects, reports that were sitting in his desk waiting for her to translate, and safety procedures.

"Thank you for the wine," he said as he stood up. He handed her the glass. "It was good to meet you."

"Thank you for the lift home."

"I'll see you Monday at the embassy." She escorted him to the door, said good night, and before he could say anything else, she closed it behind him.

DARBY KENT SWAGGERED to his car, shaking his head when the vehicle parked across the street pulled out after him. They were so very obvious. Since when had espionage gotten this sloppy? Or maybe they were sending a blatant message to State Department employees that said, "Remember, we're always watching."

At least Liz Hertford seemed to have potential. It would have been nice to have an officer with some experience, but her eager motivation had a certain appeal to an old, worn-out station chief like himself. Although he wasn't a station chief now—as she'd made sure to remind him. He was just the number one case officer in Budapest. For the present.

At any rate, her language expertise would help tremendously. He chuckled to himself, pretty confident she'd blasted him in Hungarian with an insult or two. But for the life of him, he couldn't remember any insult that used the words "lovely eyes." So perhaps she hadn't been completely unaffected by his charm, even if it was only an act.

Now, I'm to turn up the heat, so that when I finally bring you to him, he can complete the process of turning you. He says there is history between you. History that you are aware of. Have you been in bed with the enemy before, my friend, my esteemed colleague?

5

US Embassy, Budapest
May 1982

"Miss Hertford?"

"Yes, Bill?" Liz had to fight to keep from rolling her eyes. Collins interrupted her a dozen times a day.

"Mr. Kent requires a minute of your time."

"Mr. Kent..."

"He's the former head of the glassworks company that is consulting with the Hungarian government."

"I know who he is, Bill," she replied, exasperated. "Mr. Kent has been in here seven times already this week. What does he want now?"

"Uh..." She could almost see the wheels turning in his head, little squirrels racing like mad around a wheel. "I'll check," he said quickly and disappeared.

Liz shook her head and went back to work.

Bill reappeared in the doorway. "He says he wants—" He was interrupted by Darby Kent himself striding through the door.

"He wants a financial analysis translated into English. Immediately." Darby Kent shut the door in Bill's face with no apology, completely ignoring the frown on it. He spun on his heel and approached Liz's desk.

"I know he's not your favorite person," she whispered. "He gets on my nerves too, but you don't have to be so rude to him."

"He expects it. So, I have a little problem on my hands."

She put her fingers to her lips in a gesture of "shh" that made him stare at her. "*Bugged, remember?*" she mouthed silently.

"*I know that,*" he mouthed back. Then he spoke aloud. "I can read the numbers on this report just fine, but I need the information in the narrative, and it's written in Hungarian." He studied her for a moment then sent her a pointed look. "But I can see you're busy. Perhaps we can review it tonight over dinner?"

"I already have dinner plans, Mr. Kent."

He rolled his eyes and jerked his thumb in frustration toward the door. "*Out!*" he mouthed at her. Aloud, he went on, his stern expression in direct contrast with the suggestive tone of his voice. "Maybe you could reschedule them. And what's with all the 'mister' business? We don't have to be so damned formal, Miss Hertford. If we're going to be working closely together, you should call me Darby." His lips quirked into a sardonic one-sided smile. "I make a mean Hungarian goulash. Does seven o'clock work for you?"

"We can certainly discuss your report over lunch if you'd like." She reached for her jacket. "Does that suit you?"

"Since I can't wine and dine you, I suppose it will have to do. For now." He followed her out into the hallway and down to the front entrance. After holding the door for her, he stalked out into the street.

"What are you trying to pull?" she demanded quietly as they strode down the street toward the little cafe.

"Haven't you ever heard of 'talking to the walls'? The most realistic cover for us is a personal relationship, i.e., an affair. How can I convince state security of that scenario if I only see you inside that bug-ridden embassy? We have to act the part."

Liz frowned. "It doesn't mean you have to hit on me every time you come in there."

"It certainly does mean that," he said stiffly. "They would never believe I'd spend so much time with you if we weren't...you know."

Liz narrowed her eyes, zipped her lips, and kept walking. Someday the man was going to pay for all the insults he tossed her way. If she'd learned anything in her young life, it was that karma was indeed a bitch.

"So you might as well quit playing hard to get. I need your help."

"A translation?"

"No," he replied, looking off into the distance. "It's a personnel issue. One of my assets has a daughter, a young woman about your age. She's ill. The local physician says she has pneumonia. It's her third bout of serious illness in a year, and my asset wants her to have a medical assessment in England or the States. I've tried to put him off, but he says he'll quit doling out information if we don't comply with his request immediately. I need him. He's my best contact inside the commerce sector of the Hungarian government, and all the intelligence worth gathering in this country is about commerce."

"You'll have to call headquarters for this. I can't pull the kind of strings needed to get her out, and neither can the ambassador."

"Obviously." His impatient tone betrayed his frustration. "The exit papers aren't the problem. With enough lead time, I can have them forged. I'm already working on it."

"Then what is the problem?"

"My asset is throwing a fit because he says she needs medical care right now. Currently, she's living in their countryside home under the care of a woman from the village."

"Where's the girl's mother?"

"Dead for many years, and with her father here in Budapest, there's no one else to care for her. He's afraid to leave the daughter with just anyone for a variety of reasons, and I'm afraid to lose his intelligence information. The only way he'll stay in the field is if I find a qualified person to watch over her and directly supervise her care until she's cleared to leave."

Liz could see exactly where this was going. "You want me to care for her? I'm not a doctor, Mr. Kent."

"It's only for a few weeks at the outside. And you do have some medical training; it's in your dossier."

"I don't care what headquarters put in my dossier. Don't you think the KGB and Hungarian secret police will suspect something if I disappear from my job for a few weeks?"

"That's why I'm hitting on you, Ms. Hertford. A romantic getaway to beautiful Lake Balaton is the op's cover."

"That would mean..."

"I'm coming with you, yes." He opened the door of the cafe and found a small table in the corner to discourage other patrons from joining them. "Actually, I'll be there before you. I'll have the daughter moved into one of our safe houses and pretend you and I are having a secret rendezvous there."

"What logical reason would we have to leave town? Why the big secret getaway? We could 'rendezvous' right here in Budapest." She shook her head. "State security won't buy it."

"I've already thought of that. We'll put about that we have to hide in the countryside because I'm married."

"Which begs the obvious question..."

"What?"

"Who on earth would marry you?" He smiled.

"Ha-ha. Let me clarify. Darby Kent is married."

"This whole cover makes me look like the worst sort of tramp."

"Necessary evil."

"Who thinks up these stupid scenarios anyway?"

"The same bureaucrats who sent me, the heir apparent to the Soviet station chief position, to Hungary as a case officer." He picked up the menu. "So, you better put on a good flirt for me, Liz darling, because I'm whisking you off to a charming little village near Lake Balaton day after tomorrow." He leaned forward, a smug smile on his face. "By the way, sweetheart, Hungarian secret police just came in the door." He stared into her eyes, mocking her even as he smiled in a way that made her insides heat up.

45

"You're such an ass," she whispered, and took a sip of her wine, putting on a fake, sultry smile of her own. He covered her hand with his.

"And yet, you're crazy about me."

THAT AFTERNOON, Liz ascended the stairs to the embassy safe house. She had a call to make, and it had to be shielded from the outside world and its unfriendly ears.

Head down, she dug in her purse as she made her way along the plush carpeted hall. After retrieving her key and unlocking the door, she began to dial the combination lock, a second level of security to access the room. Suddenly, the force of someone behind the heavy panel nearly knocked her off her feet. She squeaked, and a familiar face with oversized glasses and sandy hair peeked around the door.

"Oh! Excuse me, Ms. Hertford! Excuse me! I'm so sorry." Bill Collins looked extremely flustered.

"Bill!" She put a hand over her heart. "Geez, you startled me! What possessed you to come out that door like a house afire?"

"Oh, um...had a call to make. To headquarters." He looked nervously up and down the hallway. "I have clearance. Certainly, yes."

"I see."

He stood, barricading the entry to the safe room, staring at her.

"Well, then." Another pause. "If you'll excuse me."

"Yes?"

"I need to call in."

"What?"

She gestured at the door. "I need to call in."

"Oh!" He laughed. "Of course. I needed to call in myself." He stepped around and held the door for her. "Forgive me."

"You know, you really shouldn't just let me in the safe room. For all you know, I could be one of those dreaded double agents."

"Oh, not you, Ms. Hertford." He cocked his head to the side and looked at her, puzzled.

"No, not me. Still."

"Follow protocol. Yes, that's good advice. Thank you."

She sighed and walked around him into the safe room. His earnest face was the last thing she saw as the door shut behind her.

Elizabeth picked up the phone and dialed. He answered on the second ring. "Wickham."

"Calling in."

"Hey, gorgeous." George Wickham's voice warmed as he recognized her.

"New development."

"Really?"

"Single Man is moving personnel to the other side."

"Asset?"

"No—family."

"A whole family?"

"No, just one person."

"Through Czechoslovakia or Austria?"

"Not sure yet. She's not well enough to travel, so it might be a few weeks. I'm to help him."

"You'll be away from the embassy?"

"Yes. I'll be out of touch. There's no secure way to contact you from Lake Balaton, I'm assuming."

"Hmm. Not sure. I'll look and try to get you a message."

"Okay."

"In the meantime, stay vigilant. It worries me that he's spiriting you off by yourself somewhere unprotected."

"I won't be alone. We're staying at the ambassador's house, and his wife will be there."

"That's for the best. We'll feel more comfortable if you aren't completely on your own with him, even if the other companion is the ambassador's ditzy wife."

"She should keep Single Man occupied at any rate. I'm supposed to be the love interest, but it looks like I'll have to wait in line. As if I'd ever consider such a thing."

Wickham laughed. "You've got him pegged, rookie."

Elizabeth grinned, even though she was alone in the room. "Gotta go."

"You bet. Keep me posted."

"Yes, sir."

"Be careful."

6

LIZ STARED OUT THE WINDOW, swaying with the rhythm of the train's clickety-clack over the rails. Back when she first joined the agency and told her mom she wanted to see the world, adventures like this were exactly what she envisioned. The bucolic splendor of the Hungarian countryside was charming, reminding her in some ways of the rural parts of Virginia she traveled between McLean and her mother's home in West Virginia. There were mountains in the background, farmland all around, and forests of oak and beech in the hills to the north.

"*Badacsonytördemic-Szigliget*," the conductor announced. Elizabeth leaned over and saw a blue sign confirming her stop. She stood as the train lurched forward and nearly lost her balance, smiling apologetically to the older couple sitting beside her. The passenger car began to empty, and she wondered how she would find the villa where Johanna Bodnar had been moved on Darby's request.

She stepped off the train and lifted her face toward the warm spring sunshine. A cool breeze ruffled her hair. She closed her eyes and took a deep breath before turning her attention to the mission at hand.

She immediately headed for the train station, a run-down

wooden building that resembled a fast-food drive-in with its ticket windows and wooden handrails designed to keep the passengers in some semblance of lines. She approached one of the uniformed men standing near the building and spoke in near perfect Hungarian.

"Excuse me, sir. Is there a map?"

He glared at her and jerked his head toward the ticket window, indicating either that he didn't know or it was beneath him to say so.

"Erzsebet!"

Liz turned at the sound of a woman calling her Hungarian name and saw Cara Hurst, the US ambassador's wife, about twenty yards away, waving her hand like a beauty queen. Darby Kent stood beside her, hands in his pockets and his typical scowl in place. With a world-weary sigh, Liz joined them.

"Darling!" Mrs. Hurst greeted her in German. "How was your trip? It must have been very trying. You look a mess. Doesn't she look a mess, Mr. Kent?"

Liz looked down at her wrinkled skirt and fought the urge to step away as she felt Cara's hand try to smooth down her wind-blown hair. She glanced up at Darby and saw him slip into Ogling Admirer mode in a fraction of a second. He smiled, and damned if it didn't make her heart speed up. Liz hated him for that.

"I think she looks lovely. Welcome to Szigliget, Liz." He took her bag and her elbow as he led her away. "The car is this way." He kept a proprietary arm around her, opening the back car door when Cara slid into the front seat. Liz smiled, imagining the elegant ambassador's wife calling, "Shotgun!" so she could sit beside him.

"Is Johanna at this Alsómező house you mentioned?"

"Yes," Darby replied. "They brought her in yesterday."

"Poor, dear thing," Cara intoned without any real sympathy. "Such a pretty girl. So pitiful."

"Someone will have to escort her to the States when she's well enough to travel."

Elizabeth was silent then, absorbing that piece of information. After a minute or two, she found herself taking in the picturesque village with its red-roofed buildings and the wide brick on the gateposts and some of the houses. A church stood proudly on a knoll at the edge of town; its steeple reaching toward the heavens as if to point the way to God.

They turned by the church and drove a couple more blocks to a golden-colored house with ivory trim, Baroque style, with a black iron fence around it. The two-story structure had an understated elegance: an orderly garden in the front, a small porch with rocking chairs, and drapes drawn to hide the rooms of the house from prying eyes. A wooden plaque carved into a rowan tree adorned the brick post next to the street.

"And here we are—Alsómező, the ambassador's little vacation house." Cara Bingley Hurst opened the gate and stepped through without waiting for the rest of the party.

Darby reached to open Liz's car door, only to see she'd already done it herself. Glancing up and down the street, he took her elbow and steered her away from the car. "I'll get your bags."

He led her up the stairs to her room, setting the suitcase and medical bag inside the door and staring at her, hands in his pockets.

She indicated the door with a nod of her head. "Guess I should see to my patient."

"Of course." He bent over for the medical bag. "Follow me." He knocked gently on the door across the hall and called out, "Miss Bodnar? I've brought your nurse."

"I'm not a nurse, Darby," she hissed.

"You are to her. She won't know the difference anyway."

Liz rolled her eyes. He opened the door and held it so she could enter. "Johanna, this is Erzsebet. She'll be taking care of you while you're here."

The young woman lying on the bed forced a tired smile, followed by a cough. She tried to push herself into a sitting position.

Liz stepped forward, pulling a chair up to Johanna's bedside. She offered her hand. "It's good to meet you," she said in Hungarian.

"Thank you for coming," Johanna replied. Liz assessed the young woman's appearance. She was beautiful in a frail, china-doll way:

light brown hair, sad blue-green eyes the color of the ocean, and skin so pale as to look almost translucent.

Darby quietly slipped from the room as Liz adjusted the covers around Johanna and reached into the medical bag he had left her. "Let's see." She took out a stethoscope. "That's quite a cough you've got there."

"Where did Mr. Kent find you? Your Hungarian is very good." A tiny smile crept around her lips. "And his is not."

Liz laughed.

Johanna's smile grew. "So how did the two of you ever begin a conversation?"

"I work as a translator. I'm not actually a nurse, but I took some medical training back at home, so I guess I was the best choice he knew."

"Where is your home?"

Liz knew better than to give her too much information, but telling her something vaguely correct would prevent having to remember a lie later on. "Washington, DC."

"The US?" Johanna perked up. "Tell me about it. I will go there. At least I think I will go. When Papa and Mr. Kent find a doctor."

Liz put the stethoscope to her back under her gown. "Deep breaths."

Johanna took two before she coughed again. Liz reached for a glass of water and handed it to her. "Here."

"Thank you." She leaned back and closed her eyes. "So, tell me all about Washington."

Liz spent the next several minutes telling stories about life in the US capital—the food, the housing, and all the things to see there—while Johanna sat enthralled, a dreamy smile playing upon her lips.

"So at one end, we have the Washington Monument—for our first president, George Washington—and at the other is the Lincoln Memorial. That one is for Abraham Lincoln, who was president during our Civil War..." Liz noticed Johanna had slipped into an uneasy slumber, her breathing shallow but no longer labored. Quietly, so as not to disturb her, Liz placed her stethoscope back in the medical bag and slipped across the hall to her own room to clean up and get ready for dinner.

IN THE EVENING, Liz returned downstairs to find a miniature dinner party in progress. Cara had her arm linked with Darby Kent's and was laughing and speaking with the other guests in rapid German. When Liz entered, Darby's eyes immediately sought her out. Extricating himself from the ambassador's wife, he joined her, picking up a glass of wine en route. He sidled up next to her, leaning close to her ear to murmur, "Some of Cara's guests are suspected police informants. We'll have to keep to the script. So suit up, Liz Hertford, you're my paramour for the evening."

"You might want to keep Cara Hurst at arm's length then."

"I only have eyes for you, Liz darling." He gave her a shadow of a smile and leaned over to kiss her temple. "How's Johanna?"

"Still sleeping. I gave her some of her meds, listened to her lungs. There's definitely some rattle in there."

"What do you think is wrong?"

"I don't know—for the umpteenth time, I'm no doctor—but if I had to hazard a guess, either she's never gotten rid of the first infection, or something's keeping her from fighting it off. Autoimmune disorder, maybe? I know we could get her better care in Budapest."

"My colleague is"—he nodded at the man passing by them on the way to the sideboard—"reluctant to admit her to the state-run hospital," he whispered in her ear. "He fears discovery and the possibility she will be used as leverage. Now, giggle for me."

"I beg your pardon?"

"It's cute when you do that 'I'm so offended' bit, but you should probably act a little more receptive by now. So, giggle, my dear, and show our guests that you like me."

Elizabeth pinched his arm as she complied and whispered back to him. "Will we be watched the whole time we're here?"

"Yes and no. There may be a state police presence on and off for the next couple of days. Cara leaving the day after tomorrow should draw most of them off."

"Speaking of..."

Cara called across the room. "Liz darling. Come meet our guests." She turned back to the local couple she'd engaged in conversation. "She's simply marvelous—you wouldn't believe it. Public university, yet her Hungarian is almost flawless. My husband says he just can't do without her, and here Darby has spirited her away from her duties for a frolic in the countryside."

Liz narrowed her eyes so that only Darby could see her expression. He shrugged slightly. Resigned, she started across the room but halted when she saw a handsome man, who was not the ambassador, enter and kiss Cara's cheek. There was a quick embrace and Cara whispered something in his ear, which caused him to turn around and spear Liz with a curious look. His face broke into an open, friendly smile, beckoning her forward, and he held out his hand as she approached the group.

"You must be Liz." He took her hand in both of his.

"I am."

"It is wonderful to meet you!"

"I'm glad. And you are...?"

Cara made the introduction. "This is my brother, Charles Bingley. A bit of a shiftless sort, but we love him anyway."

Charles let out a good-natured laugh. "Aw, Cara. I'm not really lazy. I'm writing the 'Great American Novel.'"

"You're writing the 'Great American Novel'—in Hungary?" Liz asked with a smile.

"In Hungary, Austria, Timbuktu—wherever my feet and my brother-in-law's free room and board take me. The world is my home." He spread his arms wide and winked at Liz. "Think I'll go clean up, okay, Cara?"

Cara had started another conversation and waved him away impatiently. After he left, Liz, realizing he might not know which room she herself was in and not wanting him to stumble on their secret guest, followed. She stopped when she heard hushed voices. Charles had apparently found Johanna Bodnar.

Liz panicked. No one was supposed to know Johanna was at Alsómező. She turned around sharply to ask Darby how they should handle it and bumped straight into him.

"Oof." He put his hands at her elbows to steady her.

"Cara's brother just found Johanna."

"I know."

"What do we do?"

"Nothing."

"Nothing? She's in hiding."

"It's fine."

"Fine?" Liz's voice ramped up.

"Well, it's not ideal for a variety of reasons, but..."

Charles stuck his head out the door and beckoned them inside.

"Don't worry, Liz. I know better than to talk out of school when my brother-in-law, the US ambassador, has a houseguest hidden upstairs. Johanna's secret is safe with me. We've been having a nice little chat." He reached over and patted her hand, a genuine smile on his face. She blushed and looked down at the coverlet.

Darby frowned.

"If there's anything I can do to help—medicine I can bring, people I can contact—let me know." Charles stood, and the two men exchanged a look. Liz felt a rising panic again. Would Darby betray his asset—and his asset's daughter? And was Charles Bingley what he seemed—the ambassador's carefree brother-in-law? Or was he something else entirely?

7

"LEAN FORWARD," Liz said while Johanna obediently covered her eyes with her hands and put her head over the kitchen sink. Liz rinsed the color from her patient's newly cut hair—part of Johanna's disguise for the upcoming journey. The last few days, Johanna had slept a lot, but she was starting to look better. There was a slight pinkness in her cheeks and a brightness in her eyes. The cough was better too.

"I practice English now, okay?"

"Okay," Liz answered.

"It was so good of Ambassador Hurst to allow me recuperate in his home, and his wife here to welcome me. And I enjoy getting to know you better, Erzsebet. How smart Mr. Kent is to bring you! You make my stay much more comfortable."

"I'm not sure if it's my nursing or the fresh fruit and vegetables Charles Bingley keeps foisting on you."

Johanna smiled. "He is kind, yes?"

"I think he might be infatuated with you."

"What does that mean—infatuated?" Johanna had some rudimentary knowledge of English, but they both knew she'd need more when she got to the West.

"Infatuated—um, intrigued..."

"Oh." Johanna blushed, something she did frequently when Charles Bingley was mentioned. Reverting back to her native tongue, she said, "Oh, I...no. He is...kind to me."

"He looks pretty infatuated to me." She brought Johanna's head up and towel-dried her hair. "Just comb the tangles out and we'll let it dry. I wish we had hair conditioner."

Johanna looked at her with a confused expression.

"Oh, um...to put on after the shampoo to help with tangles."

"Ah, yes. That is not used much here." Johanna reached for a comb. "It is quiet in the house today."

"I kind of like it. And I'm sure Cara Hurst was glad to go back to Budapest."

"Truly? I thought she seemed sad to leave."

"Perhaps she's only sad because she didn't want to leave Darby's bed." Liz glanced up at Johanna's furrowed brow. "I'll bet she wished you and me and every other female who entered the house miles away from him." Liz collected the towels they'd used into a pile. "I saw her leaving his room the night before she left for Budapest."

Johanna's eyes went wide.

"Mm-hmm." Liz tried to act nonchalant, but the little episode she witnessed had disturbed her. "I was in the bathroom right before dawn. I heard voices coming from his room—hers, sounding distressed—his was stern, angry. When I was in the hall, I saw her. She left the room in a rush, but then she stood outside the closed door with her forehead resting against it. I was baffled. She's always so haughty, but she seemed—I don't know—dejected maybe? I almost felt sorry for her."

"Poor Cara."

"Then she turned and saw me watching her. Put that smug expression right back on her face and stalked off. She's probably thinking I'll tell her husband. Like I care if she throws herself at Darby Kent." Liz shrugged one shoulder. "No skin off my nose," she muttered.

"Maybe I cannot blame her. Mr. Kent is a handsome man." An impish smile crossed Johanna's face, making Liz laugh out loud. Now that Johanna was feeling better, little sparks of mischief sometimes escaped her. She had a sharp wit softened by kindness, and Liz had grown quite fond of her.

"Are you ready to try a walk by the lake today?"

"Yes, I am."

"Let's don your hat and spectacles then," she said, handing Johanna the rest of her disguise: a floppy hat and sunglasses brought from Liz's apartment in Budapest.

Darby Kent met them in the vestibule. "Where are you two going?" he demanded, causing Liz to prickle with annoyance.

"For a walk. Johanna needs some air and sunshine. Don't worry, Mom, she's in disguise, and we're just walking down to the lake and back."

"I'll escort you."

"Completely unnecessary."

"Nevertheless, I'm coming with you."

"Suit yourself."

They started off toward the lake and met Charles Bingley about halfway there.

"Good morning, ladies. Darby."

"Charles." Darby looked back and forth between Johanna and Bingley, his eyes narrowing in suspicion.

"We're taking some fresh air. Care to join us?" Liz turned her back deliberately on Darby and gave Charles an inviting smile.

"We need to get off the street," Darby interjected. "It's too conspicuous."

"Yes, definitely." Charles looked from Johanna to answer Liz's question. "Louis has a sailboat at the private dock. We should go sailing."

Liz looked back at Darby. "I don't know. The motion might make Johanna—"

"Yes, we go to sail! I have not sailed in long time." Johanna's eyes were bright. "I want to go."

"I don't know if sailing is any less conspicuous than strolling down the street in front of everyone." Darby folded his arms, his eyes taking in the terrain around them.

"It's got to be better than standing around in this stupid manner," Charles chimed in.

Liz laughed. "Right you are. You know, I've never been sailing."

Darby perked up. "Never?"

She shook her head.

"Then we must teach you." His enthusiasm for the outing picked up suddenly. "You need to learn."

"I'm not so sure about that. When would I need to sail anything?"

He leaned down and whispered in her ear, "Spy Rule Number Twelve: Never turn down the opportunity to learn a new skill."

Liz shivered.

He rubbed the goose bumps on her arm, a shadow of a grin moving across his face. "Don't be a scaredy-cat."

"I'm not."

"What's the matter? Can't you swim?"

"Yes, I can swim! Very well, thank you."

"You seem nervous," he goaded her.

"Am not."

"Are so."

"Am—"

"Cut it out, you two. Let's go." Charles held out his arm to Johanna and led the way. Liz and Darby had no choice but to fall in behind.

LIZ SLOWED her steps when Johanna became winded. The waves of the lake lapped up against the rocks to their left. To their right, a ring of trees and a battered park bench beckoned. Just behind them, Darby and Charles worked on readying the boat. Liz took Johanna's elbow and pointed, and they stopped for a rest. Johanna sat down, breathing in deeply—without coughing, Liz noted, which was an improvement.

Johanna looked down at her hands, resting in her lap. "Cara's brother, he is so..." She fished for the word in English before giving up and reverting back to Hungarian. "*Lovagias.*"

"Gallant? Yes, I suppose he is. And handsome, which a man should be if at all possible."

Johanna blushed. "America must be full of handsome men."

"If only it were so."

"They are all handsome in movies."

"That's movies, though, not real life."

"I guess you are right."

"You haven't met my annoying colleague at the embassy yet, have you?"

A laugh bubbled out, and Johanna covered it with her hand. "No, but I hear you speak enough to understand that it is no matter how he looks; he makes you...annoyed. Is that how you say it?"

"That's how I'd say it."

"Can you explain something?"

"I'll try."

"I think about what you say this morning. Cara, she is married, yes?"

"Yes, she is."

"I hear that all Americans are...hmm...most have open marriage. They do not honor a marriage vow. Now, I am adult. I do not believe such things, but if Cara and Mr. Kent are...then perhaps..."

"No, of course not. I mean adultery happens, but it's not at all respectable. You know how that goes. I'm sure those things happen in Hungary too."

Johanna shrugged. "I know nothing about it. I am a sheltered girl. My father made it so."

Charles approached them. "Are you ready for an adventure?"

"Yes, definitely!" Popping up from her bench, Johanna took a step toward him and tripped over a tree root.

"Easy there." Charles caught her arm and steadied her, and they shared a moment intimate enough to compel Liz to look away. She bit her lip to hide a smile, one that truly disappeared when she saw Darby frowning at them.

"Stick in the mud. Hypocrite," she muttered under her breath.

"I WISH I spent more time on the lake when I was a child," Johanna commented. "See, my mother died. I was four, and after, Apa and I spend most of our time in Budapest. I think it is lonely for him to be here without her. My mother was from the Balaton, but we never come back—not even for holidays."

"It must have been rough." Charles put a guiding hand on hers. She was standing next to him in the stern pulpit, her hands on the wheel. He called out, "Ready, Liz?"

Liz looked back from her station by the winch. "Aye, aye, Captain."

"Hoist the main sail."

She began turning the crank, raising the sail. At first, it went quickly, but as the sail rose and caught the wind, the crank became harder and harder to turn.

"Give her a hand, Darby."

Darby appeared right behind her, his eyes unreadable behind sunglasses, a small smile playing about his lips. "Aye, aye, Captain."

"I can do it."

"Not before we get blown off course. I don't mind helping. It's the first time you've been sailing, and the fact that men have better upper body strength is just a result of biomechanics, not an evil plot to disempower you."

"I have plenty of upper body strength. I swim, and I've trained in self-defense techniques. I've even been known to lift weights when I was back home."

"A woman of many accomplishments." Darby's eyes raked over her, his chin tilting up and down to draw attention to his notice of her. "Nothing wanting in your upper body, Liz."

"Say any kind of stupid misogynistic remark you like. My courage rises with every attempt to intimidate me."

"No doubt." He nudged her aside and cranked the sail up the last couple of feet. "You did a fine job—for a girl." He tossed a grin back at Charles while Liz bumped him with her hip and took her station back.

"Women today are so much more accomplished than they were even just a few years ago."

"What on earth are you talking about, Charles?" Darby moved over to the winch and began to hoist the jib.

"They've entered the workforce in droves since the Sixties, become more interested in politics, more involved in athletics, and yet..." He glanced at Johanna. "They retain their goodness in a way men don't."

"You have a distorted definition of 'accomplishment.' Accomplished women should be intelligent and capable, no doubt. In addition, I personally appreciate it when they're pleasing to look at..." His eyes darted to Liz, staring at the horizon with her hand shielding her eyes from the sun.

Darby continued. "But a bigger accomplishment is the development of intellect through education and lifelong learning. And still, adding to all of that, an accomplished woman has to have a strong character. In other words, she has to have guts. In their recent attempts to grab the spotlight, I think many modern women have lost sight of those qualities."

"Your ideal woman is a fantasy," Liz replied. "She doesn't exist."

"Then, it's a good thing I can still enjoy less than ideal."

Liz pursed her lips in annoyance. "You don't know what you're talking about. Grab the spotlight? What does that even mean? A woman isn't grabbing the spotlight if she's naturally gifted at her job and receives her due for it. The way things are, even now in the 1980s, a woman has to toot her own horn to get noticed. How would people know if she were accomplished or not if she were tucked away where no one saw her capabilities, if she had to stay in some low-level position all her life? The glass ceiling is real, Darby Kent. And I, for one, plan to break through it."

"I would never question your determination." He swept his hand forward in a gallant bow, accompanied by a smile, but Liz had turned away in annoyance and missed it.

"I think," Johanna interrupted quietly, "that many women have qualities you speak of, Mr. Kent. Only most people do not notice them yet."

"Exactly. What she said." Charles gave Johanna a brilliant smile.

When I first met you, I thought, perhaps I'd made a mistake, taking this road of double agent. You seemed so together, so free of doubt, so unencumbered. So damned moral. I envied you that. But it doesn't bear considering now. That crossroads, between spy par excellence and double-dealing traitor happened for me a long time ago. You seem to have it all, but I realize no one is without burdens. No one—not even you.

8

June 1982

LIZ AND JOHANNA stood at the sink rinsing vegetables. Darby had offered to make his famous Hungarian goulash soup for dinner, and Johanna, being the polite creature she was, had expressed enough interest for him to go out for additional ingredients.

Liz took some tomatoes out of a bowl to wash them. "And there I was, stranded in a bar, the only female in the place who wasn't covered in leather, saying to the bartender, 'Excuse me, sir, can I use the phone?'"

Johanna laughed and pulled open a drawer. "Knives are in here? I can never remember."

"You should let Chef Darby do his own chopping."

"I do not mind. He does much for me. It is the least I can do."

"Johanna, all these things he's doing for you, he's not doing them out of the goodness of his heart. It's his job—nothing more and nothing less. Lucky for you, his job is the most important thing to him. Don't forget that."

"Oh, I think there is more to him."

"You tell yourself that enough times, and you're liable to get in serious trouble."

The door slammed, and Darby walked through, a cloth sack in one hand and a troubled expression on his face. He walked over to the counter, emptied his sack, and took out a battered envelope with dirt in the creases.

"Where have you been all day?" Liz teased him. "It doesn't take four hours to buy a few vegetables. Is Cara in town?"

He stared at her, and then walked over to the stereo and turned on the music.

Liz stilled, her face instantly sober. The music was his way of conveying that someone might be listening in. It was so idyllic here at Lake Balaton, she'd almost forgotten she was still at cross-purposes with the Hungarian government—an unwanted stranger in a strange land. "What is it?"

In response, he opened the envelope and handed it to her. She read and looked up at him, eyes wide. "How did they—?"

"I don't know. I met Collins this morning in Székesfehérvár. He told me he's heard from two sources inside state security that American intelligence officers are planning to help a female informant escape to the West. They are sending orders to checkpoints and border patrols to be on the lookout for a Hungarian woman with an American man exiting the country."

"But I am not informant!" Johanna's face was white with fear.

"It doesn't matter, Johanna. If you're arrested, we can't protect you; you're a Hungarian citizen. They will interrogate you, and if they are successful, your father is in danger—"

"Apa!"

"As well as any of us you've learned about."

"Charles..." She gasped in distress.

"He's in Vienna. I telephoned him a coded message this morning telling him not to come back to Hungary. Cara and Louis have diplomatic immunity, and that covers Liz, Bill, and me to a certain extent. But, I don't think Liz and I could make it back to the embassy now, so even that protection is iffy."

Out of habit, Liz translated this information into Hungarian. Johanna sat heavily in the chair. "So I am not going anywhere? Except maybe prison."

Liz hurried over to her, putting an arm around her shoulders. "We'll find another way out, won't we, Darby?"

"We'll have to. Since he showed up here unexpectedly, we considered having Charles be the one to escort you out, using our usual channels. But that can't happen now. One source told Collins the government believes the escape will be through Bratislava to Prague, but the other source indicates they are also suspecting alternate routes."

"And you can't take Johanna with you, Darby, because you can't pass for Hungarian."

Darby's lips twisted in a sarcastic smile. "Yep, the agency screwed me royally there, didn't they? If we'd been in the USSR or Czechoslovakia, I could blend in without a hitch."

"Perhaps I could take her?"

He shook his head. "My guess is they'll look hard at any American leaving the country now." He gestured outside to the garden. "You'll forgive me, Johanna, but I need to speak to Liz alone. The less you know about all of this, the better, in case..."

Johanna looked up, her eyes shiny with tears, and nodded.

Darby led Liz out to the gazebo in the center of the Alsómező property. He gestured for her to sit, but she declined.

"You know, you might not be able to pass for Hungarian, but maybe German...?"

"There's more."

"More?"

"I believe we may be dealing not only with a one-time information leak but perhaps with a double agent."

Her eyes narrowed. Was he trying to throw suspicion on someone in order to deflect it from himself? "What do you mean?"

"Darby Kent's picture is circulating as the case officer to look for at the border. That's much more specific information than a run-of-the-mill lapse in security."

"I see." Liz wondered if he had leaked his own identity. It would be an easy way to get back to the Soviets—but why? Why would he compromise himself to the Americans when he was placed to learn so much more information with his Darby Kent cover intact? It made little sense.

"So like Johanna, I can't get back to the embassy. Can't leave through Prague. Can't stay here—as state security could easily learn my whereabouts. This place isn't commonly known as the ambassador's vacation spot, but it isn't a closely guarded secret either. Lake Balaton would be an obvious choice if they were to come looking for me."

"Even more so because Cara flaunted her relationship with you."

He squirmed a little. "Her flirtatious behavior definitely made a bad situation worse."

Liz laughed without humor. "For all of us. What makes you suspect a double agent rather than just good surveillance on the part of the secret police?"

"I'm much better at covering my tracks than the Hungarian government is at discovering them, for one thing."

"So, it couldn't be that you messed up, could it?"

"Highly unlikely."

Typical arrogance, according to George Wickham.

"Plus, there was a..." He paused, looking uncomfortable, reluctant.

"Yes?" Would he tell her about George and Jirina? Spin it in his favor to garner her sympathy?

"A situation during my last assignment. A sloppy officer who made a mistake that cost us an...asset." He looked away. "At least, I thought it was only a mistake—until this happened. Perhaps we had a double agent even then."

Liz couldn't believe he was going to try to pin this situation on George Wickham. George wasn't even in country! "So you think the person who leaked our mission here is the same person who botched your job in Prague."

"Could be. I wouldn't put it out of the realm of possibility, but it could be a dozen others or maybe someone I don't even know."

He gestured with his hand as if to waive that idea away. "But we've got bigger fish to fry at the moment. I have an idea."

"I'm listening."

"There is a new vintner near Sopron." He looked at her with wry amusement. "Part of my job is to find and encourage Western-style commerce, within the letter of communist law, of course."

"Of course."

"Anyway, there's a grape grower in the lake region near here. He's an agency asset—has been for years—long before I came to Hungary. Part of his crop goes to the state, but he makes his own wine, too, and sells to the place in Sopron for a little cash on the side. He's also trying to break into Austrian wine country and trade with them, either his own wine or his grapes. So he has a reason to go both to the border and beyond it—and most importantly, the papers to do so. I think he can drive us out, but he needs some plausible deniability about why he's going and what's in his truck. So we'd go hidden in his cargo. That's where you come in."

"I'm the one escorting you and Johanna?"

"I know it's a lot to ask, but the truck isn't big enough to hide three of us, and you're the only one not being sought by state security at the moment."

"If I try to pass myself off as Hungarian, they'll want to check me at the border, thinking I might be Johanna."

"But you'll be with my asset, the grape grower. That should diminish suspicion. Plus, your Hungarian is impeccable." He gestured toward the house. "I forged you a passport in case of an emergency. It's in my desk drawer."

Liz nibbled on the end of her thumb as she paced back and forth.

Darby put out a hand to stop her but drew it back before he could touch her. "Look, I completely understand your nerves. Perhaps you don't believe you're ready to run an op like this. Frankly, I have some doubts myself, but our options are limited."

"Your faith in me is overwhelming."

"It isn't a matter of faith, Liz. I'm sure this is the most precarious situation you've faced since joining the agency. I need to get out of Hungary before there's enough suspicion for them to call me in for questioning. I know too much to be arrested. It would ruin my career, but even more important, if they could get the information out of me, I could compromise many of the officers in Central Europe. This escape plan is dicey and it's dangerous, and I would be hard put to successfully run this op myself. I'm reluctant to hand it over to a rookie, but I don't have any choice."

Perhaps she could see his point. But still...

"I can do it."

He smiled at her. "Atta girl. Now, here's what I'm thinking..."

THEY COULDN'T TAKE the farm truck across the border at night. Nighttime would give them the cover of darkness, but nothing would arouse more suspicion than to take wine and produce to Austria after dark.

In addition to Prague, Sopron was a popular escape route from Budapest to the West. Therefore, Darby judged the Hungarians would beef up the border patrols along those routes. He also knew that more guards at Sopron meant fewer guards at the other checkpoints along the Austrian border. It was becoming increasingly difficult for the Hungarians to man every station the way they had in the early years of Communist rule. Guard shacks and barracks were run down, Soviets were called home, and personnel were cut back in favor of other "necessities." With that in mind, he and Peter, the grape farmer turned spy, had plotted a course from Keszthely, on the western edge of Lake Balaton, heading west to Körmend, then north to Szombathely and on to Kőszeg near the Austrian border. Once in Austria proper, they would just head north to Vienna, unimpeded.

"There was some government activity on the road from here to Keszthely yesterday," Darby informed Liz while he burned their courier's message in the fireplace at Alsómező. It was a couple of hours before dawn, and they had planned to take Darby's car into the lakeside town. The music on the shortwave radio played to mask their voices, an anomaly in the early morning quiet.

"So, do we wait another day?" Liz asked.

"No more waiting—we need to get out of Hungary. We'll go another way." He glanced up at her, calm and collected as always. "By water. But we're taking a little motorboat. The sailboat is too easily recognized, and the wind too unreliable."

"Where did you get this boat?"

He let out a laugh devoid of humor. "I stole it. Peter will return it if possible. I will have to abandon the agency's car, which is unfortunate, but maybe the ambassador can put it to good use."

"We're abandoning quite a lot here in Hungary."

"True enough. I'm sorry about your apartment, Liz. Did you have anything irreplaceable there? Anything I can try and get for you?"

She shrugged. "Nothing my friend Mary can't pack up and forward out through diplomatic channels. Although I wasn't talking just furniture and things. We have to leave behind some good intelligence channels we'd begun to cultivate—and, of course, we're leaving behind our assets and other agency people. Have you heard from Bill Collins?"

"No, I decided to keep the details of Johanna's escape off the official information chain. Bill is in the embassy, so he's safe there for the moment. By the time he gets wind of what we're doing, we'll already be in Vienna. It gives him plausible deniability about our plans, which he needs sorely, the schmuck. I swear I don't know how he made it through training."

"I've wondered that myself at times." Liz preferred to talk about the subject at hand, however. "How will we find our ride, given this change in mode of transportation to Keszthely?"

"Our driver thought this might happen, so he arranged to meet us near an abandoned factory, just in case. It will be about a half-mile walk from the boat dock to his truck. Is Johanna up for that, do you think?"

"I think so," Liz said, grateful that they had been working on the young woman's stamina. Who knew that she would have to sneak her way out of Hungary this soon?

"How's she holding up?"

"Physically, she's fine."

"And psychologically?"

"She's frightened but resigned to her fate, whatever it turns out to be. But, Darby, we have to get her out safely. I don't know how she could possibly withstand incarceration, even for a short period of time."

"You've become too attached to your asset, Liz. It speaks well of your compassion, but it's a rookie's mistake—one that can have far-reaching damage, trust me. If it comes down to it, you have to be willing to leave her behind."

"Good god, Darby! Could you leave that sweet young woman behind to be arrested...or worse?"

"If it was necessary, I could. I have done that very thing. Intelligence work is a lot of thinking and planning and writing reports, but at certain times, it requires ruthlessness. You know this. Our mission is bigger than one person."

"I understand that, or I thought I did, it's just..."

"It's harder when your asset has a face." His smile was almost sympathetic, but then his expression became tougher, more distant. "But you must do it, even when—maybe especially when—the stakes are high." He turned toward the sound of steps on the stairs. "Are you ready, Johanna?"

"Yes." In spite of the early hour, Johanna was wide-awake, her blue-green eyes sad in her pale face.

"No papers on you, are there?"

"No. Just like you said, no papers, no photos—nothing but the clothes on my back."

"Good. Spy Rule Number Five: No papers on you when you're sneaking around *anywhere.* That way, if the worst happens, and we are separated from Liz and Peter, we can pretend to be an American couple, robbed and set out on the highway. I might be able to pull that off. I'll do the talking; you pretend you are dumb with shock."

Johanna looked, frightened, at Liz, who translated into Hungarian.

"That deer in headlights look you're sporting right now is perfect," he muttered.

Johanna frowned as she translated his last words while Liz stared at him, dumbfounded at his insult.

Johanna's face broke into a wry smile. "No pretending." The smile faded. "I will do my best, Mr. Kent."

THEY WALKED along a wooded path to the ambassador's boat dock, and there, tied up next to the sailboat was a small runabout that smelled of fish. Darby stepped down with one foot, and turned, leaving the other on the dock while he handed Johanna, and then Liz into the boat.

"We'll row out to the middle of the lake before we start the motor."

Liz took the oars next to her seat, and Darby smiled in admiration at her initiative. His rookie would never wait around for someone else to take over the physical work. Somehow, her typical spunky behavior settled him.

"Can you row a straight line, Ms. Hertford?"

"I may not be able to sail worth a damn, but I can row anywhere."

"Carry on then."

Fortunately, the lake was calm. The dark pressed around them, and every once in a while, there was the sound of a fish breaking the surface. Once they got out on the water, Darby started the motor, and they puttered slowly down the lake. Off starboard, the large, black leviathan of shoreline kept pace, looming over them in the cool, predawn air. Although there was no one around to hear, they kept their voices just barely above a whisper.

A sudden breeze blew Liz's hair in a swirling dark cloud around her head. Darby couldn't see her face clearly in the darkness, but that just brought the light and pleasing outline of her figure to his attention. He felt this visceral pull between them, an impulse he tried to attribute to the danger in which they found themselves. Adrenaline pumped through him, making him hyperaware to every sight and sound and to her every twitch of movement. It was odd; he'd not felt this way when he fled Prague last year. But then he was reeling from losing Jirina. This time, both his charges were right here under his watchful eye, and Wickham was an ocean and half a continent away in Washington. At least this time, Officer William Darcy was in control of their collective fate.

"Have you rehearsed what you'll say at the checkpoints?"

"I work for the state agricultural committee. We're taking wine and grapes to Austrian vineyards. Peter has the papers, right?"

He nodded. "It should be pretty routine. Peter's smuggled things out before, and he's yet to have his cargo inspected, except for a random box near the edge of the truck. Of course, he's never smuggled out people before. We'll put ourselves in the interior crates, away from the tailgate. Once they look in a couple of places near the back, if they look at all, they should wave us through. There is a trap door in the bottom of the truck, in case a timely escape is needed."

"Let's try to avoid that if we can," Liz said in wry tone. "I don't know how I'd ever find you if you left the truck—at least before state security scooped you up."

"Remember, in that case, the plan is to drive a mile down the road and wait there for...?"

"Three hours—I know, I know."

They rode on in silence. He found himself wanting to comfort her but not knowing how or what to say. He'd watched her for weeks, read her dossier, listened to her talk with the locals. She loved Hungary and regretted leaving, but it was par for the course. Maybe, someday, she could return. "Sure thing, right after the USSR dissolved," he thought with grim humor.

Their landing point, a rickety dock, loomed ahead. Darby shut off the motor and took up the oars. They careened gently into the dock, and Liz reached out a hand to grab the post. He looped a rope over and stood beside her.

"Just step out and help Johanna. I'm going to let the boat drift off into the lake. Less chance of someone suspecting anything out of the ordinary if there's no empty boat here."

"And boat owner be damned?"

"Afraid so. Peter will make it right. I hope."

They approached a truck parked behind a warehouse on the outskirts of town.

"We haven't much time before sunrise." Peter waved them toward the truck impatiently. "Here you go. Get in, miss." He indicated a crate in the center of the covered truck bed.

Johanna looked dumbstruck at the crate, which was a little over a meter square.

"What's the matter?" Darby asked, irritated.

"She's claustrophobic," Liz whispered.

"Well, hell."

"I can do it." She closed her eyes briefly and opened them again. Her voice was calm, determined. "I must do it. Therefore, I will."

She took Peter's hand and climbed into the truck. Darby was right behind her and settled in, his legs stretched out alongside Johanna's. His crate was slightly longer, which, in addition to the slats on the sides, would allow some light and air to reach them. Peter and Liz arranged the other crates around the two carrying more precious cargo and laid some tarps in strategic places.

PETER SET out along the road west. They were waved through the first checkpoint after showing the papers to the guard, but as they approached the border right outside Kőszeg, they were motioned to stop. The guard checked a memo he held in his hand. Peter handed over his papers, but then the guard eyed Liz and asked in Hungarian, "See your passport?"

She handed him her Hungarian passport, littered with false trips to Austria, Czechoslovakia, and France over the past two years. He looked from her to the passport, and back again. "This paper looks brand new, not like it's been handled during all these trips."

"I take good care of it," she replied, her Hungarian flawless.

"Need to inspect your cargo." He tapped the slats on the truck with his weapon. Liz's heart raced for fear of discovery.

INSIDE THE CRATES, Darby looked at Johanna, trying to gauge her condition. Dawn-painted sunlight from between the crates cast a reddish glow on the upper part of her face. Her eyes were wide with fright and shiny with unshed tears. Darby held a finger to his lips and kept her gaze in his. He didn't dare move another muscle, however, and she took her cues from him. He could hardly tell if she was breathing.

The guard swaggered around the back of the truck and smacked one of the back crates with his hand. Darby was afraid Johanna would jump at the noise, but she only closed her eyes and stayed deathly still. The guard's voice moved up toward Liz's window.

BESIDE THE TRUCK, the guard shifted his weapon in his hands. He approached Liz, running his eyes down her front, and stopping to admire her chest.

So that's how to play it.

"What's your name, sir?"

"None of your concern," he grunted.

"Could we keep moving? See, we don't want to be late. I know you understand. Today is our first trip to this particular vineyard. If I arrive late with opened boxes, the haughty vintner won't take them, and I'll get in trouble with the boss. You know how it goes."

"Who's the driver? Your husband?"

"Him? No. He's just a guy driving the truck. I don't have a husband."

"You're from Budapest?"

"Yes. Do you get to the city often?"

"Sometimes." He opened her door. "Step out of the truck."

Liz complied, leaving the door open so she could leap back inside at a moment's notice.

"We're supposed to be on the lookout for a Hungarian woman, which you are, accompanied by an American man."

"Which he's not, obviously." She followed the guard toward the back of the truck. "Why do they want these people?"

The guard shrugged. "Why do they want anybody? It's none of my concern." He eyed her again. "Bela."

"Hmm?"

He finally smiled. "My name's Bela."

"Erzsebet."

"From Budapest?"

"Indeed. As you saw on my passport. Have you ever tried any of this?" She indicated the box closest to the tailgate.

"We don't get to drink fine wine out here too often."

Liz picked up a crowbar and pried open the back crate. It would be a horrible mistake to overtly offer a bribe, offensive even, but if she could sweet-talk him...

She called to Peter. "Did you put any glasses back here?"

"No, ma'am."

"That's a shame." She tossed her head and speared the guard with a speculative look. "Because I know you'd enjoy it."

His grin was slow, calculating. "I would, probably. But I wouldn't know what I was tasting, would I?"

"That's why I wanted to share a glass with you. To educate you on what you're tasting." She paused to consider. "You should take a bottle or two."

"What about getting in trouble?"

"They'll never miss a couple if I pack the box right. Take some to share with your friends." She reached into the crate. Thankfully, there really were bottles of wine in it. "Save one though."

"What for?"

"For when I get back to Hungary. We'll open it together. Next time you're in Budapest."

"Where should we open this fine wine? Your place?" She gave him the street address on her passport. "I'll even have wine glasses." Her laugh spilled out over the clink of bottles as she wrapped them in burlap and handed them to the guard. He had to shoulder his weapon to take them.

She re-packed the crate and turned to give him a bright smile. "Until Budapest."

"Until Budapest then."

She got in, and Peter wasted no time in leaving the checkpoint behind.

Liz let out a shaky sigh, took the handgun out of her ankle holster, and laid it on the seat between them.

He looked down at it, surprised. "And just how were you planning to use that?"

"I actually have no idea."

"Not like you could blast your way through a check point."

"I guess not."

They'd reached the outskirts of Vienna before her panicked numbness wore off. Peter stopped the truck right outside an abandoned warehouse, and they each leaped out, pulling crates to the side and helping Johanna and Darby out into the Austrian sunshine.

"*Bécs!*" Peter triumphantly called out the Hungarian name for Vienna, grinning at Johanna. She gave him an uncertain smile in return and looked around her, taking it all in. Darby seemed wobbly, and his legs were likely stiff. He caught Liz's shoulder to right himself.

She was shaking.

"What's the matter?"

"Nothing. I'm fine." But her teeth began to chatter in spite of the warm summer morning. "That was close."

"Close, yes. But you improvised and got us out of there. You read the situation and devised a plan to deal with it. You did well, Liz Hertford."

"Thanks." She looked up at him. "It's Bennet."

"Pardon?"

"I'm Elizabeth Bennet. We're out of Hungary, and I'll never be Liz Hertford again."

He nodded, and a small smile lit his face. "Nice to meet you, Miss Bennet."

Her eyes filled, and a terrified sob bubbled up from somewhere inside her. She laughed through tears. "I've got to get myself together now." Then she turned away, hand over her mouth to stifle the involuntary crying.

He turned her back around and drew her into his embrace. "Hey," he murmured. "Hey, we're all right." She nodded against his chest, spilling hot, wet tears on his shirtfront. He pulled back and rubbed her arms. "You're okay."

"I'm fine. I mean, I'll be fine. I'm sorry. I can't believe I'm breaking down like this—and in front of you, of all people. Which stinks. But I was scared shitless, and don't you dare despise me for it."

"Indeed, madam, I wouldn't dare. Don't despise yourself either. It's a side-effect of adrenaline, not evidence of weakness." He let her go with an awkward pat. "You'll be...fine."

"Mm-hmm." She bit her lip. "Thanks, Darby."

"Darcy. William Darcy."

She laughed at the James Bond allusion, a cautious display of mirth. His gallantry surprised her. She had rather expected him to roll his eyes at her outburst or at least scowl at her, but the situation must have strung him out, too, because he was looking at her with the strangest expression.

WILLIAM DARCY KNEW he was heading for trouble. Nothing caught his admiration more readily than guts—and guts was something Liz Hertford—no, Elizabeth Bennet—had in spades. He had never been as bewitched by any woman as he was by her, and if it were not for the fact that she worked for him, he really believed he might be in danger of falling for her.

PART II

Beware, my friend. It might be seen in your eyes, the way your head turns toward the object of your desire, how you speak of her when she's not around. Eureka! After all this time, I believe I have finally found it—your fatal flaw.

Humbling, isn't it? To know that someone exists who can lead you so far away from yourself or what you thought you were. Is it obsession? I suppose it is. It proves you're human. Imperfect. Like...me! You're like me after all. Don't fear it so much. Don't be such a wuss. Ironic that we should be in love at the same moment, isn't it? So much we share. Yet so different our lives turned out to be. You with your golden badge of privilege and the status that comes with wealth and family. That privilege bought you career advancement too. Gave you a leg up that this old boy would never get. Never. The old man made sure of that.

9

East Berlin, Germany
August 1982

APPLAUSE THUNDERED THROUGH THE THEATER. Liam Reynolds glanced at the man next to him, and after exchanging looks, they both rose to join in the ovation. From his third row seat, he saw all the actors as they came up to take their bows. His eyes were riveted, however, to one Beth Steventon, known to him now as Elizabeth Bennet, his translator and fellow CIA officer from Budapest. She was right when she told him she'd never be Liz Hertford again, just as he would never be the smooth American businessman Darby Kent again. New city, new assignment, new pocket litter in his jacket—scribblings, tickets, and cards to convince the Stasi about the veracity of this new life.

New assignment but not where he wanted to be. Liam was frustrated with his lack of progress toward the top post in the USSR. East Berlin was on the front lines of the so-called Cold War, but he was still a case officer with a non-official cover, what the career embassy officers called a "damned NOC."

Beth avoided eye contact with him in his third row as she should;

they were supposed to be strangers. But somehow, he took a perverse pleasure in trying to draw her attention.

Last week, Reynolds was floored when he walked into the British Embassy and saw Beth chatting up his longtime friend and MI6 contact, Richard Fitzwilliam. Honestly, Liam assumed he'd probably never see Beth again after they parted ways in Vienna. Yet there they were, starring in their very own *Casablanca* moment. His lips quirked into a wry smile, thinking "of all the gin joints," etc.

Her hair was different, shorter, a new auburn color—becoming but not too conspicuous. She laughed heartily at something Fitzwilliam said, making Liam's insides twist in an odd way.

"Reynolds!" Fitzwilliam called him over with a wave.

He approached the pair, waiting to see whether she could cover her surprise at seeing him in East Germany, assessing her poise. He was oddly disappointed when she turned to face him without a hint of recognition whatsoever.

"Fitz," he acknowledged his friend. "How's the BBC?"

"Good, good. Glad to see you. What brings you to East Berlin?"

"I've got a traveling position, working for the Goodwin Theater Company—looking for new ideas, fresh talent."

"How long will you be here?"

"Unknown. Depends on what I find, I guess."

"I guess." Fitzwilliam's eyes twinkled. As if suddenly remembering he wasn't alone, he turned and gently took the elbow of the woman next to him. "Speaking of fresh talent, I'd like you to meet Beth Steventon. She's an Oxford grad student on a theater fellowship at Humboldt University this semester. Beth, my friend, Liam Reynolds."

She held out her hand. "Pleased to meet you."

When their hands joined, he felt the old familiar tingle in his arm, the same one he felt when he first spun her around the dance floor in Budapest. That instant spark, unfortunately, hadn't dulled at all. He rubbed his palm with his other hand to try and displace the feeling.

"Beth is a dancer in the new show at Rosengarten."

"Oh?" He'd had no idea she could dance well enough for professional stage work.

"It's a small role." She looked away as if to downplay her part. "Just an extra really. But that's what you expect when you're a student —and an outsider. It's been a good learning experience."

"I'll have to look for you when I attend the show on opening night."

Fitzwilliam jumped in. "Liam's organization, the Goodwin Theater Company, is one of the oldest in the States."

"I'm familiar with the name," she answered. "You'll have to let me know what you think of *Stolz und Vorurteil*, Liam." She twisted the ring on her finger, a well-established signal she was giving him a message with her next words. "The female lead is a talented actress. Make sure you see the show—for her performance if nothing else."

"I will."

"I'd be curious to know what you think of her and the play in general. I hear they're having a cast and crew party to celebrate opening night. You could keep her out of trouble; ask her to dance."

SO HERE HE WAS, attending the East German Rosengarten Theater with an eye bent to the show's leading lady, a woman named—he glanced down at the program—Anneliese Vandenburg. She was apparently the new asset, according to that brief talk he had with Beth last week. Fitzwilliam had wrangled him an invitation to the cast and crew party after the show, a party that included government dignitaries and press. From the third row, he could tell Anneliese was a striking woman—tall, blonde, fair—actually, quite beautiful. He wondered what information she had or could get that would be useful to the CIA.

The after-party was taking place in the director's house, located in the Prenzlauer Berg district, so Fitzwilliam offered to drive his Trabant to the festivities. Liam peered into the house's entryway, lit up with a glorious chandelier, laughter spilling out of the kitchen and into the vestibule. He rolled his shoulders and took a deep breath to relax. There would be no Beth at a gathering like this, so there was no need to be cognizant of squelching his compulsive tendency to follow her with his eyes.

Instead, he would focus on his new asset, the mysterious Anneliese Vandenburg. According to the dossier Collins had left him, Anneliese was relatively new on the theater and cabaret scene, born and educated in Dresden. She was a fast rising star in East Germany's state funded arts program. Liam would meet her, maybe spend some time with her socially, but let Beth function as the cut-out, handling Anneliese's intelligence information through a dead drop. Hopefully, after a few encounters, Anneliese Vandenburg would never remember Liam Reynolds was alive, which was exactly how he wanted it. After his recent experiences in Prague and Hungary, he needed to be extra cautious. Even with his new artist look, he was leery about being recognized. He'd toned down his splashy, polished spy persona for this tour in East Berlin. Hungary's Darby Kent, the embassy man with the suave smile and expensive suits, was long gone. Flashy arrogance was too conspicuous for the Stasi and for the East German people. It wouldn't do to have the luxuries they didn't have or wear the clothes they couldn't get. That would draw extra attention to his Western background, something he surely didn't need. He'd grown his hair into a dark mane sprinkled with gray, long enough now to pull into a tail at the nape of his neck. He sported a Gallic-looking beard as well, and he had lost some weight, making him appear every inch the brooding artist.

Fitz brought a couple glasses of champagne and led Liam over to introduce him to Anneliese. She peered at the two of them over the rim of her glass. Her smile was chilly; her bright blue eyes glittered in a way that almost set his teeth chattering.

A cold, beautiful woman. Cold as ice.

But ice could feel as if it were burning when one touched it for too long, and Anneliese gave off that kind of searing bite when she looked at him. "Herr Reynolds."

"Fraulein Vandenberg."

"You work for Goodwin Theater Company, I hear?"

"I do."

"I've always wanted to see the inner workings of Broadway theaters." She smiled grimly. "On a temporary basis, of course."

"Of course."

"The tyranny, the uncertainty, the capitalist corruption."

"The overnight success stories, the money, the free exchange of ideas."

"There is that too, I suppose. But I'm only concerned with acting the plays, not writing them."

He decided to leave American posturing aside for the moment. A little was expected after she baited him like that, but neither of them could speak their minds here anyway.

"I enjoyed your portrayal of Elsbeth tonight."

"*Danke.* Will my Western thespian colleagues get to hear about it?"

"I could tell you that they definitely would, but I'll be honest and say the development director has the final say."

"An honest theater man." She tossed her head, laughing. "What a novelty!"

"Honesty is a virtue."

"And a virtuous one as well! Those are scarce around these parts. I should beg for an audience with you."

"It's a date." Why on earth was he trifling with this woman? Her demeanor gave him the impression she'd as soon put his balls in a vice as look at him.

A stern-looking matron in an East German military uniform approached them from behind. "Anneliese." Although her voice wasn't loud, it still sounded like she barked the name. "Who is this?"

"Mother," Anneliese said. "Meet Liam Reynolds, assistant to the artistic director at the Goodwin Theater Company. It's in New York."

"Western thespian."

"I am indeed, madam."

She studied him a long minute and then held out her hand. "Oberst Catrina Vandenburg."

"Pleasure," he said politely. His brain clicked through the various reports he'd read on East German military staff. No wonder Vandenburg sounded familiar. This was the prize Anneliese had used to angle into US intelligence. Her mother was a border commander—and even icier than her daughter if he was any judge of character. There was no family resemblance he could detect except for a grim wariness he saw in many of the East German people these days.

"Liam is reviewing *Stolz und Vorurteil* for his company. Isn't that exciting?"

"Mm."

"Should I let him review me as well?"

"It will have to be approved by the bureau, of course. I'll need to read some of your earlier work, Herr Reynolds."

So will I. Thank goodness there isn't much yet to read. He was only the second officer to assume the Liam Reynolds cover since it was created in the late Seventies.

"Of course." He turned once again to Anneliese. "Can I find you at the theater later this week?"

"Rehearsals each day at two, but I'm always there, it seems."

"I'll drop by." He turned toward the doorway, and—

There she was.

He hardly knew what name to give her: Liz, Erzsebet, Beth. The only appellation that came to mind was "She." *She* of the fine eyes and the bright smile, her hair pulled back in a sleek knot at the nape of her neck. *She,* wearing black pants that hugged her hips and a silky top with a plunging neckline. *She,* who glanced at him and turned away, nonplussed. *Tear your eyes away. Someone will notice if you look too long. Stop staring; stop—*

"Do you know that young woman?" Anneliese asked, following his gaze to the door.

Damn it! "No. I...I thought I did, but no."

"One American looks like another, I suppose." Anneliese's brittle smile returned, and she leaned into him. "Yes, she is American: one of the dancers in the show. Graduate student—from Oxford, I think —but she is from the US originally." The sharp, powdery scent of

Anneliese's perfume reached his nose, making it twitch in an attempt to keep a sneeze from erupting.

"I could arrange an introduction if you would like. She is a friend of mine."

This was a disaster! He needed to distance himself from Beth Steventon, not associate himself with her in Anneliese's mind. "She's not really my type."

Anneliese eyed him, speculation in her gaze, then shrugged. "Come meet our director. He is over by the wine, talking with the playwright and the Minister of the Theater."

To have the leading lady show him around wasn't conforming to his plan to observe and disappear, but Anneliese seemed determined to parade him in front of the entire cast and government officials in attendance.

"I suppose I should let you speak to your lovely American comrade now. You have met everyone else." She hooked her arm in his.

"We don't call them comrades in the States."

"What do you call them?"

"I don't know...countrymen?"

Anneliese drew her brows together in confusion.

"I know, I know—she's not a man."

"Ah, well. Your American *country man* then." She shook her head. "It is a pity I have to introduce you to her."

"Why?"

"Why encourage you to look at the competition?" She heaved a dramatic sigh. "The girl could at least have the decency to be ugly."

"She could hardly be considered a great beauty."

Anneliese nodded toward Beth. "But apparently, she is attractive enough to draw the attention of a man on our crew. You have missed your chance."

He forced himself to stare into his drink instead of whipping his head around to see who had dared approach *his* rookie. He emptied the glass while Anneliese prattled on about the East German reviews for *Stolz und Vorurteil*.

Once he saw Beth had her eyes trained on him, he gestured with his glass toward the kitchen.

"I seem to be empty," he said to Anneliese. "Can I get you something?"

"*Danke*," she replied. "But no alcohol for me. Bad for the voice, you know."

He walked through the house and out the back door, confident that Beth would follow. Silently, he indicated a hedgerow several feet from the house and turned as she approached him.

"Why are you here?" he demanded.

"*Guten Abend* to you too. I was invited. I'm in the cast. Geez, Liam! I'm the cut-out remember? Between you and our new friend."

"Does Anneliese know you're the liaison?"

Beth shook her head. "She's not supposed to. Collins set it up before he left town."

"Collins. Hmmph. He left a shitload of redundant documentation I have to purge. Where did they send him again?"

"Back home to Uncle."

"Best idea they've had in months. Maybe home will suit him better than the field."

"It sounds boring to me."

"Exactly. But then, you aren't Collins, are you? You're qualified for your work."

Beth shot him a quizzical look, her eyebrows drawn together. "What?"

"Waiting for the left-handed compliment to drop."

He reached for her hand then drew it back. "What I mean is, you have an aptitude for what you do, and it shows."

The sound of a door closing drew her attention. "Someone's coming," she whispered.

Liam cleared his throat. "So, how do you like East Germany, Miss Steventon?"

A short round of small talk ensued, ending with the appearance of Fitz, warning Liam that Anneliese was on the prowl, looking for

him. Beth Steventon disappeared into the crowd, and the three officers parted ways for the rest of the evening.

10

Several weeks later, Liam Reynolds cut across the Volkspark Friedrichshain in East Berlin, glancing behind him for telltale signs of being followed. The Stasi had been merciless when he first arrived, but now there were a few windows of time where he was truly alone, often in the mornings. He had received a message to meet Fitzwilliam here.

As he started to cross the bridge, he spied the MI6 operative, sitting on a park bench, elbows resting on his knees, a cigarette between his fingers. Liam started toward the bench when he caught a movement out of the corner of his eye. He paused mid-stride and then stumbled when he saw who the interloper was. He stood, just watching, as *She* cantered over to the bench—with a little skip on the last two steps—and sat down beside Fitzwilliam. They talked in low voices, smiling, with the occasional chuckle. They had formed a friendship, and there was a rumor circulating about a romance—a rumor the three of them encouraged to put distance between Beth and Liam.

Tamping down his resentment, Liam continued toward the pair and saw his friend glancing up as he approached. "Mr. Reynolds!" Fitzwilliam leaned back, crossing one ankle over the other knee and spreading his arms wide to span the back of the rickety bench. "We were just discussing you."

Beth had been facing Fitz but turned when she heard the man call Liam's name.

"Oh, really? I'm sure it's a fascinating subject." *So she discusses me when I'm not around—interesting.* He picked up his pace.

Beth raised her eyebrows and looked at Fitzwilliam with an I-told-you-so expression.

He turned his attention from Fitz to Miss Fine Eyes. "And what could you possibly know about me, Ms. Steventon? We hardly know each other, after all."

"My American friend said she knows you from the States, and I said I wanted to know how you behaved on your home turf."

"It's shocking, I tell you." She folded her hands in her lap and looked at Liam the way a disapproving schoolmarm would dress down a misbehaving student.

He loved that look. "I'm not afraid of you." Liam sat down, sandwiching her between himself and Fitz.

"All right then, you asked for it." She turned to Fitzwilliam. "I was in this class of new...thespians. Reynolds here gave a pompous speech to the group, and none of us underlings could stand him. We talked about him for weeks afterward."

Liam pondered while Fitzwilliam chuckled. *Is she making this up? I met her at the ambassador's party in Budapest, right?* "I'm sure that's not correct," he replied cautiously, not sure what game she was playing.

"Heard him tell the professor he had better things to do than to wet-nurse a bunch of runny-nosed brats and greenhorns right off the farm."

The farm? The Farm? His eyes widened. *She was in that class? That group of recruits I'd been railroaded into instructing right after I returned from Prague?* "Well now, that's hardly fair. Maybe I was having a bad day." *More like a bad month, a bad year. If I recall, I left that talk to go straight to a twelve-hour debriefing.*

"I couldn't believe it when I walked in the door at that cast party the other night and saw him staring at everyone in the room with that awful scowl on his face, just like he did at our *theater* class."

Fitzwilliam looked at her sideways, amused. "Liam and I have worked together before—Paris, London, West Berlin. He knows his stuff and can certainly be lively enough when he chooses. But maybe a throng of budding *thespians* is too much for him to handle all at once."

"I've never had the gift that some have—of being at ease in a crowd, especially if the attention is on me."

"Should we ask him why?" Beth asked Fitzwilliam.

"What do you mean?"

"Why should a man who has traveled the world, represented a well-established professional theater company, and met people in a dozen or more countries—why should that man be ill at ease in a room full of new people?"

Liam held Beth's gaze long enough that her teasing smile began to fade.

"When I walk into a crowded room"—he paused—"I can't screen anything out, not the emotions on people's faces, the way their gazes move from place to place and person to person—not even the way they hold their damn wine glasses."

"It's your training, perhaps."

"Perhaps. An *artist* is trained to be observant, of course. Sometimes, it takes me a minute to sort it all, to find my place in it, to decide how or who I will be. We'll call it...an occupational hazard. Perhaps I've been living like that too long to behave any other way."

"There are many tasks in my profession that I don't perform as well as I should, but I've always assumed that I'm just as capable as anyone else but that the situation to use that skill hasn't yet arisen. You've practiced your observational skills. Perhaps if you practice, you could also learn to live in the moment. In some cases, it's less conspicuous than glaring at everyone from the side of the room and deciding who you should be today."

"I believe I'm a lost cause." Liam's smile warmed with the realization she had hope for him yet. "But you've used your time and talents much better. No one who has seen your work could find anything wanting."

BETH LOOKED AT HER FEET, uncomfortable with his praise. It made it harder to investigate, harder to look for his transgressions, harder to keep him and his Bohemian persona out of her dreams at night. Why did those sad hazel eyes and that long dark hair tied up in a queue appeal to her? *Remember Jirina*, she castigated herself. *This is all an act. He's not really eccentric or shy.* Like she'd told Johanna Bodnar, his priority was the mission—always. And anyone who'd been an operations officer and a station chief all those years knew how to immerse himself in any situation he chose, crowded room or not.

Beth glanced around the park before sliding a newspaper from underneath her thigh, brushing his hand with hers. She pitched her voice low. "The envelope inside is from our friend. Copies of border guard reports."

Liam surreptitiously opened the envelope and scanned it, covering the report with the newspaper, lips held firmly together to keep them from moving.

Fitzwilliam rose and stepped behind Liam to read over his shoulder. "Looks like they're watching one of our chaps. Damnation, I warned him not to flaunt his cigarettes and extra deutsche marks."

"What do you expect from a twenty-year-old kid who's never had a deutsche mark to his name?" Beth murmured.

"It'll go bad for him if he's caught."

"Bad for him, and bad for us too," Liam said.

"He doesn't know any of our people by sight. That's fortunate."

Liam pulled out a lighter.

"Don't—" Fitzwilliam interjected, but it was too late. The flash paper disappeared almost instantly.

"I was looking at that," he complained. "Not everyone has your bloody photographic memory."

"Spy Rule Number Eleven: A written intelligence report that is also an accurate intelligence report is not your friend."

Beth glanced around the park. "I've got to get to rehearsal. And figure out how to shake off Karl."

"Who's Karl?" Liam narrowed his eyes at her.

"Stagehand who's taken an interest in the new foreign girl."

"If you need assistance..."

"Whoa, back down, Big Brother! I can deal with it. I've been using the 'Fitzwilliam's my new man' cover." She laughed and punched Fitz lightly in the arm. "Right, cutie-pie?"

"Happy to oblige."

Liam tamped down his annoyance once again. "I'm stopping by the show tonight anyway. I—"

"Stop by the show if you want but not on my account. I can handle myself. See you around, Fitz."

"Bye, love."

The two men watched Beth disappear around a bend in the path.

"East Berlin isn't a good assignment for her."

"What do you mean?" Fitzwilliam struck a match on a tree and lit another cigarette.

"She looks worn out, frazzled. Don't you think?"

"Hadn't noticed."

"Anneliese has been pursuing a friendship, running her around at all hours of the day and night."

"Maybe our Beth can make some use of that connection."

"You know, Fitz, I can't figure out why 'our Beth' is here in East Berlin at all. Makes no sense. Her specialty is Slavic and Uralic languages."

"Maybe so, but her German is first-rate."

"The company sent Collins here originally, but then he was out, and she was in. Makes no sense."

"Yeah, you said that. Maybe she asked for the transfer. Don't rock the boat. I'd rather work with her than some bloke any day."

"Yeah," he said moodily. "Me too, I guess."

A female voice sounded from around the bend.

"Liam!"

He recognized the harsh timbre, the Germanic turn of the vowels. She appeared over the rise, waving a paper in her hand.

"I have it. I told you I could get it."

He waited until she was close to minimize how far her voice carried. How he despised a loud-mouthed asset! "What did you get, Anneliese?"

"Permission to travel to West Berlin this Saturday night to see *Universally Acknowledged*—and an overnight pass, courtesy of my mother. I can go with you now. I am supposed to stay with my great-aunt on my father's side, but once we are over there, we can stay wherever we want."

"I've already made other plans," he said. "Fitzwilliam here is covering the play for the BBC. He's along for the ride."

"Oh." She paused, frowning. "Then I'll get Beth, that American girl in the chorus line to go. She has a pass once a month to visit a family member living in West Berlin. Cousin of some sort. She and Fitz are an item, and that leaves you free to escort me."

"She may not want to—"

"Oh, she'll go." Anneliese gave him a steely smile. "She owes me a favor."

My heart. My light and my life. This is almost more than I can bear. Who knows when she and I will be together again? I know that you will be seduced, as I was, by her beauty. You will lie with her, and I will hate you for it. I hate my love for it as well, but some things have to be. I've done my best to protect our interests in East Berlin, but damn it, I can't protect what's mine from you.

11

West Berlin
October 1982

BETH CURVED her hands around the warm cup in front of her and sighed lustily. She took a sip and closed her eyes. "Mmm," she purred. "God, I've missed this."

"Stop it. You make it sound like drinking the coffee is better than sex." Wickham laughed at her expression.

"Right now, it is. I've almost forgotten about sex."

"Now, that's a real shame."

Beth shook her head and grinned. Wickham was the worst kind of flirt. "Occupational hazard." She took another drink. "I do miss coffee something fierce though. We can't get anything this good over the border."

"How long is your travel pass?"

"I have to be back in East Berlin tonight by 2100 hours."

"Where did you stay last night?"

"Hotel."

"You could have stayed with Lidia and me."

"No thanks. I'm sure your new German conquest would not want you to bring some random American girl home with you."

"She's hardly a conquest. We've been together four months now."

"Does she know what you do for a living?"

"Absolutely not. She thinks I work for Polaroid."

"Taking a slight chance there, aren't you?"

"They're making us all NOCs these days. Chances come with the territory."

"But using a well-known company for your cover? Cuddling up with a local?"

His lips twitched as he tapped his cigarette against the side of the ashtray. "I can handle Lidia. Besides, I'm not good at foregoing female companionship."

"A common trait among agency men, I've discovered." Beth gazed outside the glass that fronted the upscale coffee shop in West Berlin. Early evening shadows were beginning to deepen, and the neon signs above the street level began to flicker on and shine into the gathering night. She pointed out the window. "This is one of the biggest differences between East and West."

"What is?"

She nodded toward the street. "The lights. Going across the border is a little like a trip through a time portal. Some of the buildings have hardly been touched since the Second World War bombings."

"Is that so?"

"And there are other differences."

"Such as?"

"It's hard to get some things." She lifted her cup again. "Like coffee. Fruit."

"That explains your insistence on getting a banana split earlier."

"Never cared much for bananas before I lived in East Germany, but now they're the most delicious food on earth."

"Sorry. I know it's not the best of circumstances. But the director sent our man to East Berlin because he wanted to see him on the front lines of the Cold War without the protection and restriction of diplomatic immunity. See if the constant tug between East and West would draw him out—lead him to make a mistake."

She shrugged. "I know. It's not the worst situation by any means. I'm doing without things I'm used to, but that time portal I was talking about isn't all bad. You know, East Germany still has some of the innocence of simpler times. There's a sort of wholesome charm about the place—at least the part the government lets me see."

"Wholesome? Not sure I'd see it that way. Seems kind of backward if you ask me."

"Yeah, well, that's an unfair generalization; it has its pleasant moments. However, I do realize they can't get some technology items without a black market and can't trust *all* their neighbors not to rat them out to the Stasi if they step out of line. I think the fact that they can't go anywhere without permission is the biggest sticking point for many of them, even more than the lack of luxuries. Human beings weren't made for that kind of confinement."

Wickham blew out a stream of smoke. "God, how do they stand it?"

"It seems unbearable to us from the US, but perhaps it's just different than what I'm used to. I have to admit though, even as Pollyanna as I am, I find it pretty bleak at times." She glanced out at the cheerful hustle and bustle on the other side of the window. "I miss the West. It's odd. I spent all that time studying Eastern Europe, couldn't wait to get here, and now..."

"Now, you're craving bananas."

"Yeah."

"And Darcy? What's the latest development there?"

She smiled and shook her head. "Darcy, aka Liam Reynolds. Hmm. Let's just say you're not the only one with a new German girlfriend."

"You don't say?"

"He spent last night with that actress, Anneliese Vandenburg. They're talking at the theater most nights after rehearsal, and he's hanging around after performances. Many nights he walks her home."

"How do you know that?"

"My place is between hers and the theatre. They're behind me five nights out of seven. It's awkward: I'm supposed to be the cut-out, and she's leaving the coded information about which border guards their military is keeping an eye on. He doesn't let on that I work with him. So he works with me, but his Liam Reynolds persona pretends he doesn't really know me. He makes time with Anneliese but pretends he doesn't really work with her. I can't figure out if they're comparing notes or not. I don't think so."

"Darcy's never been one to fall for a honey trap if that's what you're thinking. But if he's in with the KGB, Vandenburg's the one in danger, and she'd never even know any better."

"Crazy, isn't it? So she's feeding information to him through me, yet presumably, she doesn't know her information is finding its way to his hands, even though she's spending her nights with him. I don't think she knows I'm the one running her because she originally set up the drop with Collins before he went back to DC. It all makes my head hurt."

"Darcy hasn't done anything suspicious at all? No extra expenditures, no clandestine meetings?"

"No."

"Are you following him?"

"Geez, George. I don't need to follow him! He's always at the theater, waiting around outside until we're finished rehearsing or performing, even if it's midnight."

"Come on, I'm sure he's not *always* at the theater."

"Okay, not always, but the times I've followed him, either he's seen me and struck up a conversation, invited me to join him and his MI6 buddy, or he's gone straight home. As an American, I'm not allowed to wander around all night following people, but then, neither is he."

"The Stasi will begin to look askance at Anneliese, spending all that time with a Westerner."

"Even more now as we all spent last evening here in West Berlin."

"I still can't believe they let her go."

"Her mother's convinced Reynolds can make her—and East German theater—famous, and the woman is a ranking military officer. I'm sure she can call the Stasi off her daughter at her whim."

"To a point, yes, but..."

Beth set her cup down with a click. "You know, I can't help wondering, how sure are you and the director about your suspicions? Are we on some kind of wild goose chase here? Because it's been months now, and I've not seen one indication Darcy is any kind of double agent."

Wickham gave her a frosty look, followed by a vaguely amused smile. "Interesting. Never thought I'd see *you* get all hot and bothered for Darcy."

"Never thought I'd see *you* think a woman wants to bed every man she works with. I'm not hot and bothered!"

"Methinks the lady doth protest too much."

"You're wrong, completely wrong about that. I know to keep the target of an investigation at arm's length. But I see what I see, and I know when I'm not seeing it. I've always been able to read people and their motives pretty well."

"I'm sure that's true, but in this case you're just not looking hard enough. Something isn't right with Darcy. You know, he was missing for about ten days before the company sent him to Budapest?"

"Missing?"

"Nobody knew where he went. Took a commercial airliner to Miami, but then he just disappeared off the grid."

"That is odd."

"He's hiding something, and if you dig hard enough—"

"But—"

"Be the exceptional officer I know you are"—he laid his hand over hers— "and you'll nail him."

"Fitzwilliam thinks he's top notch."

"Fitz is a good guy, one of Six's best, but even experienced officers can be duped. Don't let that happen to you." He blew out a sigh of frustration. "Jesus, everybody thinks Darcy's the perfect spy. He's got them all fooled. But then I suppose I've seen a side of him that few people ever see. All I can say is, thank goodness, the director sees it too."

"I'm not discounting your experiences or the director's hunch. Maybe I've been in the field too long, staring at one problem until I'm myopic, but this doesn't make sense to me. True, he sent you to accompany Jirina at the Prague meeting instead of going himself, but that could have been a precaution or even a fluke. Then he's identified by state security in Hungary, according to Collins, but if he's a double agent, why would they ID him as CIA? Wouldn't they want him to stay in Budapest? He was in the center of that network and cultivating new assets as well."

"The KGB might not want to keep him in the midst of goulash Communism if there was another position that was more advantageous for them. If he's the hunted, we're less likely to think he's the hunter. Or perhaps they think we're too close to the truth. Or they might think he'll be put in a higher-ranking position in another place. Personally, I think he's being groomed for the Soviet station chief position by both sides."

"The director would allow the agency to put a man in line for the Soviet station chief chair with this kind of suspicion hanging over his head?"

Wickham smirked. "He might allow Darcy to think that was a possibility, at least for a while."

Beth sipped her coffee, thinking. It didn't sit well with her. She understood the need to catch moles and double agents, but ruining a man's career based on supposition and hearsay? "What evidence does the director have that started this ball rolling to begin with?" Maybe if she could trace it from the beginning, it would make more sense.

"Sorry, it's..."

She snorted. "I know. It's *eyes-only* information. I'm starting to really hate that phrase."

"Sorry." He stubbed out his cigarette and finished off his espresso. "Look a bit harder at his communications. Search his flat."

"Yeah, okay." She capitulated, but her heart wasn't in it. Darcy was a womanizer and an arrogant ass, no doubt about it. She just wasn't sure he was a traitor as well.

12
_____

ABOUT A WEEK after the West Berlin field trip, Liam Reynolds was awakened before dawn by incessant phone ringing. Still groggy, his eyes half-closed, he grappled for the phone.

"Reynolds."

A frantic female voice answered. "Liam, I think I am in trouble."

"I'm sorry, who is this?"

"What do you mean 'who is this'?" Now, he recognized the clipped vowels, the harsh tone.

"Oh, Anneliese. Sorry, it's early. Ah, what can I do for you at"—he checked his bedside clock—"six in the morning?"

"I need to go to West Berlin. Today."

"That is a dilemma, and not one I can help you with. Why don't you consult your mother for her advice?" He started to hang up.

"She can't help me now." Her voice broke. "God, Liam! I have been talking with some people, thinking I could get out of here if I helped them, and now..."

"Why are you telling me this?"

"Maybe you know people." She paused. "You *must* know people."

"I *must* know nothing of the sort."

"The Stasi found out what I am doing. They have to know

because I am being followed. When I came home last night, I realized they searched my apartment."

"Then go to the people you've been helping. I can't do anything for you."

Her voiced turned shrill. "If they pick me up, I will implicate you."

"I'm only a businessman, I—"

"I will implicate you—and every American I can think of. The little theater student. The authorities will believe me. They are suspicious of any foreigner, and we all went to West Berlin last week together. It would not be much of a stretch. She is always sneaking around after you anyway."

His heart stopped even as his mind began to race. Had they been so careless? Could Anneliese have seen him with Beth at the theater? Or outside the director's house that night of the cast and crew party? He'd put even more security in place than usual. Reduced his number of personal contacts, watched his own back—and Beth's —religiously.

"You will not help me then? Fine. I will contact your intelligence people, your embassy. If the Stasi get me beforehand, it is on your head!"

"I don't know what you're talking about." He hung up. Scrubbed his hands over his face. *What the hell is going on? Prague, then Budapest, and now East Berlin?* The GDR was a more dangerous assignment, sure, but damnation! If he were the director, he'd start looking for systematic leaks. For...

A mole at Langley? Is there an enemy, not just out in the field but burrowed in the heart of the CIA?

He replayed Anneliese's phone call in his mind for any clue as to who her contacts were, or at least who she believed they were. She must have thought he knew something, and the only other person she'd implicated was Beth, who might be in terrible danger if she went by the drop this morning. If Anneliese gave Beth's description or the drop location to the Stasi, they might be waiting for her there. He reached for the phone then put it back down. He couldn't risk a call to Beth. He'd have to drive over, wake her, and warn her in person.

He got in his car, wound his way around the city in a convoluted survey detection route to make sure he wasn't followed before slipping into her building. He'd never been in her apartment here so as not to cast suspicion on her. He knocked once. Knocked again.

"Beth?"

The door across the hall opened.

Damn it!

"She left early." The elderly woman in the opposite doorway looked him up and down as if memorizing his features. No matter, he wasn't planning to hang around East Germany anyway. He thanked the woman and left.

Perhaps she was at the theater. Or perhaps she'd gone early to check the drop. He stopped dead in his tracks and made a beeline for his car and Volkspark Friedrichshain. It broke every protocol, but he had to know—warn her if possible. Or if she'd been taken, he had to know that too. Gorge rose in his throat. Just like Jirina, and yet, not like Jirina at all. This was a whole new type of terror. Jirina's capture had released a flood of regret in him. But the possibility that *She* was in custody, being held in a Stasi interrogation room, made the breath back up in his lungs. He could envision it all too clearly: her eyes wide and frightened, stammering her innocence, sitting on her hands so the dogs could come in after and catch her scent from the chair pad. He saw her being released and followed by hounds and men. Saw her capture. The idea that *She* might be hunted down and imprisoned, beaten, drugged, and interrogated clawed at him—a rage unlike any he'd ever experienced.

He stopped the car about one hundred feet from the drop. Sure enough, a chalk mark indicated a message was waiting. He checked around him for surveillance, and finding none, he stepped up to the hollow stones under the pine tree.

A bough slipped from his fingers, whipped toward his face. His head snapped back, and he was stunned as the sniper's bullet whizzed past and lodged itself in the tree trunk. He dove for the ground, taking cover behind the trees. Using the foliage to hide, he fled down the other side of the knoll. He scanned the street and started running, trying each car door until he found one unlocked. He hotwired the Trabant and took off toward his own apartment.

No suits loitering about his building front door, no suspicious characters he could see. *Thank god for small favors!* He sprinted up the steps to his flat. He had to find a way to contact Beth and get them both out of East Berlin. He tore through the well-ordered heap of useless but damning information left by Collins weeks earlier. Reynolds chastised himself for not prioritizing that mess. It was tortuous boredom to wade through the copious notes, but now they were costing him dearly in escape time. If there was anything worthwhile in there, it was about to be lost in his haste to destroy it.

He heard footsteps on the stairs. Beth! She might have figured out the mismatch between the signal and no message at the drop. *No, no, no! It's dangerous for her here! She mustn't rush over here to investigate!*

He yanked open the door and looked straight into Anneliese's harsh, beautiful face. Then he glanced down.

"Son of a bitch," Liam said under his breath, staring down the business end of a silencer. "Are you the reason I had an unexpected visitor on my morning walk?"

"You think you're so damned smart. *Super Spy Darcy.* Thought you didn't need to bother with protocol because nobody could tail you. Never even considered that I don't need to tail you because I know all about you and your little American friend. Theater student, my ass."

"I don't know who you're talking about, Anneliese." He eased back into the room, hoping she'd follow him. It would give her less opportunity to cover the flat and the building's entrance if they were inside the room.

"It's Natalia, not Anneliese."

"You don't like the name the Stasi gave you?"

She shook her head, smiling grimly.

"And Oberst Vandenburg is not your mother, I presume."

"She was a means to an end, that's all. A means to your end as the heroic CIA officer. She's been in on this from the beginning. The very beginning."

"Then it appears that I am amazingly stupid." She was twitchy, he realized, and that might give him an opportunity to escape. "I thought we were on the same side. I even broke protocol for you because I thought you were in trouble. I thought we all were. I wanted to help you, maybe I still can, but I couldn't say such a thing on the phone. I had to get—had to warn..."

"The chorus girl?" She snorted. "Don't look so shocked. I know you pretended to be passed out drunk that night we spent in West Berlin so you could avoid sleeping with me. And I have seen the way your eyes follow her everywhere she goes. A smart woman intuits these things. But she is expendable, no one of consequence. I knew all along it was *you* they wanted. Wilhelm told me..."

"Who?" Reynolds demanded in spite of himself. "Who told you?"

"Shut up!" she said in Russian and cocked the pistol.

"You don't want to do this."

"Not particularly, no. I like you, Darcy. But he wants you—alive and working for us if possible, but if not, just gone will work. Either way, your time here is over. You are coming with me."

She blinked, a tell signaling what was to come, and that gave him the split second he needed. He dove to the left, behind the metal desk, drawing his handgun out from the holster strapped beneath his jacket. A searing pain tore through his right arm, and he switched the gun to his left hand.

Damn it to hell, damn it to hell!

The Stasi would be along any minute. He heard footsteps storming the hallway. But the voices he heard weren't German, they were Russian.

Of course, Anneliese would have a KGB partner on this little expedition. They'd never send her in alone. He was probably the sniper, the sniper that had missed him on purpose and driven him here, right into their trap.

"I told you to wait!" The male voice hissed out a Russian expletive.

There was a silence, and he knew she was giving her comrade the location of her prey. Darcy drew in his attention and focused on the two shooters. He listened for the disturbance of air and the scent of fear that would give away the man's position. Inching around the metal trashcan, he fired a shot that caught the guy in his knee. As the big Russian bear fell back against the wall, Darcy rolled out from behind the desk, and in one fluid motion, he triple tapped him, two bullets into the man's chest, one into his head. He whirled around just as Anneliese took aim, and before she could pull the trigger, he pointed and fired, right through her forehead.

Her finger reflexively pulled the trigger as she fell, and his side exploded with pain.

He screamed—out loud? Or just in his head? The scream burned in his throat, echoed in his mind.

He reached for the phone. Dialed.

Holy hell, am I in trouble!

13

DARCY FRANTICALLY GATHERED files and rifled through them, pulling out the occasional stray paper and stuffing it into a beaten-up leather briefcase while he damned Bill Collins and his organizing ways to hell and back. Destroying all this paper was sucking away valuable escape time.

Spy Rule Number Four: An undercover man's worst enemy is a set of neat, orderly files. "Stupid fool." Darcy muttered under his breath.

The voice on the other end of the line was drowsy, reminding him of the time difference between East Berlin and the States.

"Who is this?"

"You know who this is!" he hissed in a violent whisper that evolved into a gasp. He looked down at his bloodstained shirt. It had bloomed significantly in the last minute or so. *How much time do I have before I pass out from loss of blood?*

"Good god, man—it's four in the morning!"

"Well, it isn't four in the morning here, and they'll be able to spot me a mile away in the bright German sunshine."

"Where are you?" His colleague's voice changed from a yawn to a semi-awake mumble. "And what's the security status of this phone line?"

"I'm in a dive in East Berlin, where I had to set up shop after Budapest—and this may be my final destination if either the Stasi or their KGB handlers find me and finish me off."

All sleepiness faded as the man's voice leapt from drowsy to aware in a fraction of second. "Tell me."

"This morning I got a frantic—and unsecured—phone call from Stonewall."

"What did she say?"

"She was in trouble. The Stasi knew everything. She wanted out."

"She wanted asylum? We can't give everyone asylum. You know we're supposed to keep the assets in place. Convince this one to stay put and let us assess the situation first."

"Don't quote me agency clichés from the safety of your uppity Georgetown address. I've got a real emergency here!"

"Stonewall called *you*? And didn't contact the cut-out through the drop? That's not procedure."

"I know, I know. But it's complicated. Because Stonewall isn't an asset. She's a damned KGB officer who's played us all. She's the actress, and her so-called mother is in on the whole operation. Stonewall threatened me, all of us here: the staff, my—"

"Okay. What's been done so far?"

"I think the other officer is safe. She should be at work this morning, and she wasn't at the drop when I got there."

"Hold it. You went to the drop in person. You, yourself?"

"There wasn't time to do anything else. I couldn't risk her..." A fresh rush of pain washed over him.

"You there?"

"Yep, I'm still here. But god, I'm so screwed! There was a sniper waiting for me at the drop. I think he missed me on purpose—to drive me into the trap."

"Don't tell me you've blown your cover—again!"

"It appears that I have."

"What's your status right now?"

"I was followed, and they got me. This place will be crawling with

Stasi any minute. Call USBER. Tell them I'm on my way to West Berlin, and I'm going to need to get through Checkpoint Charlie in the next couple of hours." He winced. "Tell them to be waiting outside Café Adler."

"A couple of hours?"

"There's someone...no, something...something I have to find first."

"No, your identity's been compromised. You're wounded. I can send a team to your location. Just stay where you are."

"Negative. It's suicide to stay here, man!" *We saw what happens after the mess in Prague: interrogation, torture. Who knows how long I could withstand torture in this state? Thirty-six hours...forty-eight? What would they get from me? Officers' names? Asset names? Drop locations?* "Can't let the others be compromised. Have to get out of here—now."

"I can have our people there in ten minutes. Or I can contact our man from MI6. Stay put."

"I don't have ten minutes! Call Mission Berlin. I'll meet them at the rendezvous." He hung up.

"Damn it!" He clutched his side as he ignited papers stained with his blood and threw them into the fireplace.

Spy Rule Number Seventeen: A good fire covers a multitude of sins.

He took one last look around as he yanked the phone out of the wall. Already, he could hear sirens in the distance.

The fire escape clanged as he let it down, and the last rung unfortunately stuck about ten feet above the ground. Darcy strapped his leather messenger bag across his good shoulder and shimmied down the ladder. He missed half the rungs as he went, and fell the final distance to the ground. With a groan of agony, he stood and began the eight-block trek to the infamous Wall, the demarcation line between East and West, holding one hand to his hastily bandaged gunshot wound.

"BETH?" Karl came up behind her and put a hand on her arm. "Are you all right?"

"I'm fine, Karl." She reached down to straighten the seam in her stocking, dislodging his hand in the process.

"I was relieved when I saw you here this morning."

"Why?"

He looked around before bending to whisper in her ear. "Anneliese is missing."

"Missing? What do you mean missing?" It came out in English first; then she shook her head and lapsed back into German.

"Shh! Not so loud, okay? She didn't come to rehearsal earlier, so Heinrich sent a messenger to her place. She isn't there."

"Maybe she's sick. Have they contacted her mother?"

"I'm sure they have, but I haven't heard anything. Heinrich's got the understudy warming up."

Beth made a quick scan of the theater. If Anneliese had been picked up and was being interrogated, she might finger Beth as her cut-out.

Karl leaned over and spoke in her ear. "I thought you'd want to know because you two seemed close."

"Close?"

"You hang around together sometimes, and you took that trip West together with that Brit and that American."

"Well, yes, but..." People were associating her with Anneliese because of that stupid trip. Not good.

"I thought maybe they got you too."

"Wait, Karl, did the Stasi get Anneliese?"

"People talk, but you never know if what they say is true or not."

"Why would they pick her up? She's an East German theater darling from Dresden. Her mother's a military border guard officer."

"You're right—it's probably nothing. I just wanted you to know I'm here for you. If you needed help, or..." He lifted his shoulder in a half-shrug. "I have friends."

"Oh, Karl." She wondered what kind of friends he had—ones that would turn her in, turn him in, or truly work to get her out. She wondered whether he even knew what kind of friends they were, or whether he himself would be the informant. If he was sincere about helping her, well, it was kind of sweet. If poor Karl only knew she could take him down in seconds flat, concoct half a dozen ways to poison him, or slip over the East-West border virtually unseen with an hour's lead time...

But he didn't know, and for his sake, she'd make sure he never would.

And yet, she worried. She could evade and elude the authorities pretty well, but all bets were off if the wrong government officials got suspicious and plucked her off the street or out of her flat without warning. Suddenly, Beth Steventon knew way too much for comfort. As soon as she could, Beth would check the drop for news from Anneliese—maybe check in with Darcy, or Fitz at the British Embassy. A sense of foreboding raced up and down her spine.

After Karl went off to check the lighting, Beth slipped out the back theater door, scanning for anyone tailing her. There was a Sunday matinee at two o'clock; she couldn't be gone long. Satisfied that she wasn't being followed, she rode her bike by Volkspark Friedrichshain. Sure enough, there was a chalk mark on the sidewalk, indicating a drop had been made. She walked up behind the fir trees and, bathed in their evergreen boughs, leaned down to lift the bottom layer and open the hollow stone.

Empty.

Empty?

Meaning someone had been there before her and retrieved the message but hadn't erased the chalk signal. The message *should* have been coded, but if it wasn't...

Her head began to pound as the possibilities poured through her mind like water over a dam.

She peered out of the boughs of the tree and headed down the back side and out the west entrance of the park, pedaling as fast as she could go.

Beth approached Darcy's flat, slowing when she saw the suit standing outside.

"Not good, not good," she muttered. If Anneliese was gone, a message was missing from the drop, and the Stasi were outside the flat, something must be going down. But she couldn't rush in there or rush away. She veered smoothly across the street and ducked into the cafe without being noticed. She'd grab a seat and watch. Maybe Darcy wasn't even in his flat. Maybe they were just searching it, and she could warn him in time. Or confront him. Catch him in the act of double espionage. She'd finally have the evidence Wickham was looking for.

And then what? If he were innocent, they'd both be in hot water, surrounded by East German secret police. If he were guilty, she'd go the way of the mysterious Jirina. Beth shivered. She'd wait it out and see what transpired.

She'd been idling at the outdoor cafe about five minutes when a shot rang out in the crisp morning air. The agent rushed into the apartment building, and Beth had to swallow her heart back down because it had leaped into her throat at the sound of more gunfire. Surreptitiously, she exited the cafe and, leaving her bike out front, began the four-block walk to the British Embassy. There, she'd find Fitz or use the embassy's safe room to call Washington for further instructions. About a block away, at the sound of a siren, she turned around and saw a lone, tall figure make his run toward Brandenburg Gate. She recognized him at once. William Darcy had been compromised by either East or West and was on the move.

At the back of her mind, a niggling voice whispered. *If he's a double agent, why would he run?*

TWO BLOCKS DOWN, *six to go.* He walked fast, scanning left and right and taking a quick peek behind him. Two men stood at the street corner near his flat, smoke rolling out the window above their heads. The Stasi officers pointed in his direction, and as there was no need for secrecy now, Darcy kicked it into gear and took off up the street.

His heart raced with either adrenaline or the necessity of

pumping the blood he still had to his vital organs. There was an old safe house in this area. Ducking around the corner of a building, he searched along the alley for the rowan tree above the door—an ancient symbol of protection, marking safe houses that had been in use long before Darcy had come to the divided city.

What would he do after he found the place? He had no mobile communication device on him to call for help.

Halfway down the alley, he found the safe house door. He made quick work of the nine-pane window above the doorknob, breaking the pane closest to the door handle with half a brick. Reaching inside, he unlocked the knob and winced as he cut his hand on the glass.

Wrenching the door open, he eased around the corner, making sure the dark room was empty. Apparently, the safe house had been a bakery at some time in the past; it still smelled faintly of dust and yeast. The flour had been swept up, however. No footprints in white powder would leave a trail for the Stasi to follow, although the blood dripping from his hand might. He stuffed his hand under the opposite sleeve to staunch the wound. He could hear his own harsh breathing in the still of the Sunday morning. Most people were sleeping in, although a few might be subverting the government by attending church services. Darcy tried to remember the last time he slept in or was in a church for that matter—to attend a service, not to drop off money, or instructions, or meet an asset or a defector—but the memory eluded him. Pulling aside the curtain hanging at the doorway of the pantry, he wriggled his way inside the small room. Beyond that back panel lay temporary living quarters. It was a tight fit, but hopefully, it would shield him from prying eyes and passersby until...

Until what? He was starting to become dizzy now, light-headed, cold, and clammy. "Hypovolemic shock." He mumbled the textbook definition in an attempt to hold onto rational thought. "Symptoms are anxiety, confusion, weakness, pallor, rapid breathing, sweating, unconsciousness." *I wonder who will find me?*

Given the day he'd had so far, she'd be a harsh, beautiful KGB officer—someone who'd kick his body where it lay.

Women—the bane of his existence in one way or another. From his cold, distant mother to the tempting blonde with the ice blue eyes who'd caused today's disaster. They were all out to get him, or get something out of him.

"No," he whispered to the silent room. *Not fair—there was one. One who was innocent and trusting.* One girl—he called her a girl, rather than a woman, because she was little more than a child—a little sprite with brains and kindness and bravery.

"Jirina," he whispered softly and for the umpteenth time, "I'm so sorry."

In many ways, she was the great regret of his life. Not because he'd never been her lover, because he didn't care for her in that way. He had, however, let her get away. Or rather, Wickham had—the slimy bastard. It was Wickham who made the self-serving decision that cost the agency one of its most promising assets, and cost her... well, everything. And now the Amazing Jirina, as Darcy had once jokingly called her, was no more. Her joie de vivre, her brilliance, her life—forgotten by all but a few.

Pain roared through his brain and body with renewed vengeance, consuming his attention. His mind wandered, he realized. He began to see little spots behind his eyelids, and his breath came in shallow pants. He tried to swallow them back as he heard harsh German voices pass the front of the safe house. And he hid, desperately fighting the oblivion threatening to overtake him.

Think! he demanded of himself and tried to remember his train of thought before he let the spirit of Jirina overtake him.

Women.

Not that Darcy didn't like women. He did—very much so—which was probably part of the reason he was in his current predicament. Some of them were brainy, talented, or helpful in their own way. And some were all of the above. Like *She*, the new, little minion who turned up in Budapest. An accomplished woman in all the ways that mattered although she could certainly be an annoying little shrew.

That smart mouth of hers shouldn't be so charming. However, she knew her languages like a native, and she'd gotten them out of a jam in Hungary when he couldn't do a thing to help her. He hoped she could tap that quick-witted resourcefulness now. If she was going to make it out of East Berlin, she was definitely going to need it.

His vision began to darken. He heard shouts again, a man's, no... there was a female voice in the mix.

Hate. My mind is filled with hate. You and your kind have taken everything from me. And now? Now, you've taken my love. Quite literally, taken her forever. Why did you do it? You didn't have to do it. My handler has summoned me, but I'm not going to him. He says I'm still to bring you to him, but I don't know if that's possible anymore. I don't know what to do with this rage inside me. But I swear on all that is holy, I will make you pay.

14

West Berlin, twelve hours later

"STUPID, ARROGANT JERK!" Elizabeth Bennet muttered for the umpteenth time as she alternated between pacing the hallway outside the operating room and flopping into a chair and gnawing on the tip of her thumb, a childhood habit that reappeared under times of extreme duress. *Why didn't he stay away from the drop like he was supposed to? Why didn't he stay put in his apartment like Fitz said the deputy director told him? They had been less than five minutes away from him for Pete's sake!*

By a stroke of pure luck, she met up with Fitz barely a block from the little café across from Darcy's flat. Somehow, he had obtained carte blanche from MI6 to provide Darcy assistance and rescue if need be. Fitz was the one who remembered the old safe house location, so thank god she had run into him. On her own, she might never have found Darcy in time. And who knows what would have happened to him? Or to her, for that matter. Bottom line? He never should have gone to the drop in person. She could almost hear his haughty voice, *"Spy Rule Number Eighteen: Let the cut-outs do their work, and you do yours."* It was unlike him to make that kind of mistake. Unless, of course, it was no mistake.

This would be a black eye on the whole field office and taint her by association. She and Fitz had saved Darcy from the Stasi at least, but Fitz had to burn an asset, one of his precious border guards on the take, in order to do it. To add insult to injury, this particular border guard had been a Stasi-planted officer, put in the guard to spy on his comrades. That is, until Fitz had turned him into a British asset. It was a tremendous loss; that officer helped the British spirit a lot of people back and forth between East and West Berlin.

She put her hands on her knees and stood—resigned yet determined to face the music. It might not be her screw up, but she knew there would be consequences to this latest turn of events—significant repercussions on her career, regardless of what part she had or hadn't played. She made her way to the elevator, descended to the lobby, and headed out into the night. After rounding the corner, she entered a public phone booth and made her call.

"*Müller*," said a friendly female voice on the other end.

"Good evening. I need to speak with George Wickham," Elizabeth said in German.

"Mr. Wickham is having his dinner," the voice replied, considerably less friendly now.

"Well, tell him it's urgent, will you?"

"Something wrong at the factory?"

"Fraulein, you can say that again."

Elizabeth heard the woman cover the phone with her hand and call for George.

"Wickham."

"George. I hope your pretty German mistress isn't listening in on the line. She seemed none too pleased to call you to the phone."

"Well, hello, darling. I thought I told you never to call me here," he said, his voice laced with amusement.

"Ha-ha. Look—we have a problem."

"Oh? A problem with what?"

"With the target."

"Did he muss his tuxedo? Spill his martini? Lose his medal?"

Elizabeth ignored the sarcasm. "As we speak, Single Man is in a West Berlin hospital in critical condition because an asset tried to kill him this morning. Damn near succeeded too."

"You don't say?" Wickham actually sounded intrigued at the news.

"In addition, getting him out cost MI6 one of their best border guards."

"Unfortunate, but it happens on occasion."

"Don't joke about this! I could have been arrested today!"

"You're right." Wickham lowered his voice in an attempt to soothe her. "You're absolutely right. Now, tell me what happened."

"Darcy told me there was a sniper waiting for him at the drop, but the shooter missed."

"Why was he at the drop anyway?"

"Why?" Elizabeth paused. "Hell, I don't know why!"

"Piss-poor sniper if you ask me. Then what?"

"He went to his flat. That's where he was shot."

"By who?"

"The asset, Anneliese Vandenburg. At least, I believe it was her. Darcy called her 'Natalia' but—"

"What makes you think it was Vandenburg?"

"She didn't show up for work today. Believe me, it would take some earth-shattering event to keep her out of that theater when she was the star of the show. I knew something was up, so I went to look for him. I saw the goons outside his building. I heard the shots, for heaven's sake!" Her voice began to wobble.

"Okay, okay. So then you went into the flat?"

"No, Fitz and I found him in a safe house a few blocks away. Before he lost consciousness, Darcy tried to tell me there's a traitor on the loose. He said his assailant said a name—Wilhelm."

Silence on the other end.

"Did you hear me?" Elizabeth asked with impatience.

"I did."

"You know what that means, don't you?"

"What do *you* think it means?"

"That this whole line of internal investigation is for naught. We've been barking up the wrong tree all this time—since Budapest." She kicked the wall of the phone booth.

"Did we recover this dead Natalia? Can we verify her identity?"

"No, we left her behind. Had to. We barely got him across the checkpoint still breathing."

"Unfortunate."

"Do you mean about the shooter left behind, the border guard lost, or about Darcy still breathing?"

"Tsk, tsk, Ms. Bennet. That's no way to talk about our hero. Of course, I mean the girl. The border guard is MI6's loss, not ours."

"Just making sure I understand. Still not sure I believe you."

"We still don't have any information that would clear Darcy of suspicion."

"Go on."

"Here's what I think *really* happened. I told you that day in West Berlin that Vandenburg was the one in danger, remember?"

"Well, yeah, but—"

"So Darcy arrives in East Berlin and within days, he puts the Stasi on Vandenburg's trail. She's a traitor to her country, right? They'll want her stopped. Over the next month or so, they plan to get rid of her, but then she gets wind that the Stasi are on to her—she thinks she's being followed, sees her place has been searched—and she contacts Darcy for help. After all, he's American, he's her lover, and she thinks she can trust him."

"Yes, okay."

"Now the Stasi have to move immediately. She's getting ready to flee the country. So Darcy gets his orders. He has to dispose of her before she goes to the West again."

"I suppose it could have happened that way."

"You're the cut-out, but Darcy knows where the drop is, right?"

"Right, but the sniper—"

"Damn it, Lizzy! He *made up* the story about the sniper! The sniper was for Anneliese; he set the whole thing up to ice her when she checked the drop. But then the stupid sniper missed her. She runs to Darcy's place, so he has to do the dirty work and finish the job himself. He kills her in the end, but she goes down shooting and takes a piece of him before she goes."

Elizabeth considered. It made a certain amount of sense, but something felt off—from the vehemence in Wickham's tone to his unwillingness to consider any other scenario. "Again, George, why? The name she gave him was Wilhelm. He told us that. If Darcy's the double agent, why would he give us his own name?"

"A diversion—to throw us off his trail."

"You didn't see him today. I doubt he had the wherewithal to even consider his trail. He was going into shock when we found him."

"My opinion? The KGB told him to kill her, so he did. Darcy is ruthless. Don't forget what he did to Jirina."

"Yes, I've heard the story."

"You know what she meant to me."

"I've heard that too, several times—how wonderful she was, how brilliant, how you loved her."

"Darcy may not have actually pulled the trigger, but he was responsible for Jirina's death nonetheless. He led her on with misinformation designed to cover his own tracks. He sent her on a wild goose chase that got her killed."

She didn't want to get him started on another one of those rants. "So what do you want me to do now? I can't very well gather information on a comatose officer. Seems pointless."

"You can, and you will. Wait around the hospital. See who tries to contact him. Guard him from the KGB. We want him alive so he can pay for his crimes when the time comes. I'm going to arrange it with the director for you to remain in West Berlin and follow our target wherever he ends up after he recovers—if he recovers. My guess is they'll bring him back to Washington as soon as they can. Keep your secrets close to your vest. We don't want to chance him knowing we're so close to the truth."

Elizabeth snorted in frustration. She was tired of this—tired of Darcy and tired of Wickham's tunnel-vision vengeance. There was a real secret war out here, and instead of helping win it, she had spent the last eight months babysitting William Darcy, an egotistical, demoted station chief, and nursing the bitter spirit of George Wickham, a demoted case officer.

But Wickham—and the director—had plucked her out of a whole class of recruits for this counterintelligence mission, one that any new graduate would be thrilled to get. She owed it to them to finish the job, and finish it she would.

"I guess this means I'm going back to the States."

"I'll keep you posted. For now, just relax. You're safe and sound in West Berlin."

"You're the boss."

"I thought we were a team."

"Sure." But she was starting to have her doubts.

"Lizzy?"

"Yes?"

"Stay alert. Keep your eyes peeled. Keep those reports coming. I know it's a lot of watching and waiting, but it will be worth it in the end. You're serving the agency well. We need people with their heads on straight, and that's you in a nutshell. Good luck."

"Yes, sir." Elizabeth hung up.

Exiting the phone booth, she crossed the street and entered a quiet pub. It was raining when she emerged from the hospital, and even though it had stopped, the street was dotted with puddles that reflected the streetlights like mirrors. As the cars went through them, the sound of water being displaced hissed into the cool dark.

Sitting alone at the window, she watched the evening traffic drift by. If Wickham was right about Darcy, they were closer to finally snagging an agency mole, someone who threatened the lives of every officer in the European division. So why couldn't she dismiss this nagging apprehension in the back of her mind?

Sure, Darcy rubbed her the wrong way from the start. Like she'd told Fitz that day in Volkspark Friedrichshain, Elizabeth first laid eyes on him when he gave the lecture at The Farm. If she were honest, she'd admit she let her eyes linger on him too. She would have been dead *not* to notice the tall man with the rangy build, the brooding expression, and a rich baritone that rumbled in a girl's ears. Then he insulted her and the entire class. Strike One against the London Fog.

Months later, when Elizabeth arrived in Budapest, she was determined to show him she had the right stuff to be a field officer. Oh, *she* remembered *him* from that day at The Farm, but when they met again at the Hungarian ambassador's party, he hadn't even recognized her. It annoyed her even more. *Strike Two.*

The first night in Hungary was memorable, an exercise in personal and professional embarrassment. She was in her first grown-up cocktail dress. Darcy wore a tuxedo and ordered a martini, like an overused spy novel trope. The beautiful ambassador's wife at his elbow made the stereotype complete.

Just out of training, Elizabeth's head was filled with her new orders from the director. Part of the cover story included Darcy "meeting" her at this party and striking up a conversation. That meant he'd have to publicly ditch the stunner with the flaxen hair and svelte figure, which was a stretch in Elizabeth's opinion. Even though she never thought of herself as ugly or even just plain, men didn't turn away blonde bombshells for cute, little Elizabeth Bennet with her ski jump nose dusted in freckles, and her average bust size and height.

Darcy played his part well, however, doing a double take when he saw her at the other end of the bar. She played her part too, pulling out a cigarette and turning expectantly to the portly bearded fellow beside her. The poor man blushed a bright shade of red and dug frantically in his pockets for a light, but it was Darcy, aka Darby Kent, who gallantly stepped between them and offered a burst of flame, both from his sterling silver lighter and his bedroom eyes. The small-town girl hidden inside the newly minted officer giddily accepted the light, the conversation he initiated, and the invitation to dance a few minutes later. She felt extremely proud of her undercover expertise so far.

But he ruined her spy-girl buzz when he tugged her close against him, leaned down and murmured low in her ear, "If you're going to pretend to smoke one of those cheap, foul-smelling cancer-sticks, you'll have to do more than sit there holding it while it stinks up the air around the entire table. For god's sake, take a drag off the thing every once in a while."

Strike Three.

Her look of shock must have been priceless, because he grinned at her and pulled her back against him, whispering, "Masterful expression of 'shocked, yet intrigued.' You look like I just proposed you do something salaciously scandalous." He trailed his fingers down her bare back and flattened his palm against her spine just above her derriere, making her blood simmer.

Jerk.

After the dance, he led her off the floor, gave a flick of a gesture to his host, and hustled her out the door and into his car.

That was Elizabeth Bennet's first up close encounter with "the London Fog."

From that moment on, the tone of their interactions was set. He lorded his knowledge and experience over her head with all his stupid-ass "Spy Rule Number 8000 whatever." She, in turn, needled him like an annoying insect every chance she got.

The first month had been rough, but over time, she thought he'd started to depend on her. He needed her to communicate with Hungarian assets and enemies, and he'd come to rely on her pithy wit for his amusement. At least, that was her impression because he appeared to enjoy goading her.

During the ensuing months they worked together in Budapest, and later in East Berlin, she had developed a grudging respect for Darcy's skill as an officer, even if he might be a double agent. Most of the time, she didn't know what to think. He often seemed on the up and up, but that would be the mark of a good mole, would it not?

And then there was the way he changed his entire appearance between assignments. That lean, dangerous, intellectual persona he cultivated in East Berlin fascinated her. She caught herself watching him as he talked to Anneliese outside the theater, or when he appeared suddenly to "walk her home" after rehearsals. Seeing him interact with Fitz brought out glimmers of a complex man underneath all the subterfuge. Darcy was arrogant, blunt, and dismissive, but he could also be kind, sympathetic, and complimentary. Who could blame her if she found all those contradictions sexy as hell?

Of course, Wickham always gave her a good dose of reality whenever she checked in. William Darcy played the espionage game better than almost anyone, and Wickham wouldn't let her forget it. She was grateful for that reminder. It helped keep her priorities in line—and her naughty dreams at bay.

Darcy had almost gotten himself, and quite possibly her own self, killed today. "Stupid, arrogant jerk," she muttered again, all her resentment bubbling back up to the surface like the sticky foam on her dark German beer.

Elizabeth finished her meal, paid her check, and made her way back to the hospital waiting room.

The doctor was speaking with Fitzwilliam—in a mixture of English and German—about Darcy's condition. Fitz turned to her as she approached, and he nodded toward the double doors at the end of the hall.

"He's still in recovery, but if you identify yourself to the nurse and the guard outside the door, they'll let you in to see him."

When she entered the room, the beeping of the monitors and machines filled the air. She approached him, taking in the long, lean form stretched out on a white hospital bed. Tubes came out of his mouth. An IV flowed from his wrist. Bandages covered his right side just below the rib cage, and his right arm was immobilized. He was deathly pale, his dark hair matted against his head, stubble just beginning to appear on his jaw.

A nurse came in and fed something into the IV tube.

"Your husband?" she asked Elizabeth in German.

"No."

"Brother?"

"No." She chuckled. "He's my 'colleague' for lack of a better word. How is he?"

"Critical but stable. Very lucky man. Two gunshot wounds—the one in the upper arm will give him more trouble in the long run. The one in his side just grazed the skin."

"It sure bled a lot."

The nurse came over and patted her shoulder. "He will recover with medical attention and with time."

"What did you just give him?"

"Antibiotic. We want no infections."

"No, we don't."

The nurse wrote some notes on the chart at the foot of his bed. "I'll be back to check on him."

Elizabeth stepped up to stand beside Darcy's left side and gently touched his uninjured arm. As she looked at him now, so ill and helpless, it was hard to imagine him ever selling government secrets or shooting a woman who was trying to flee to the West.

But earlier that day, with ruthless efficiency, he had likely killed the woman he himself had code-named Stonewall—a woman with whom he had been intimate.

Elizabeth shivered and left the room.

15

DARCY'S EYES POPPED OPEN, the rush of blood pumping through his veins as he gasped himself awake. His eyes darted to and fro, trying to figure out where in the hell he was. *Room, hospital room.* He smelled the antiseptic and heard the beeping of a heart rate monitor. He turned his head and thought the motion would make him sick to his stomach. The staccato sound of the monitor began to accelerate. The young woman sitting in the hospital chair by the window looked up at the change in speed.

She.

Relief washed over him. *She had made it out of East Berlin. Wait, surely we're out of East Berlin, right?* His eyes darted around the room again, processing. The facilities certainly seemed better kept than the local hospitals in the GDR.

His eyes connected with hers, and the monitor betrayed him as his heart sped up even further. Not only had she made it out, she had made it out unscathed and sat before him bathed in glorious sunlight that gave her a halo of reds and golds surrounding unruly auburn hair. He couldn't drown himself in her fine eyes from across the room, but he remembered them. So many times over the last few months, he'd caught himself staring at her, and then he'd yanked back his self-control—quickly, before she could read the fascination in his expression.

She set her newspaper aside and shot him a brisk, business-like smile. "Welcome back." She rose from her chair and approached the bed. "Wide awake and raring to go, if your heart rate's any indication." She eyed the monitor. "Really raring to go. Maybe that's just a result of waking up. I'll call the nurse."

He protested, or tried to, but his throat was raw and his voice came out in a hoarse moan.

"Don't try to talk. You were intubated until last night."

He tried to shift in the bed.

"Be careful moving around too. They just changed those bandages this morning."

"Where'm I?" he croaked.

"Bethesda. Walter Reed hospital."

"States?"

"Yes, genius, the States."

He tried to work up a smirk, but it surfaced as a grimace instead. "You?"

"I'm in the States too." She grinned at his wobbly attempt at an eye roll. "I'm fine—no thanks to you and your unscheduled trip from East to West." She put her hands on her hips and glared at him.

"But...why?" he whispered.

"Why am I here?"

He nodded.

"I still work with you, so I go where you do. Apparently. Lucky me."

No, lucky me. Or unlucky, depending on how one looked at it. He was in for another battle in this continuous war with himself, fighting his attraction to her. At the moment, however, it seemed like a blissful kind of torture.

She picked up the call bell. "Time to get the nurse. They said to buzz the minute you became conscious."

He stayed her hand by grasping her wrist. "You got me out."

"Fitz was mostly responsible." She stared at his hand.

"You treated my wound." His voice was getting stronger, so he tried to pull himself upright.

"Hey, wait a minute." Her tone was patient but firm while she reached over to help ease his struggle. "Maybe you shouldn't sit up yet."

He sank back into the bed. With eyes closed against the fluorescent light, he brought her hand to his lips and kissed it. "Thank you."

When he opened them, he saw the surprise and confusion in hers. He saw her blush. She pulled her hand away. "No problem. You'd have done the same for me."

"I would," he replied in a solemn voice. Behind the barrier he kept in place to protect himself, he silently admitted the truth. *I would do anything for you.*

"DAMNATION, Bennet! Are you trying to kill me?"

"It's tempting!" Elizabeth expelled a growl and let go of Darcy's arm. "The physical therapist says you need range of motion on that shoulder."

"She's trying to kill me too," he mumbled under his breath. "All the pretty women are trying to kill me."

She fought the urge to smile and ignored his griping. "Three times a day." She punctuated the order by holding up three fingers in front of his face. "No excuses. Isn't that what you'd tell me if the situation were reversed?"

He sat back and crossed his arms over his chest, wincing as he did so. His bottom lip stuck out a fraction, the perfect imitation of a pouting toddler.

"I want to laugh and shake you at the same time."

"I wish the powers that be would tell me what in the hell they're doing. I'm sick and tired of this place," he snarled, gesturing around inside their CIA safe house near Langley.

"I can't imagine you're going anywhere, banged up as you are."

"Anything's better than this sitting around, doing nothing." *And staring at your ass all day—that is, when I'm not sneaking looks down your blouse.*

"It's only been two weeks. You're rehabilitating, not 'doing nothing'."

"So why don't they let me go home? I've a nice house in Georgetown. It has an office. I could rehabilitate there."

Elizabeth sighed in resignation. "I don't know, Darcy. They won't let me go home either."

He stopped. "Where is home for you, anyway? I'm not sure I ever knew."

"I thought you said good agents don't talk about their personal lives. That was Spy Rule Number Twenty-two or some such nonsense."

"I'm just making conversation. You don't have to tell me exactly, just give me an idea: small Southern town, big noisy city, California suburbs, Midwest farming community."

She reached for his arm and began the range of motion exercises again. "Illinois. My father was a foreman on one of those big commercial farms."

"What did they grow?"

"Corn mostly. Soybeans sometimes."

"Farmer's daughter? Yeah, you look like one of those."

"What the hell is *that* supposed to mean?"

"You know, you look—"

"Yes?"

"Oh, what's the word? Ah, wholesome, I guess."

The phone interrupted them, and Elizabeth glared at him while she picked it up. "Bennet." Her face drained of color. "Yes." More silence on her end, voices on the other. "Tell him we're on our way. Thank you."

"What was that all about?" he asked as she put the phone back in its cradle. "You're white as a ghost."

"Deputy director's office. He wants us there in an hour."

"What for?"

She looked at him and they locked gazes. "The secretary didn't say, but I think we finally might be getting out of here."

A CAR WAS WAITING downstairs to take them to Langley. They rode in silence, Darcy brooding as he gazed out the window, and Elizabeth chewing on her thumb and trying to remember not to chew on her thumb.

The Suit-of-the-Day, as Elizabeth had begun calling their security detail, drove through the gate, showing credentials to the guard before he dropped them off outside the front door.

"You need help, Mr. Darcy?" The Suit asked.

"No," he snapped. He hoisted himself and his bandaged arm out of the car, slamming the door. Elizabeth hurried out the passenger side and up the stairs ahead of him. She turned to see him white-faced and drawn.

"You're still not a hundred percent." She laid a hand on his arm. "And you shouldn't expect to be."

"You're not my wife, and you're not my doctor. No need to dish out the warm, fuzzy sympathy."

She drew her lips into a thin line, paused as if she were about to say something but thought better of it, and turned back to the door. She yanked it open and walked through, forcing Darcy to let himself in with his good arm.

The deputy director's seventh-floor office was opulent but messy. Elizabeth had never met the man, but Darcy told her they had been co-workers back in the day, and the two men were still friends. She didn't know how Darcy's former colleague could be so completely opposite of him in work habits—Darcy's surroundings were Spartan —but the space seemed functional for the unknown officer-turned-administrator who was only a year or so into this position.

Elizabeth stopped just inside the door, frozen in shock.

"Darcy!" Deputy Director Charles Bingley came in from another door behind his desk—looking remarkably well, Elizabeth thought.

Better than he had the last time she had seen him, his arm around a fragile Johanna Bodnar in Vienna.

"Hello, Charles."

"I have to say, I'm damn glad to see you in one piece and on the mend."

"I'm glad to be seen."

"I was afraid that phone call from East Berlin might be the last time we spoke." He turned to Elizabeth. "And you've brought your go-to-officer in the field."

"Which you already knew, given that you sent for both of us."

"True enough. How are you, Liz Hertford? Or should I say, Elizabeth Bennet?"

"Charles?"

He gave her that quick, handsome grin of his.

"I...I can't believe it. You're Ambassador Hurst's idle brother-in-law. Not..."

"It's a good cover, isn't it? Even the case officers don't suspect me. Having Louis so high in the State Department has really helped, in more ways than one. Of course, it's hard to hide from seasoned guys like this one." He put a hand on Darcy's good shoulder.

"What's happened to our Alsómező friend?" She had been itching for news of Johanna Bodnar, and now she could get an update straight from the horse's mouth.

"Ah, doing well, as far as I know," he said hurriedly, glancing at Darcy.

"Is she in the States? Perhaps I could see her."

"I think we could arrange something." Bingley deftly changed the subject. "I feel compelled to thank you." He pressed her hand in both of his. "Your service to your fellow officer here, and to the CIA, does you credit."

"Thank you. I'm just glad it didn't result in a star on Memorial Wall."

He smiled. "Yes, we're all pleased about that. Let's sit down, shall we? We have a lot to discuss." He led them across the office and opened a set of double doors leading to a conference room. A number of officers and security men gathered in groups of two or three, talking in soft tones, and a long table monopolized the space.

"Coffee please, Bridget," Bingley murmured quietly to his assistant as he gestured Darcy and Elizabeth into the conference room with his arm. "After you."

Darcy stepped in, and this time it was he who froze in his tracks. Elizabeth felt the resentment rolling off him in waves and the toxic vibe returned in equal measure. At the other end of the table sat George Wickham.

Well, this meeting is full of surprises. Playing her part as Darcy's colleague rather than Wickham's, she took a seat and turned to hold out a chair for Darcy. He plopped in it, glaring furiously at Wickham, at Bingley, and then at the table in front of him.

Bingley joined them, pulling his chair up to the table.

"I appreciate you all being here today. Darcy, you especially—I know you still have some recovery ahead of you."

Darcy nodded.

"We have had a situation arise—one that needs our immediate attention and, I think, a change in operations, at least for a while. George?"

Wickham cleared his throat. "There's been some chatter over in the West German intelligence channels. Some rumors about a mole in the CIA. Those kinds of rumors aren't new, but in light of recent events, they deserved some attention. In the messages from East to West Berlin, they refer to this mole as Wilhelm..."

Darcy interrupted. "That's the name I was given by my assailant."

Wickham went on as if Darcy hadn't spoken. "While it's possible that name was a plant of some kind to throw us off base, I think we have to consider that this Wilhelm may be a real threat. Not only that he might be real"—Wickham speared Elizabeth with a brief look —"we think he may be here."

"Here—as in here in the States?" she asked.

"Here—as in here at Langley."

"Impossible," a voice piped up from the other side of the room. There was a collective roll of the eyes.

"Nothing's impossible, Collins," Wickham declared. "We know your favorite asset has weighed in on this, but other sources—"

"My Soviet contact in East Berlin, Ekaterina, insists that there is no Soviet intelligence officer within the walls of Langley. Due to her contacts within the KGB, she has intimate knowledge of the workings of the highest levels of the Soviet government. She..."

Elizabeth let her attention wander. Collins was always spouting off in one way or another about this "contact" who, in truth, was nothing more than the widow of a mid-level bureaucrat. Her information was rarely even relevant and almost never confirmed by the agency's other sources.

"Uh, Collins, is it?" Bingley interrupted. "Be a good man, would you, and get a copy of your original report for me? I want to take another look at it."

Several smirks were exchanged around the table. Elizabeth saw Collins take in the looks and almost thought she saw wheels turning for a second. His expression tightened into a mask of contempt that flickered and then died so quickly she might have imagined it. He beamed at Bingley. "Of course, sir, it's in my office in the other building. It may take a while."

"It could be important, so take your time, and bring me the complete report—and your notes."

"My notes, sir?"

"Yes. I appreciate your effort."

"Yes, sir!" He left the room.

"Thank god," Darcy mumbled under his breath.

Bingley waited several seconds then buzzed his assistant. "Bridget, if he comes back before we're finished, implement Code Eighteen."

"Code Eighteen?" Elizabeth asked, confused.

"Director is playing a round of golf with some high-ranking official."

Darcy sat back in his chair, eyeing Charles carefully. He still refused to make eye contact with George.

"This information could have been conveyed by phone or message. Why bring us down here?"

"There's a new wrinkle in the situation."

"Spell it out, Charles. I'm growing old waiting for you to give it to me straight."

Charles sat back and studied his old friend as he spoke. "This attempt on your life, along with what happened in Prague and the close escape in Hungary, as well as other information I'm not at liberty to share with you yet, has led our analyst here"—he indicated Wickham—"to recommend that we put you under protection."

"What?" He whirled around on Wickham. "Son-of-a-bitch! You're recommending they take me out of the field?"

"Sit down, Darcy." Bingley spoke sharply then softened his voice. "Please." The men standing at the corners of the room tensed, ready to intervene. Darcy observed them and then looked around the room, realization dawning.

"You think I botched those assignments in Prague, in Hungary— on purpose? You think I'm Wilhelm? I'm some kind of...double agent?"

"Relax. No one thinks that."

Darcy pointed at Wickham. "He does. He has for months, ever since Ramsgate."

Wickham held up his hands, a show of surrender, but Elizabeth caught the smug little spark in his eyes.

Bingley interceded again. "I don't think you're a double agent— not by any stretch of the imagination. We are concerned, however, that you may have been the intended target of the abduction in Prague and a victim of the leak in Budapest. Obviously, you were the target in East Berlin. We need to get you out of the line of fire for a while until we can sort this out—figure out why in hell they want you so much."

"I know a lot of people working across Europe. If the KGB could get that kind of information out of me..."

Wickham snorted.

"But this is Langley! What makes you think they would come

after me here? I understand if I'm out in the field, but they won't try to get to me in the US."

"We think they might. And with a mole inside, they might succeed."

"That makes no sense."

"It does if you can help us identify this Wilhelm."

"I can't."

"But once we debrief you and Elizabeth and put your information with ours, it's possible we can. Wickham's intelligence sources say the former Prague station chief is believed to know Wilhelm personally. You were the COS, Darcy. And if they think you can help us identify their mole, they'll want you dead—no matter where you are."

"But—"

"Plus there may be some retribution for the deaths of their agents in East Berlin."

"I don't believe this."

"If your identity has been compromised, and on the chance that the KGB can track your assignments and location, you're a danger, not only to yourself but to anyone who works with you. We can't risk it. We have to take our analyst's recommendations."

Darcy slumped back in his chair. His expression was glum. "Very clever, Wickham. That's the one scenario you knew would work on me—putting the others at risk."

"No left-handed compliments are required," Wickham said. "I would never assume you'd consider anyone above yourself. I simply recommend what needs to be done."

Darcy snarled and turned to Bingley. "So, do you have a plan, Deputy Director?"

"We have a safe house in northern Virginia. The cover is set. We pretended to put the house up for sale, and you"—he looked down at the folder on his desk—"Dr. William Eliot, Civil War historian, on sabbatical to write a book on Civil War weaponry, are now the proud owner of a Federalist style fixer-upper. That is, you"—and here he grinned mischievously—"and your lovely wife."

"Wife? What wife?"

Bingley looked at Elizabeth, his eyes twinkling.

"Oh no," Elizabeth declared. "No way! Pretending to be his wild Hungarian fling is bad enough. I'm certainly not posing as his wife." She tossed a frantic glance at Darcy, once up and down, and turned to Bingley with a pleading look on her face. "Look at him," she whispered. "The very idea of being married to me is about to make him toss his breakfast all over your expensive mahogany conference table."

Darcy did indeed look shell-shocked.

"Don't fret. It's temporary. He needs a believable cover, which you can help provide. You know the area, correct?"

Darcy spoke up. "But you said you were from Illinois."

"I lied, okay?" She turned back to Bingley. "My dad's family is from Taylorsville, but I haven't been there in years—since my grandmother died."

"You won't be in Taylorsville. You'll be in Fredericksburg, hidden in plain sight. You know enough of the area, the community, the social structure. So it's perfect." The deputy director laid a hand on her shoulder. "There's something else you should consider."

"What's that?"

"If the KGB broke Darcy's cover, then they almost certainly have broken yours as well. And if they've sent an assassin to the States for him—"

Elizabeth paled.

"Your life's at risk too, Elizabeth. You simply can't function effectively as a field officer at the current time. The decision's been made. Think of it as a vacation."

Elizabeth's eyebrows shot up. *A vacation? Is he serious? A vacation is a couple of weeks on a tropical island, lounging on the beach with a romance novel in one hand, a piña colada in the other, and a sweet but not too bright bronzed Adonis at my feet. Not a cold, miserable existence in the middle of nowhere with the London Fog, who never looks at a woman except to find a fault.*

Darcy scrubbed his hands over his face. For the first time in her memory of him, he looked...weary. Still handsome, of course, but not polished and debonair the way she first saw him in Budapest or competent and shrewd as he had been in East Berlin. He rested his chin in his hand and smiled at her weakly.

"Guess you'd better go pack, honey."

"No, no," Bingley interrupted. "You aren't going back home for any reason. We packed you. Your bags are waiting in the car. If there's anything else you need, let us know, and we'll get it for you."

Darcy sat back in his chair, resigned. "Don't chew your thumb, darling. It's a nasty little habit, and people will think you are an unhappy wife."

She grimaced at him and stalked out of the conference room.

"Sorry, I can't be there for the housewarming party, Darcy." Wickham gathered up his papers and stood. "Enjoy the thriving metropolis of Fredericksburg. Good day, Deputy Director."

"Wickham."

After Wickham and the others left, Darcy turned to his boss and friend. "Trusting that man is a mistake, Charles."

Bingley sighed. "You're probably correct in a general sense. But in this case, I think he has the right of it. You were quite chummy with Anneliese Vandenburg, and now she's been eliminated by your hand. I'm not sure the KGB will let that slide."

"It was self-defense. She held me at gunpoint. And she shot me, damn it!"

"I believe you."

"You know I wouldn't have done it if there was another way."

"I do. I still can't figure out what pushed her to threaten you. What did Anneliese know about you?"

"Nothing, at least, I thought she knew nothing. Sure, I spent time with her, but I didn't make time with her. I didn't fall into a honey trap. I'm smarter than that."

Bingley turned cool blue eyes on him. "No one's smarter than that if the right situation comes along."

"Charles, if this is about Budapest..."

"But no, I don't think you gave Stonewall classified information. Unfortunately, I have to convince the men at the top. Just give me some time on this, won't you? I'm hoping we can get you back out there soon."

"The chief of station in Moscow has been there for three years come January. Maybe..."

"Maybe." Charles looked troubled. "That's not my call though. If you'll excuse me, I need to make a couple of phone calls."

"Yeah, okay." Darcy glanced back as he stepped through the doorway. Charles was looking out the window again, sipping coffee as if he had not a care in the world. For the first time in years, Darcy was on the outside looking in.

It was a lonely place to be.

Now, I wait. The CIA brass are baiting the trap, but I'm too smart to take the bait. I watch and wait, hidden in plain sight. And I've been thinking. I don't think it's enough of a punishment to turn you, to make you like me. Now, I think you must die. But how to do it? Sure, I could just take you out, no problem. Because you're weak now. Injured. On my own, I made a try for you while you were in the hospital, and once again, my plans were thwarted.

Now, I wait. Perhaps that is for the best; that was impulsive on my part —impulsive, vigilante retribution for the wrongs you have done me. I'm better than that. I'm smarter than that. I don't have my love anymore, but my mother always said money can buy excellent substitutes for happiness.

So I'll make myself a rich man. I've already got a good start on that. Oh, my handler isn't pleased that I took matters into my own hands. He still thinks there's a chance you can be turned, but I see now, you are too weak for it. Too weak, too stupid.

16

The National Mall
Washington, DC

ELIZABETH APPROACHED the blonde reading as she sat on the park bench. "*Szia.*"

Johanna Bodnar glanced up, and a delighted cry escaped her lips. "Hello to you too, Erzsebet!" She embraced her friend, clutching her around the neck as if it had been years since they had seen each other rather than five months. Elizabeth's bodyguard advanced and then retreated when she waved him off.

"I did not know it was you I was meeting in this place today!"

"Neither did I." Elizabeth grinned. "I suspect a mutual friend with some connections arranged it. So, how have you been? Have the doctors been able to give you some answers?"

Johanna sat and patted the bench beside her. "I am on the mend. It is not all good news though. They say I have lupus."

"I'm sorry, Johanna. That's difficult news. But it's treatable, right?"

"Yes. It is serious, but there is medicine. And I have to take care of myself. Papa is insisting I stay here for treatment, but I miss him so much. Sometimes I want to go home, even if medicine is here."

"I'm so sorry you've been lonely." Johanna did indeed look unhappy, although her color was better than Elizabeth had ever seen it. "Have you not made any friends here?"

"A few," she acknowledged. "At first, Charles and Cara were regular visitors. He, especially, came to me."

"I see." Elizabeth tried not to smile too much. "I knew you two would hit it off."

"I admit, I thought we did."

"Thought?"

"All of sudden, one month ago, all that ceased. I imagine he was out of country. He travels much, you know."

"I know." *And now I know why.* Although, Elizabeth was pretty sure that Johanna didn't know her American crush was a deputy director in the CIA.

"But I thought Cara and Louis might still be in town, so I called her on the phone. Twice. I had almost given up entirely when she finally returned my call."

"What excuse did she give for not calling you back?"

"That she had been so busy she hadn't gotten the message."

"Hmm."

"I asked after Charles. She said he was well. Traveling, not under her watchful eye this time, so no telling what debauchery he was up to. I thought perhaps you might have seen him. Cara said he was in Mr. Kent's company. I do not know if you and he still work together."

"Oh, I haven't seen Darby Kent in quite a while," Elizabeth said, mindful of the ironic truth she spoke. "If those two were in cahoots, the debauchery would make sense, wouldn't it?" She looked up at Johanna's stricken face. "Oh no! I didn't mean it that way, Johanna! I was just taking a jab at Darby Kent. I'm sure Charles isn't—"

"I have no claim on him, Erzsebet. He brought me to the US, came to see me several times. But he made me no promises. Except for a few wonderful dinners and sightseeing trips, I have not met him. I simply read too much into his attention, as one might expect of naïve, lonely foreigner. He only pitied me and most likely pities me still."

Elizabeth remembered Darcy's disapproving stares directed Charles and Johanna's way, and wondered whether Darcy had a hand in Charles's recent vanishing act. She would expect interference from Cara, and maybe she could see how a sister would feel justified butting into her brother's life, but Darcy needed to stay out of other people's business.

"I saw how Charles treated you in Alsómező. It didn't look like a case of pity from my point of view. He's probably just working—you know, on his novel. Cara's trying to cast doubts on his feelings for you, that's all. She's a snob."

"She is kind to me. Maybe she warns me Charles does not feel the way I do."

"I think you're giving her too much credit."

"I will know if I do not hear from them after this. I will know if he is gone on to other places, other people. I will not be sad. It is the way of the world."

"It will work out. I know what I saw between you, and not even Cara's snobbery will stop it forever." She hugged Johanna. "Now, I've got to go."

"Where are you off to now?"

"Amsterdam."

She squirmed slightly at the lie. Elizabeth liked Johanna, but her new location was dangerous information to have.

"You must write me."

"I will, if I can."

"*Isten áldjon.*"

"God bless you too, Erzsebet."

"Thank you, and *Jó egészséget!*"

"To your health as well."

They embraced again, and Liz joined her bodyguard. He escorted her to the black sedan that would take her back. From there, she and Darcy would go directly to Fredericksburg, her next assignment on this bizarre mission.

17

As far as hideout partners go, I certainly could have done worse. Darcy considered his situation as he and Elizabeth rode in the nondescript black sedan. He still wasn't cleared to drive, which was annoying, but being restricted to passenger status did give him ample opportunity to observe the lady behind the wheel as she took the winding roads with a consummate skill, born of familiarity with the region.

"Who taught you to drive?" he asked.

"Please spare me any smart-ass comment about women drivers. That's where you're going with this, right?"

"Absolutely not," he replied, pretending to be offended. "I'm simply curious. You're a very good driver." He paused. "Did you drive the car when we left East Berlin? I don't remember."

"I think you're excused from the memory lapse as you were barely conscious." She glanced over at him. "And no, I didn't drive. Fitzwilliam did."

"Good old Fitz. But you took care of me."

"As best I could."

"I don't know if I ever thanked you."

"You did, right after you woke in the hospital. Then you kissed my hand." She blushed and fixed her eyes straight ahead.

"Well, I meant it. Thank you."

"My stepfather."

"Pardon?"

"My stepfather taught me to drive."

"You said your father's family is from Virginia. Do they live close to the safe house? To where we'll be staying?"

"Yes and no. There are some cousins floating around the area, but I hardly know them. My father's buried in the Taylorsville Cemetery." She counted on her fingers. "Three counties over."

"I'm sorry."

"Thanks, but it was a long time ago. He died when I was three. My mother remarried, and her husband was wonderful to me. I grew up just fine."

"For certain."

There was an awkward silence.

"Does your mother know what you do for a living?"

"She knows I work for the agency. She knows I'm a linguist. She's not happy about it."

"I'm wondering what, if anything, we should tell her. Secrecy is of the utmost importance here—to keep us safe."

"It won't be an issue because we won't see her. She and Jim live in West Virginia."

"No siblings?"

"Twin sisters who are a lot younger than me. They're still in high school."

Another pause. "What about you?"

"Hmm?" He jerked his attention away from the curve of her neck, the little slope of collarbone visible above the neckline of her top.

"Siblings—do you have any?"

He hesitated a long minute. "A sister. Like your sisters, much younger than me."

"Where does she live?"

"A large metropolitan area on the Atlantic Seaboard."

Elizabeth's cheeks reddened. "You always nail me on that."

"Nail you?" He sat up straight, trying to force the sudden, vivid images of nailing her out of his head.

"You get me to tell you things about myself, and then you clam up about your own life. You always ask but never reveal."

"That's Spy Rule Number Eleven." He grinned at her, loving the annoyance his remark stirred in her expression.

"Even in a situation like this, you're always in some kind of disguise."

"I'm a master of disguise. That's why I'm the boss."

"You're not my boss, Darcy."

"Closest thing."

"What's the next turn off?"

"Your predisposition toward sarcasm?"

"Ha."

"Highway 53." He eyed the distance on the map. "Looks like about a mile or so." He paused. "See there? That proves I'm the boss. I'm telling you where to go."

"I'll tell *you* where to go," she grumbled, and he burst out laughing.

"I bet you would, Ms. Bennet, with barely a moment's hesitation." He looked down at the map again. "After that turn, take the next left onto Hunsford Street. Looks like our new place is in town."

Minutes later, she turned into a gravel drive beside an old, Federal-style town house.

"The honeymoon suite," Darcy remarked with a sigh of resignation. It was going to be a challenge, living with this woman under the same roof, even for a short while. Working with her had been trying enough; now he would see her all the time—every day and night. This small-town setting was different from the exotic places in which they'd previously found themselves and far removed from the trips they took in his dreams. Those flights of fancy were full of snowy ski slopes and warm brandy by a hot fire. Or sunny beaches and umbrellas, and walks at sunset along the ocean's edge. Yet here they were, in real life, staking claim to an old house along an old Virginia street. Darcy and his lovely colleague were hiding out like cowards while some slimy traitor who wanted them dead was probably free to roam the nation's capital, maybe even roam around the offices at Langley. It pissed him off.

"Stop frowning, Darcy. It's not that bad."

She took the key out of the ignition. With her typical business-like efficiency, she stepped to the back of the car, unlocked the trunk, and began unloading the suitcases.

"I can get my own bag if you don't mind."

"Got something to hide?" she joked without thinking about the conversation in Bingley's office that brought them here.

Rage churned inside him, quick and hot like a pot arriving at a rolling boil. "I wouldn't put too much stock in George Wickham's opinions. Let me give you some good advice, Elizabeth. He talks a good talk, but when you ask him to walk the walk, he'll walk away every time. Don't trust him. Just don't."

"Deputy Director Bingley seems to."

"If Charles really does trust Wickham, he's gravely mistaken. I've known George a long time. I've worked with him too, and he's a weak-willed, self-centered mockery of a man. Let's just hope he doesn't get someone killed before this is all over."

"I think Wickham's just making a recommendation he thinks is in the best interest of the agency."

"He bends the facts to suit his own purposes and cast himself in the best light."

"That's quite an accusation. What on earth did the man do to you, Darcy?"

He glared at her, slammed the trunk, and walked toward the house with his suitcase in his good hand.

She followed. "Fine. Be that way if you want. I'm just trying to get a handle on him. And get a handle on you, too, for that matter. You can't blame me, as much time as I've had to spend with you over the last few months."

"I don't know what you mean," he said over his shoulder as he walked away.

"You're so full of contradictions. Everyone seems to see a different man when they look at you. I can't make you out at all."

"I don't think these are the right circumstances under which to evaluate my character. I suspect it's not a good time for me to assess yours either. We're under enough stress as it is."

"True enough," she muttered.

"Neither of us is at our best at the moment."

Darcy ascended the steps that connected the sidewalk to the front stoop and had to stop and get his breath. He'd always prided himself on his physical stamina, but that damn side wound sucked the wind right out of him whenever he exerted himself. And his arm hurt like hell today! Probably due to the blasted weather—cold, rainy, miserable November afternoon! He set his bag down, and she swooped in behind him, picking it up in her spare hand.

"Here, I'll get that."

He grunted a thank you.

"You could open the screen door if you don't mind." He pulled the wooden framed door and held it open while she set her own suitcase down and unlocked the door behind it.

"Not very secure," he remarked as he eyed the door. He leaned back to take in the windows along the front of the house. "Too much glass."

"Well, I'm sure the original owners didn't have safe-house décor in mind when they built it."

The entrance foyer had a black iron chandelier suspended from the ceiling. A staircase rose along the wall to the left, and an office and sitting room were off to the right but closed off from the foyer by a set of French doors. The kitchen was tucked at the back of the house.

Elizabeth wandered through ahead of him.

"There's a master bedroom downstairs to the left just past the stairs. You can have that one so you don't have to go up and down so much."

"I appreciate your concern, but if you want it..."

"I don't. I'll have the whole upstairs to myself—almost like an apartment—and that works for me. You can have your privacy."

The idea of having privacy didn't suit him nearly as well as it usually did. Darcy put his things in the bedroom and wandered back into the kitchen.

She was exploring the place, opening cabinets and peering inside. "I'm hungry. How about you?"

"I could eat."

"Looks like they stocked the kitchen some. Staples, equipment, a few basics." Elizabeth opened the refrigerator door. "We'll have to shop tomorrow. I'm not much of a cook, I'm afraid."

"Are there eggs?"

"Yes."

"Cheese, sausage, peppers?"

"No sausage, but there's ham. Cheese—check; peppers—check."

"I make a mean omelet."

She turned in surprise. "Really?"

"Yes, really. Don't look so shocked. Omelets are easy. And I did attend two weeks of culinary school when I was undercover in Paris."

"Can you cook with that bum arm of yours?"

"If you help me."

"You're on cooking duty then. I'll clean up."

Elizabeth busied herself making coffee and chopping while Darcy stirred and cooked, using his left hand as well as he would have his right. They worked side-by-side, speaking only to say, "Excuse me" or "Hand me that." The companionable silence and domestic scenery had his pulse skipping. It was too intoxicating—to pretend she was his, she was happy to be here with him, that he might find her in his bed tonight.

"Here you go." He set a plate in front of her, and she smiled her thanks. He lowered himself gently into a chair across from her. "So, what's the verdict?" He gestured toward her plate.

"Surprisingly good."

"And why is that a surprise?"

"Just never thought of the *London Fog* as the domestic sort."

He rolled his eyes, and she laughed.

"I hate that name, you know."

"Really? You're famous for it. How did you get it?"

"Truth?"

"Truth."

"I was stationed in England, my first assignment. Some smart ass MI6 agent of your acquaintance—"

"Good old Fitz, I presume."

"Gave me the name after I let a target escape by mistake. He said I was like a fog because the targets saw me but I didn't really stop them."

She laughed heartily, and a tiny grin escaped him.

"Go ahead. Laugh at my expense."

"And here I thought it was because you wore a trench coat or something."

"I made up for the mistake later, and most people started to think I had the name because I could *evaporate into thin air* or some such nonsense, but it stuck, as nicknames tend to do. Do you have one?"

"A nickname? No. I'm not near interesting enough to have a nickname. Well, my mom calls me Lizzy."

"I think 'Elizabeth' suits you."

She tilted her head, puzzled, but he didn't elaborate. Just put another forkful of omelet in his mouth and smiled at her.

They lingered after dinner. Elizabeth found a bottle of brandy, which seemed a strange pairing with omelets, but it went down easy and smoothed out the rough edges he still felt from the day. As they lounged in the sitting room late into the evening, Darcy couldn't remember the last time he had felt so relaxed in a woman's company. Or maybe he had actually never been relaxed in a woman's company. At least, not in this particular way—this warm, fuzzy, euphoric state where his attraction simmered under the surface. He could almost float on the bubbly conversation and exciting undercurrents in the room. There was no agenda, no assignment rushing him, no phone calls to make, no information to gather. It was a strangely perfect ending to what had started out as a very messed up day—one he hated to see end.

"Do you like working undercover?" He had always wondered.

Elizabeth didn't seem the type to enjoy subterfuge.

She stared into her brandy snifter. "It's fine. I originally signed up for Science and Technology, but circumstances change."

"I didn't know that. It would be a good place for you with your training in languages."

"Well, the powers that be had other ideas. They handpicked me out of my recruiting class to work with you in Hungary."

"I needed someone who could speak the language well enough to pass herself off as a local, and you needed experience, so it fit nicely. You did a fine job—played the part to perfection. No one would ever predict that you were from anywhere but the Hungarian countryside."

"You know, I think that's the first compliment you've ever given me."

"Oh, surely not."

"It is."

He chuckled. "The brandy must be going to my head."

She finished hers off and stood up. "It is getting late. Here..." She took his glass and set it on the coffee table. His pulse spiked as she reached for his hand. "Let me..."

She paused and he looked up into her eyes. Her gaze fluttered down as she took his elbow in her other hand. "Let's do one more round on your shoulder exercises. We missed the middle of the day."

Disappointment flooded his system but didn't tamp down the excitement having her hands on him elicited. He smelled the oranges and gardenia that typically surrounded her—a scent he associated with her now—a scent that washed over him, leaving a terrifying lull of happiness in its wake.

Silently, she moved the shoulder in a series of positions, while he played a silent game of trying to catch her eye. When he finally did, she lowered her gaze again.

"Your eyes are blue."

"They are," he said. "They made me special colored contacts to wear in Budapest and East Berlin."

"I can see why."

"Oh?"

"I was shocked when you first opened your eyes in the hospital. They're quite striking." She blushed and concentrated on moving his arm.

Darcy smiled in spite of himself. "Too memorable, too conspicuous. Occupational hazard."

She applied gentle persuasion until she met resistance. He winced.

"Sorry," she murmured.

"It's okay. Talk to me. Get my mind off it."

"What do you want me to talk about?"

"I don't know—anything. You said earlier that your mother wasn't happy you joined the CIA. Why not?"

"Mostly because of my father, I guess."

"I thought he passed away when you were three."

"He did." She hesitated. "Truth?" she asked, mirroring his turn of phrase from earlier in the evening.

"Truth."

She considered what to say, frowning as she studied his arm. What followed was a rush of words that tumbled from her exquisite mouth. "My father worked for the CIA."

"He did?"

"It's not common knowledge, although there are still a few old hands around Langley who remember him. I prefer to be known for my own accomplishments."

"I can understand."

"He was killed in the line of duty, around the time of the Bay of Pigs. He has a star on the Memorial Wall."

Darcy startled. "Bay of Pigs? He trained the rebels in Guatemala?"

"Among other things."

"Do you know how he died?"

"Not the details, no. One of the commercial suppliers found his body, which was a comfort to his parents and my mother—to know for sure. So many families don't know for sure."

"What was his name?"

"Thomas Bennet."

"You kept his last name—even though your mother remarried?"

"My mother never bothered with changing it when I was younger. Later on, I insisted on keeping it. Another way to honor him, to be close to him, I guess."

"The Bay of Pigs—the CIA's big disaster."

"It was. But I'm proud of my father, of his service."

"Of course you are. So that's why you joined?"

"It was a factor." She brought his hand straight up above his head, and he grimaced again.

"That motion still hurts a lot, doesn't it? Can I see?"

He nodded, and she unbuttoned the top three buttons on his oxford shirt, pulling the sleeve over to the side to examine his sutures on his arm, just below the shoulder.

"No signs of infection," she said, almost to herself. "Maybe it's just swollen in there, which impedes the movement."

She dug her fingers deftly into the tissue surrounding the shoulder joint, above the stitches. He felt the dual edge of pleasure and pain as she tried to ease the shoulder into position. Somehow, instead of destroying his arousal, the agony only sparked his libido further. *Intriguing. Never would have pegged myself as a masochist.* He closed his eyes, his mouth in a grim line, and she eased back.

"I think that's enough for tonight." She let go of his arm, and of their own free will, his fingers skimmed her cheek as his arm descended.

"Elizabeth," he murmured as he opened his eyes.

She stood in front of him, her eyes reflecting the firelight, her hands folded awkwardly in front of her. "See you in the morning." Without another word, she fled the room, leaving him all alone, staring into the gas-log flames, and sipping brandy.

He sat before the flickering firelight another half hour, pondering the exotic dance between men and women, and the bonds between fathers and children. No matter what the bureaucracies built or the technologies changed, it seemed those fundamental connections between people were what bent and shaped the entire world.

18

The Park: Coffee Shop and Bookstore
Washington, DC

"Welcome to The Park, my dear. Table for one?"

"Oh no. I'm meeting someone." Elizabeth peered around the kindly older man holding a menu and silverware wrapped in a cloth napkin. She pointed. "There she is. Right over there."

"I'll escort you," he said, his eyes twinkling. "It makes me look good to walk a lovely lady to her seat. Is that her over in the booth?" He pointed to a tall, lanky young woman with expressive brown eyes and sharp features.

"Yes, thanks," Elizabeth said as he showed her to Charlotte's table.

"Hey there, E!" Charlotte stood and embraced her friend as the older gentleman retreated from the table.

"Charlotte, it's good to see you. Thanks for meeting me."

"I would have driven to you if I'd known where you were."

"It's better this way. Convenient to the Hoover Building and hidden in plain sight, which follows Spy Rule Number Seventeen."

"Huh?"

"Never mind."

"How are you?"

"I'm doing pretty well, surprisingly."

"I couldn't believe it when you called! I had no idea you were back in the States. When did that happen?"

"Just a few days ago."

"I won't ask where you were."

"Probably wise." A young man in a coffee-stained apron put down his bus tub and took pen and paper out of his apron pocket.

"Coffee?" he asked.

"Yes, two please. With cream."

"My pleasure."

"I won't ask," Charlotte said as he ambled away, "but I know you were in Europe."

"FBI sees all, knows all?"

"You bet." She caught Elizabeth scanning the room. "See somebody you recognize?"

"Hmm? Oh. Um...no. Habit I've developed. Scoping out the place. Sorry."

"You're a real CIA gal now, I suppose."

"Yup."

Charlotte Lucas eyed her college friend with a penetrating stare. "The CIA's not what you thought." It was an observation, not a question.

"Oh, I don't know. In some ways, it's very much what I thought."

"And you can't talk about it." She folded her hands on the table. "I have some of the information you asked for."

"You do? Charlotte, you're a wonder!"

"I am. I truly am. This wasn't easy to come by either."

"I know, and I'm grateful to you. I needed some help—from a disinterested party."

"Disinterested?"

"No...I mean...I know you're interested. What I'm trying to say is I needed help from outside Langley."

"And they say your kind and my kind don't mix, at least not on the job. FBI and CIA don't have a reputation for playing nice with each other."

"You and I...we're different, though, aren't we? We're friends. Our employers have different missions, so I get it. But this guy I'm looking at—he's a US citizen, and I thought you might be able to shed some light on a corner I can't seem to get to."

"Gathering intel on officers inside Langley—sounds like you've worked your way into counterintelligence."

Elizabeth fidgeted in her chair. "Look, can we keep this just between us for now? I could get into real trouble for it. I figured if my supervisors found out, it would be easier to beg forgiveness than ask permission."

"You know you can trust me. We are friends, but beyond that, you have my respect. And I have yours or you wouldn't have called me for this." She took a nine-by-twelve envelope out of her bag. "Here you go. But I have a feeling this just scratches the surface on the guy."

Elizabeth frowned as she scanned the documents.

"There's some background to start: education, work history, military record, travel history, family, financials. The guy's loaded. Did you know that?"

"No."

"Old money on his mother's side. Founding Fathers-type lineage. A lot of the money was hidden, especially because he's CIA."

"I knew you could find something."

Charlotte grinned. "You do know me well, but there's more where that came from."

"More?"

"You can read through it yourself. The only thing that looks wonky to me is this little disappearing act he did right before Budapest." She leaned forward and leafed through a couple of the pages. "Right..." She pointed. "There. Right there. He flew commercial to Miami, but then—poof. He's off the grid for two whole weeks."

"I'd heard about that."

"No hotel, no rental car, nothing. He was at the airport, and then he wasn't."

"Private aircraft?"

"Maybe. He has a pilot's license, which is on page two by the way. But there's no record of a flight plan."

"That is weird."

"Yeah, a flight plan's not mandatory, but most people file one in case of emergencies. You really piqued my curiosity with this. So I called in a couple of favors. An unidentified plane did land on a private air strip in Barbados."

"Was it him?"

"Not sure. The FBI keeps tabs on people in the States who are suspected of espionage, but that's way out of our jurisdiction."

Elizabeth's gaze shot up from the page just in time to see the older gentleman return to take the tray from his waiter and approach their table.

Charlotte sat back as he put the coffee cups carefully on the table. "No, no. We're not tracking your guy. But we did pick up another guy here in DC earlier this week." She plucked another file out of her bag. "This was found on him. See for yourself."

"Anything else, ladies?"

"No, thank you." Elizabeth absentmindedly picked up a spoon and twirled it in her cup, swirling cream and coffee.

"The message is coded."

"Translation is on the next page." She smirked. "We have code breakers too, you know."

"Orders based on intel from Wilhelm to kill some asset at the Soviet Embassy in DC."

"He got the guy too. Poor son of a bitch. Found him lying in a pool of his own blood outside his doorstep."

"I could have gone all day without that visual. God, Charlotte, that's gruesome."

"Espionage is gruesome—except when it's boring."

"'Wilhelm' was the name Darcy got from his assailant before she died. George claims the similarity in names is more evidence against Darcy because his given name is 'William.' But—" She looked suddenly at her friend.

Charlotte grinned. "You see it, don't you?"

"Wilhelm names a second target: 'CIA officer currently recovering at Walter Reed from gunshot wounds. Officer can ID KGB asset.' Holy shit, Char! This Wilhelm even gives Darcy's room number!"

"Yep."

"Thank god for the Suit-of-the-Day," Elizabeth said to herself. "The date. This was written October 19. I was with Darcy that whole day. There's no way he wrote or received this. He was still unconscious."

"Yep."

"Wickham hasn't seen this, or he hid it from me."

"Who?"

"Nobody. Colleague. Whatever."

Wickham's insistence on keeping me with Darcy was fortuitous—just not in the way he wanted. "I *knew* something wasn't adding up!"

"Your Mr. Darcy is no angel, perhaps, but he's not Wilhelm either."

"He's not my Mr. Darcy, Charlotte."

"Figure of speech, Elizabeth." Charlotte gave her friend a speculative look.

Elizabeth studied the page a few more seconds. "I think you just solved my first case." She lifted her cup in a toast to her friend. "It looks like the London Fog is innocent. And I have a report to write."

"Here's something else you may not have considered. It may not be as simple as guilt or innocence. Just because Darcy's not the mole doesn't mean there isn't one."

"And with that in mind..." She pulled a file out of her bag. "Here are some other names: officers around Darcy during all of this. I want them checked out too. Same information: family, financials, etc."

"Elizabeth, if there is a mole, someone who's either in Langley or has connections inside, there's a decent chance he or she knows Darcy's current location—and yours." Charlotte drew her eyebrows together in a worried frown.

"I know. That's why they've got us holed up together—to keep an eye on each other. Sometimes I'd rather take my chances out in the open."

"Come on. A hidey-hole with a major cutie beats a cubicle any day."

"This cutie is grumpy, has a short temper, and sports an ego the size of Cleveland."

"You admitted he's cute though."

"'Cute' isn't the right word."

"What is?"

"I don't know...intriguing?"

"Hmm."

"And I need to get back. I left him at the safe house unprotected."

"He can't take care of himself?"

"Maybe he could if he was one hundred percent, but I should go." She started to dig in her purse.

"I got this."

"Thanks. Thanks for everything, Charlotte."

"You betcha. I should have some information on this"—she indicated the envelope—"in a couple of weeks. Good luck, girl. Stay in touch."

ELIZABETH ROARED down the street and bounced up the gravel drive to the detached garage. A strange car was parked out front—DC plates, rental car. She checked around her before bounding out of the sedan, hand on her .38 Special. Up against the house, with a stealth she'd practiced a hundred times, she eased around the back corner and inside. She heard voices but couldn't discriminate who or how many.

"I bet you brought down the wrath of Darcy on him."

"I did not."

"I know you, old chap. Even if Bingley's sort of your boss these days, you'd tell it to him straight."

"Of course, I'd tell it to him straight. He doesn't need that kind of distraction."

Fitz! Liz relaxed, put away her revolver, and started into the room to greet their friend.

"By distraction you mean the Hungarian bird?"

"She was some asset's daughter, for chrissakes."

Elizabeth halted in her tracks.

"He listened to you?" Fitz asked.

"He always listens to me about those types of things."

"You're as meddlesome as an old woman."

"Look, I don't pretend to know everything there is to know about women."

"Sure you do. I would say, perhaps he didn't have that much of a thing for her, but that would lessen the triumphant look on your face. You must have had some strong objections to the lady."

Elizabeth felt her cheeks heat up. How dare he? She remembered the forlorn expression Johanna Bodnar wore that day she met her in DC. How dare Darcy humiliate her, laugh at her with Fitz behind her back, and warn Charles away from her because she was *just* an asset's daughter. She threw her keys down on the kitchen table and started through the house.

"I'm back!"

"So you are, love." Fitz rose and took both her hands while kissing her cheek. "It's good to see you."

"You too." She pulled away, flustered and angry and not in the mood for small talk.

"What's the matter? Your face is all red. Are you well?"

"Um, yes. I'm well, thanks, Fitz. I..." She didn't dare look at Darcy. "I'm getting a cold, I think. I've got some kind of headache."

"I've never seen you ill." Darcy stood, concerned. "Do you need anything?"

"No, no. Just some rest."

At the top of the stairs, she glanced back. Fitz and Darcy stared at each other. Fitz shrugged and returned to his beer. Darcy met her gaze for a second or two before he sat back down to the conversation with his friend. Elizabeth went into her room and shut the door.

19

A FEW HOURS LATER, Elizabeth was in bed reading when a knock sounded on her door.

"What?" she barked.

The door opened a crack, and cerulean eyes speared her from the doorway. She looked back at her book.

"Are you feeling any better?"

"I'm fine, thank you."

"Good." Darcy opened the door wider and came in, sitting on the bed and looking at her expectantly. "Fitz brought some news."

"Really?" She wondered whether Darcy would ever fess up about his role in splitting up Charles and Johanna. Or if it was way toward the bottom of his Care-O-Meter—like the way he completely forgot he met her before Budapest. Or the way he tossed Cara Bingley Hurst out of his room.

"Brightman is coming back."

"'Brightman is coming back.' That means nothing to me, Darcy."

"Brightman is the Soviet station chief."

"Should you trust a grunt like me with such sensitive information?" She glanced up, gauging his reaction to her sarcasm.

He grinned at her.

So handsome, that slow, lazy smile.

Jerk.

"Not only that, but I've been called in to the office tomorrow."

"Why?"

"Most likely to get a new assignment. It looks like everything is falling into place."

Elizabeth set her book to the side and sat up straight. "You're talking in riddles. Just say what's on your mind, and put me out of my misery."

He inched closer to her and grasped her hand in his. She stared at their intertwined fingers, too shocked to pull back. "I think they're going to offer me the Soviet station chief job. In a way, I'm surprised —with all this hiding out business, I thought I might be too easily recognized, but with a disguise and the protection of the embassy, it could work. It might be a deputy position at first, but it's a step in the right direction. Finally—it's the big time, darling."

Darling? Her gaze bounced up from his hands to his face like a rubber ball. *What the hell...*

"Don't give me that look. You know I won't leave you behind. When I meet with the director, I'll insist you transfer with me so we can be together. It's unusual but not unheard of."

It was as if a foreign language was coming out of his mouth. She stared, bewildered, her color rising, her mind completely blank.

The silence only seemed to encourage him.

"I've wanted you for...god, it seems like forever. I can't seem to rid my mind of you, and now, I won't have to. I know you're only a case officer, and I'm way above you career-wise, but it doesn't matter to me. People will probably scoff a little about the station chief and the hot, young officer, but I'm prepared for that, and so should you be. The talk will die down eventually.

"I'm not quite sure how you did something no other woman has managed to do, but you snagged me. I did try to forget you, but when you showed up in East Berlin, I guess my fate was sealed. I'm crazy about you—hell, this whole thing is crazy. I can't believe this is me."

I can't believe it either.

"Say something, darling."

She shook her head in disbelief.

"I know. It's hard to know *what* to say. Moscow! The most challenging, sought-after post in the agency. The top of the heap." Some heat burned in those icy blue eyes. "You can thank me later."

He started to lean toward her—was halfway to her mouth—when she realized what he was doing and put a hand on his chest to stop him. "Hold it."

"What?"

For a fleeting moment, she almost felt sorry for the rejection he was about to suffer. They had been getting along okay, given their forced togetherness here in Fredericksburg. But then words like "I tried to forget you" and "she was just some asset's daughter" flashed though her brain. He was so cocksure, so ready to believe she'd throw herself into his arms without considering his past, her career, or her friends.

"In a case like this, I suppose you think I should be grateful. But even if I shared your feelings—which I don't—you won't get any thanks from me. I never wanted to 'snag you' as you say, and given that 'this whole thing is crazy' anyway, I'm sure it won't take you long to get over it." She picked up her book and pretended to concentrate on the page.

His complete and utter shock initially drained all his color, but then his cheeks reddened with fury. His lips pressed in a firm, angry line while he struggled with a response. For Elizabeth, it was dreadfully awkward, but finally, he gathered his thoughts enough to speak.

"So, that's it? That smart-ass response is the only answer I'm going to get?"

"Given that you've spent the last few months trying to forget me, you should be relieved I'm not interested. You know, Darcy, insults like the one you just tossed my way are reason enough for my so-called smart-ass response, but I have other reasons as well. Do you honestly think I'd start an...an affair with a man who intentionally prevented a relationship between two people just starting to care about each other, only because he could?"

"Who? What are you talking about? Is it Fitz? You have a thing for Fitz?"

Elizabeth gritted her teeth in frustration. "Don't be such a dolt! I'm talking about Johanna and Charles! You know you talked him into dumping her, and don't you dare try to deny it. I overheard you discussing it with Fitz when I came back today."

He listened to this revelation with surprise but not remorse and even gave her a small smile of incredulity that infuriated her further.

"All right then, you little eavesdropper, if you must know. I have no wish to deny that I did my level best to protect my friend. I took better care of Charles than I did of myself apparently. Talk about irony."

"But even that interference, egregious as it was, isn't the only reason I dislike you. I've spent the last several months with you, and I've observed you up close and personal. But even before that, I knew how you operate."

"And how would you know that?"

"Wickham told me everything." Not exactly true, she realized. There were still things she didn't know, but she was on a roll now. "You had him demoted. Sent him back to the States after that debacle in Prague."

His voice grew deadly serious. "What, exactly, did he tell you about Prague?"

"Your decisions caused him to lose the asset, someone he cared about, someone he loved. The loss devastated him. And when he called you on it, you blamed *him* and ruined his career."

Somehow, his quiet, white-lipped fury was more arresting than any shouting match could be. "Even after I warned you about him, you've worked up no little sympathy for Wickham."

"Who wouldn't feel sorry for him? At the very least, you used your station chief's position to punish him."

"At the very least? What do you mean by that?"

"At most, you—" She hesitated. "Come on, Darcy! You had to know that little stunt would look irregular to people in high places."

"At most, I what?" he said, contempt infusing his voice. "What do you know about any of it? Nothing. You know nothing. You weren't privy to any of the relevant particulars. It was before your time."

"And a new, wet-behind-the-ears officer's observations aren't worth a shit?"

"Is this about those things I said during your class at The Farm? All those months ago? God, Elizabeth, get over yourself already!"

"That remark is only one cog in the Darcy Wheel of Disdain."

He drew up to his full height and leaned over her. "And this is your opinion of me? This is what you think after working with me all this time? According to you, I'm a real son of a bitch. Thanks for the full-length dissertation on my various and sundry faults." He paced to the window and back, stopping well before he reached her. "You know, disguise is our business, yours and mine. But I always thought I could be honest and straightforward with you, and you would appreciate it. You were a colleague; but more than that, I considered you a friend—no, someone I wanted to be even closer than that, so I was honest with you because I thought you felt the same for me. I can't help but think you might have been a little more receptive to my offer if I'd fed your vanity rather than spoken the truth. If we were a couple, Elizabeth, there *would* be talk. No way around that. Maybe there would be other ramifications too—dangerous ones—but I thought my feelings for you were worth the risks. It's not a good idea, for a variety of reasons, for me to saddle myself with female companionship."

"Didn't stop you in Budapest with Cara, or East Berlin with Anneliese."

He stared at her. "I don't know what you thought you saw when we were overseas, but you were way off base in both instances. Cara's been after me for years, but she's trying to rekindle a flirtation that died a long time ago after I came back from Nam. And East Berlin was all about appearances, like your so-called fling with Fitz. I was doing my damn job, and I managed to do it without compromising myself or engaging in inappropriate dalliances."

She snorted her disbelief.

"If I'd approached you today with compliments and flattery,

hidden the real struggles that prevented me from making my feelings known to you, this might have gone over just fine. If I'd spouted some romantic drivel that you were actually *good* for me in every way possible, you might have accepted it. But although disguise is my business, in my personal life, I abhor it. Should I rejoice in your inexperience, in your lack of career connections, in your substandard public education?"

Elizabeth felt her anger ratchet up another notch but tried her best to keep her composure. "You're mistaken if you think that your arrogant tirade has affected me in any way. Except, I will say, you've spared me any concern I might have felt when I tell you that, when you walk into Bingley's office tomorrow, he might not tell you what you're expecting to hear. I don't know where you're going next, but I do know the deputy director is most likely going to inform you that—based on my counterintelligence report—you have been cleared of suspicion of committing espionage against the United States while engaged in the service of your country."

She saw him startle as if she'd slapped him, and she felt mean enough to keep going.

"I had you under surveillance, you arrogant prick. All this time, *you* were my assignment. So you couldn't have made a play for me in any possible way that would have tempted me to accept you."

He still stared at her, saying nothing, mortification pouring over him as if she'd doused him with a pitcher of ice water.

"Aren't you fortunate this naïve girl with no connections and the substandard public education has some integrity? I reported the truth even though I don't like you. I never saw any evidence that you were a double agent, and believe me, I looked. But ever since that night in Budapest when we met for the first time, your manners, your condescending arrogance, your selfish disdain for those you deemed unimportant to you laid a foundation of dislike so immovable that there could never be anything personal between us."

"Enough. I've got it now. I understand. And all I have left is to be embarrassed at my mistake." He opened the door. "I'm done here."

He slammed the bedroom door behind him, and Elizabeth heard

him race down the stairs and slam the front door so hard it reverberated through the entire house.

Angry tears coursed down her face. She probably shouldn't have told him about the investigation. She should have let Bingley do it tomorrow morning. But he pushed her piss-off buttons like no one she had ever met before. And as her stepfather had often told her, angry people are not always wise.

Perhaps there was no good way to tell a proud man like that she'd been spying on him from the get-go. To learn he'd been attracted to her, to the point he wanted to be her lover and take her with him on his next assignment, was simply unbelievable! He said he wouldn't flatter her, but in an offhanded way, he'd handed her the biggest compliment of all.

But the words he used and the feelings behind them were appalling. He said he wanted her, but he despised all she was. He interfered in other people's lives without considering their thoughts and feelings. He'd ruined Wickham in retribution for his own mistakes. All these considerations overcame the pride his interest had momentarily sparked.

She went into the bathroom and washed her face in cold water. Her eyes were still red and puffy, but she tried out her voice until it sounded normal. Returning to the bedroom, she picked up the phone and dialed.

"Connect me to the director's office please. This is Elizabeth Bennet. He's expecting my call."

She wrapped the cord around her finger as she waited, trying to calm herself from this bizarre emotional reaction. She thought that coming clean with Darcy would ease her mind, but her burdens weighed on her heavier than ever.

"Good evening, Director. You asked me to let you know if I told Single Man about the report that cleared him. Well, as of 1900 hours today, he knows."

20

"Mr. Bingley is available now."

"He damn well better be!" Darcy growled as he barreled toward the office door.

With a defiant glare, Bridget managed to skirt in front of him, her hand on the knob. "I'll show you in, sir," she said in her prim bureaucrat's voice.

Bingley was standing at the window, hands behind him, looking out on the headquarters complex below and the Virginia countryside beyond. He turned at the commotion by the door, vague melancholy in his expression, before covering it with a smooth smile.

"Darcy."

"I'm in no mood for your shenanigans this morning. I've been up all night, driving around the beltway, trying to figure out if I can even stomach this place after what I've learned."

"I'm not sure what you mean. I would have thought you'd drive up from Fredericksburg this morning. I said we'd meet today, but I wasn't expecting you until later."

"I left rather suddenly last night after receiving a disturbing bit of news."

"Really?"

"I've discovered Ms. Bennet's real mission for the past several months."

Charles turned to the sideboard and got himself a cup off the serving tray. "Coffee?"

Darcy seriously considered telling Bingley to take his coffee and shove it, but then he sighed, resigned to the pleasantries that were required when an officer found himself back in the labyrinth of CIA headquarters. "Sure."

Bingley poured as he talked, added too much sugar and cream. "Have a seat." He gestured as he handed Darcy his cup.

"You owe me some answers, Charles."

"Yes," he said thoughtfully. "I suppose I do."

"I know you're my supervisor right now, but I've always considered you my friend as well."

"And I've always considered myself your friend and colleague, not your boss. This current situation where you report to me is uncomfortable for both of us and, to my knowledge, was always supposed to be a temporary state of affairs."

"Nevertheless, you've managed to please the top echelon of agency men enough to be in this office, whereas I, for some reason, have not."

"Yet I am still your friend, maybe more than you know."

"You had Elizabeth Bennet watching me."

"I did *not* have Ms. Bennet watching you. The director did."

"What the hell for?"

"He came to me before the glue was dry on my nameplate over there, insisting he had substantiated reasons for investigating you."

"The debacle in Prague?"

"Yes, and...other developments."

"Meaning Wickham's half-truths and omissions found a sympathetic ear in counterintelligence."

"You went off half-cocked after that mess in Prague. You made an enemy of George Wickham."

"I had my reasons. With friends like that..."

"Yes, well. There were other questions too. Not by me, never by me. But from others."

"Meaning the director. Regarding...?"

"Family matters. Your background."

"What?"

"Some of the intelligence reports said the mole had family of Eastern European descent."

"You're kidding me? This whole double-agent fantasy scenario was credible because my father's mother was from Latvia?"

"I don't know the specifics."

"She immigrated years ago as a little girl. She was a US citizen. Her father served in the military. As, I might remind you, did I."

"No one's questioning your years of service."

"Someone sure as hell is questioning it! They're questioning my loyalty, my service, my integrity—everything that makes me William Darcy."

Bingley stared out the window for another second before speaking. "I was asked to meet with you today and assure you there is no evidence to indicate you're working for the Soviets. You have the lovely Ms. Bennet to thank for that. Wickham was none too pleased with her report."

"I'm sure." It rankled that he had Elizabeth to thank for exonerating him.

"And I wanted to give you your next assignment in person."

The idea of going to Moscow held a lot less appeal than yesterday, given that now he would go alone. Like a good agency man though, he'd take the job and run with it. He'd worked for the opportunity to head up the Soviet division for years. Plus, his career was all he had left anyway.

"As soon as you can pack and get out of here, you're the new station chief..." Bingley drew out an expectant pause, beaming. "...in Trinidad."

"Trinidad?"

"It's a great assignment. Amazing weather. Not a hot bed of intelligence activity, so you'll get some good relaxation, some extra recuperation time for that arm."

"What about me being in danger? What about Elizabeth Bennet's safety?"

"We think you *are* safe. Nothing has happened. No attempts on your life or hers. Even though it was common knowledge where you were. They must think we'd have figured out who was the double agent after we debriefed you if we'd had the right information."

"What's being done to find the mole?"

"CI's business, not mine."

"If there's a mole, it's everybody's business."

"It's not a good idea for you to go sniffing around CI these days. Get out of town for a while. Go to Trinidad."

"What about Moscow?"

Bingley shuffled some papers on his desk. "Station Chief Brightman is staying in place."

"In Moscow?"

"They tell me he's staying...for now."

"I see."

"I know you thought you might want Moscow."

"No, I *knew* I wanted it. I've been working towards it for the last five years."

"You can't always get what you want. My advice? Take Trinidad. Take the sun and the palm trees and the slower pace of living. Go sailing. Let yourself settle a little."

"I don't believe this!"

"This is a position that's on par with your skills and experience. It's a station chief's job. Not some case officer like you were in Eastern Europe. Not some NOC. Those assignments were beneath you. This is much more in line with your rank and experience. Right now, Trinidad is the best place for you, my friend."

"And it conveniently keeps me out of the way. No chance of anything truly sensitive or useful coming from Trinidad."

"Will..."

"So being cleared isn't enough. The London Fog still has the stink of suspicion on him."

"I don't know what to say to that."

"How about the truth?"

"I..."

"Have I done anything to make you suspicious of my loyalty?"

"Me personally? No, Will. That's a promise."

"I don't understand this. Not at all."

Bingley looked at him helplessly and shrugged. The two men stared at each other, neither giving way, neither quite sure how their friendship could survive this chasm unaffected.

"Well, I guess this is goodbye then."

"Best of luck to you." Bingley held out his hand. "Take care of yourself. We'll be in touch."

Darcy shook his friend's hand. He turned as if to walk out, but stopped when his hand was on the doorknob. "I do have a favor to ask though."

"Name it. I'll do it if I can."

"The files on Operation Ramsgate."

"Yes? What about them?"

"I want Elizabeth Bennet to have security clearance to access them, if she wants. The videos too."

Bingley frowned. "Are you sure about that?"

"Yes, I'm sure. Or can you not make that decision either?"

"Of course, I can. There's nothing in there someone with her clearance couldn't see, except, of course, for what was kept under wraps at your request."

"It may not sound it at the moment, but I do appreciate your faith in me, Charles."

"You'll always have it."

"Thanks." He paused. "If only it were enough to save my career."

Darcy closed the door behind him with a soft click that belied his temper. The agency bureaucrats might shuffle him off to Trinidad, but he had some things to wrap up first.

This is rich! The London Fog has been burned under the glaring light of suspicion. A long time coming in my opinion. A very long time. I know where you're going, and it's a cheap imitation of an assignment. How humiliating for you! How deliciously, gloriously humiliating. I couldn't have planned this any better. What sweet serendipity! You can't stop me now. Not from so far away. You have no power here anymore, and you can't stop me. No one can. This is a whole new beginning for me. I'm entrenched here in the States now. The money the KGB pays me gives me autonomy. I understand the power of money now. Perhaps the love I thought to have wasn't anything but a base, tawdry, unrequited lust. You know about unsatisfied lust, don't you?

21

ELIZABETH ROSE LATE the next morning, the result of a fitful alternation of sleeping and waking through the night. After she called the director, she tried a dozen ways to relax—a bath, returning to her book, making hot cocoa—but nothing worked. She half-listened for the door, signaling Darcy's return. He had things here after all, although they were nothing a man of his means and lifestyle couldn't leave behind. He left everything, and everyone, behind.

She was in the kitchen when she thought she heard the mailman on the porch. Stepping to the window, she peered out, seeing only the blur of a tall figure striding away. Retrieving her revolver, she waited several minutes, and when he didn't return, she stepped out with caution, the handgun still in her grasp. After several more seconds of scanning the area, her gaze landed on the mailbox. A goldenrod yellow envelope stuck out of the top. Darcy must have left it for her, and the tall figure must have been his, but like his nickname persona, the London Fog had disappeared into the cold, gray Virginia morning. She snatched the envelope from the box, tearing it open as she went back inside.

"Huh?"

It was a notice from The Park, the bookstore and coffee shop where she'd met with Charlotte yesterday, stating that the item she'd ordered had arrived and was waiting for her at the front desk. An involuntary chuckle bubbled out of her. She knew the bookshop package was a ruse and knew a message—probably filled with Darcy's typical multisyllabic vitriol—was waiting for her there. There was nothing for it. Curiosity demanded she drive up to DC and take whatever he was dishing out.

———

SHE ENTERED The Park with a clang of the doorbell. Closing the damp outside, she shivered. Most of her colleagues loved it here—the dark wood, the well-worn chairs and dining tables, the smell of books and coffee and cinnamon—but she always shivered when she came in the place.

The same older gentleman with twinkling blue eyes from her last visit looked at her over his bifocals. "Can I help you, miss?"

"I have a package?" She approached the counter and held out the notice. She didn't want to say a book, because she wasn't exactly sure what Darcy had left for her.

The man tilted his head up and down as he read the notice. "Ah, yes. I found it in the shipment this morning." He turned around to scan the shelves behind him. "You must be anxiously awaiting this." He plucked a brown paper-wrapped book out of a sea of them, and gave it to her.

She tore the wrapper and glanced at the contents. "*The Parsifal Mosaic.*"

"Robert Ludlum. An interesting spy novel about a man betrayed by a beautiful woman. It's been very popular in recent months. I guess we sold out before you could get your own copy."

"Yes. Thank you for ordering it." She dug in her purse. "What do I owe you?"

He blinked those twinkly blue eyes at her. "Don't you remember, my dear?"

"What?"

"It says here you've already paid for it."

"Oh, um...that's right. Pfft. Bad memory."

"Let me put it in a bag for you." He paused. "Unless, it's a gift? I could wrap it in Christmas paper."

"No, no. It's for me." She took the bag from him. "Thank you so much."

"You're welcome."

ELIZABETH REPEATEDLY GLANCED at the book as if it were a ticking time bomb sitting in the passenger seat of her car. Knowing she'd never get the thing inside Langley without a search, she drove to Scott's Run. Sitting in her car in the park, she finished tearing open the package and began thumbing through the pages. The title page contained an inscription written in a strong, close hand:

For Elizabeth—a mistress of subterfuge. Regards, William.

About one-third of the way through, she saw the cassette tape, embedded into a cut out space in the pages. She opened the glove box for her Walkman and, with her fingers trembling in an absurd manner, placed the headphones over her ears, pushed the tape inside, and pressed play. Darcy's rich baritone rumbled in her ears and down into the pit of her stomach, making her squirm in her seat.

"Ms. Bennet."

"Awfully formal of you, Darcy, considering..."

"Don't be alarmed at receiving this message. It's not a mission, or a desperate love letter, or a repetition of any of the sentiments that you found so disagreeable last night. I'm sure we'd both like to forget that whole unfortunate incident and move on with our lives.

"I do feel compelled, however, by professional courtesy and a sense of

justice, to defend myself against the charges you laid at my door. One accusation was definitely more egregious than the other, but each was unfair in my opinion. The first was that I interfered in the personal lives of two of our acquaintances without any consideration of the feelings of either. The second was that I used my position and influence to derail the career of an officer I managed, a man whom I recently learned has been a colleague of yours for some time. What other relationship exists between you and the man in question, is, of course, your own business. But if what I have to say offends you, so be it. It's a necessary evil. I'll apologize for it this once, but no matter what happens between the two of you after this, if you trust him, you won't have my sympathy. I've warned you. Twice now."

"Leave it to you to think I have to be sleeping with the guy to work with him. And don't think I feel guilty about investigating your arrogant ass either. That's what you get for throwing your weight around the CIA."

"You most likely don't want to hear me out, Elizabeth. I can hear you now, muttering to yourself about what an arrogant ass I am, but your integrity and your need for fairness demands you consider my information. Arrogant I may be, but I recognize a person with a kindred sense of justice. And I see that in you. I'll address the issue of our mutual friends on the tape, but for the story surrounding my professional relationship with that other man and the incidents in Prague, I'll refer you to the CIA classified report dated January 8, 1982. File number 82374. I've made sure you have the security clearance to access the files. Read, watch, and learn, Elizabeth, for your own safety and education if nothing else. Now, as far as the two supposed lovebirds, let me be perfectly plain..."

She snapped off the recording and jumped out of her car, taking off down the easiest trail. The cold, fresh air of late fall would do her some good. She knew the tone in his voice—full of condescending opinions as she expected—and she was in no mood for it.

But the Prague report, now that was intriguing. Referring her to a classified case file meant there was more to the story than she had been told. She'd often had the sneaking suspicion her supervisors kept her in the dark. Perhaps the report could shed some light on Wickham's motives, or even the director's, and explain why she'd spent the better part of a year on a wild goose chase.

While she walked, she might as well hear what he had to say for himself in regards to Charles and Johanna. She depressed the play button again. The tape chirped as she rewound the last sentence.

"...let me be perfectly plain: Of course, I saw the interest developing between them. Like you, I've been trained to observe people's actions and intuit their motives. Charles is charming and agreeable. It's one of his most useful qualities. No one expects a man so open and friendly to be in our line of work. He's also an unabashed flirt, and at first, I thought his time spent with Johanna was just his typical MO when dealing with women. It wasn't until they returned to Washington that I had any true suspicion he was contemplating something more...serious. I called him the weekend we were in West Berlin. He mentioned Johanna several times in a context that made me realize they had been spending time together socially. When I goaded him about falling for an asset, he never denied it. It concerned me. To be honest, I couldn't figure out what he saw in her. She's a pretty girl, but she's vulnerable physically, emotionally, and politically. Why would he want to get tangled up in that mess? Plus, she smiles too much."

"Annoying know-it-all."

"As for Johanna herself, of course, she'd welcome any attention from Charles. He's become a powerful man in a brief amount of time, and he can offer her the protection very few men can. However, he doesn't yet know how to handle people who might be trying to use him."

"Yeah, but she doesn't even know who he is, you jerk."

"I watched Johanna while we were in Hungary, and she never seemed truly interested. But it isn't just a suspicion of her motives that incited my

objections to a relationship between the two of them. Even if she is genuinely fond of him, being with her puts him in danger—definitely career-wise, but perhaps literally in danger as well.

"For example, what happens if she goes back to Hungary, even just for a visit? She'll be under suspicion from the moment she sets foot in her own country. If government security picks her up for questioning and gets her to talk, they'll be able to nab her father and possibly Charles himself.

"Conversely, if the other side gets wind of a love affair between them, even if they're here in the States, she's still a liability Charles cannot afford. The KGB could get to her here and say they'll pick up her father if she doesn't spy on her American boyfriend and his brother-in-law in the State Department.

"We've got a whole web of officers surrounding the Bingley siblings. Do I turn my back while he puts all of them at risk for some...fling? Cara sent me a message to call her after that weekend in West Berlin. She was beside herself with worry.

"So, yes, I steered him out of Johanna's path. I discussed with him the various evils of his choice. He still might have put it all aside and continued to pursue her if I hadn't pointed out that he was sealing off her opportunity to go back to her homeland—maybe preventing her from ever seeing her father again. Charles has empathy for assets, probably more than he should. One of the reasons he belongs here in Washington, I suppose. It was scarcely the work of a moment to convince him to let her go. It was for the best, and, again, I refuse to apologize for doing what was best."

She could see his point, which annoyed her. She'd had more access to Johanna than he had, though, and thought she'd read her pretty well. As for Charles, he was a big boy and could take care of himself. How officious was it of Darcy to insinuate himself into the situation? And why could he not give Johanna a break? Why was it always rules, rules, rules with him? What about flexibility? What about seeing two sides of an issue? *Jerk.*

"As for Wickham..."

There was a pause. She heard him draw a deep breath, could almost see him closing his eyes, gathering his composure. In her mind's eye, she saw his lips draw into a firm line and then glide into an almost pout. Quickly, she shut the tape off. Before she heard his side, she wanted to see the CIA's files on the Prague incident. It was time to head to the archives department.

"OFFICER BENNET?"

"Yes, that's me." She held out her badge.

He looked at her identification and then paged through a file filled with green and white computer printouts. "Okay, you're on the clearance list. Just since this morning, though."

"That's soon enough," she intoned sweetly as she held out her hands for the files.

"There's video as well. You want a viewing booth?"

"Yes, please."

"Hold on." He picked the phone off the cradle and buzzed back into the labyrinth of archive rooms. "Right this way."

He led her through to a small cubicle with a table and chairs, painted a drab celery green and white. The only other object in the room was a rolling cart crowned with a television and dressed with a VCR below it. The librarian plugged in the cord and tested the setup. "You're good to go."

She thanked him and settled herself into the metal chair. Leaning forward, she pushed the tape in and pressed "play."

Blue screen, white lettering:

CIA debriefing: William Darcy 08 January 1982 East European Division: Prague Incident: 1981–149

The lettering disappeared to reveal Darcy, sitting in a cubicle much like the one where Elizabeth sat now, his hands folded in front of him, physical exhaustion emanating from both his facial expression and his body language. His hair was longer than he'd worn it in Budapest but not quite the length he'd sported in East Berlin. The ice-blue eyes had dark circles under them, and he was unshaven, casting the lines and planes of his face into dangerous shadow.

A disembodied voice from off camera spoke. "Please state your name and rank, sir."

Darcy lifted weary eyes to the camera. "William Darcy, Station Chief, Prague, East European Division."

"Tell us about your primary mission in Prague."

"From mid-1979 until a few days ago, I was the chief of station in Prague, Czechoslovakia. I was assigned to the State Department as an undersecretary to the ambassador, which gave me some diplomatic immunity and the protection of the embassy. I ran a shop of case officers and assets placed in the government, in the state run media, even in the household of the chief of the secret police. One specific mission in Prague was to discover the fate of some of the dissidents who had signed the document often referred to as 'Charter 77.' We also tried to engage the portion of the citizenry—artists, students— thought to be most amenable to Western influence. That's a cold way to say it because there's considerable economic and personal suffering in Prague, but as station chief, it's not my place to be warm and fuzzy."

"The majority of our questions today will be directed toward the incident of December 28, 1981."

"I understand."

"But before we delve into that, please tell us how the CIA acquired the asset known as Jirina Sobota? What was the first point of contact?"

Darcy leaned back in his chair and folded his arms across his chest. "As word got around the artistic community that we were interested in the Charter 77 dissidents, we began getting a few unsolicited offers of intelligence information. Jirina Sobota was one of those. She was a young college student who walked into the US Embassy on..." He leaned forward and consulted his notes. "March 18, 1981."

"A young woman just waltzes in off the street and offers to spy for the US government?"

"That's what happened. Sometimes truth is stranger than fiction."

"What did you do? How did you handle her?"

"The same way we always handle that kind of thing. We whisked her off to a safe room and began an intake interview."

"And who conducted that interview?"

"Officer George Wickham."

"Tell us what information he obtained from her that day."

"It's in his reports. I'm sure you have them there."

"We want to hear your take."

Darcy sighed. "Of course you do." He settled back in his chair again as if preparing to spin a long yarn. "I was called in to watch Wickham conduct Jirina's intake interview from behind the two-way mirror."

"She never saw you."

"No. She had questionable validity as an asset, and I was station chief. We didn't want her to be able to identify me."

"Go on."

"She gave us quite an interesting history."

"Meaning, a fictional one."

"Not necessarily. We're still investigating some aspects of it, but some facts have been verified."

"Let's start with those."

"Miss Sobota was the daughter of a popular Czech pianist, Adriana Sobota. Jirina's father was MIA but was rumored to be an American. Jirina had only seen the man once, when she was about fourteen. This was about a year after her mother died in an automobile accident. The father had visited Jirina in secret, and during that conversation, he confided to her that he was married to a woman living in the States. During a period of estrangement from his wife, he had fallen in love with Jirina's mother. He didn't know of Jirina's existence until her mother's death, and when he found out Adriana had a child, he did the math and confirmed that the timing was right for her to be his daughter."

"Do we know the identity of this father?"

"Still searching for him."

"Go on."

"Since her mother's death, Jirina had been residing with her mother's sister, a woman married to a deputy minister in the Communist government. Jirina's father could not get her out of Czechoslovakia without endangering her life—and his, most likely—so he left her in the care of her aunt and uncle, promising to get her out when he could. He also told her, if anything should happen to him, that she had an older half brother in the States. We haven't been able to locate him either."

"So her story really is speculative."

"At this time, not all of it can be verified. What is known is that Jirina's father never returned for her—never contacted her again. However, she was convinced he had told her the truth, and she wanted out of Czechoslovakia. She came to the embassy offering the only collateral she had. She was a student living with a Communist politician. She was also consorting with dissidents—artists and other friends of her mother's—and trying to connect them with students who were interested in changing Czechoslovakia's future. She offered to provide us with that information, so we could have the names and covertly attend meetings. In addition, she also offered whatever government information she could glean from living in her uncle's house. Her price for this information was passage to the US and help finding her half brother. Her father had used an alias while he was in Czechoslovakia, so she didn't even know his real name.

"We had a dilemma with Jirina Sobota. Her goal was to escape Prague, and our goal was to keep her there. What good is an asset if she isn't in the field?"

"True enough."

"I had to balance her safety and her willingness to spy for us with our requirements for information. The higher-ups in the agency were very interested in the student factions of the anti-Communist underground groups, so I got a lot of pressure from Washington to keep her in place."

"So you were her handler?"

"No. I kept Wickham as her case officer, and he reported to me. After all, the fewer people she connected with, the better it would be for all concerned. I kept tabs on her though and developed some admiration for her, I suppose."

The man off-camera cleared his throat delicately. "I see."

"It wasn't a romantic interest. Perhaps I have a jaded reputation, but I am capable of purer motives than what's in the best interest of my libido."

"Of course."

"I admired her courage and her determination as I admired many of the people in Czechoslovakia. She was young and idealistic and full of hope."

"Tell me about the Ramsgate op."

"Ramsgate. A name synonymous with FUBAR from this point until forever."

The voice didn't respond.

"Yeah. When Jirina asked me, through Wickham, to attend a meeting of the dissidents, I agreed to go...at first. Later, I reconsidered that decision."

"Why did she want you to go?"

"So she could plead her case, would be my guess. To ask for my assistance in getting her to the States so she could find her half brother."

"And why did you change your mind about going?"

"Another trusted asset reported that state security knew the Prague COS would make an appearance at this meeting. We never could confirm this rumor though, so I made an executive decision and put about that I would be in Brataslava on the day in question. Jirina could still attend the meeting and get the dissidents' names and a lead on their plans. Wickham was to take her to the meeting and pick her up at a prearranged place afterward."

"And that's where things began to go wrong."

Darcy frowned and put his fist in his hand with some vehemence. "I *told* him to be careful—to get there early so he and Jirina could evaluate the situation before entering. I was suspicious enough that I even arranged for another officer to be on site, one who had dossiers on the most likely KGB agents. He was stationed as a concierge in the hotel where the meeting was to take place. He was to signal Jirina if the meeting had been infiltrated by KGB by jingling his keys in his left hand and then twirling the ring around his index finger before putting them back in his pocket. Jirina never got the signal instructions. I left a message with that information for Wickham, but he was late getting her to the hotel and didn't check for last-minute details, which was standard procedure by the way."

"Why did you not contact him by phone or in person at the embassy?"

"He wasn't at the embassy, and I knew the chances of finding a secure line in Brataslava were slim to none. I sent a trusted messenger—"

"And who was that?"

"Bill Collins. He's not the sharpest tool in the shed, but if you give him a message, he can manage to deliver it. When one of the assets we left behind checked the drop, it was there."

The interviewer's pen scratched across the paper as he took down the name. Darcy leaned forward and checked the notes, and then went on.

"My concierge friend gave the signal, but Jirina went in anyway, not knowing any better. He, not knowing where her pickup point was, waited outside. She reappeared a few hours later, much to his relief, but he also saw that she had picked up a tail, so he followed them. Jirina must have also realized she was being followed because Novák said she picked up her pace, almost running by the time she approached the cafe where Wickham was to pick her up. The KGB nabbed her right outside the cafe while Novák stood there, helpless to intervene. He watched as she screamed, tried to get away, and he watched as Wickham let them take her."

"You blame Wickham for that."

"Hell yes, I blame him! I mean, I understand he could hardly expose himself to capture at that point—he knew too much—but neither of them would have been in that position in the first place if he had just done his damned job! He was careless, and that carelessness cost me an asset and Jirina Sobota a hell of a lot more than that."

"What happened then?"

"Wickham called my office in a blind panic, accusing me of all kinds of wild things—of trying to get him killed, of being a double agent, of letting the KGB take Jirina so I wouldn't have to get her out of Prague. I tried to talk him down when we regrouped at the US Embassy. He didn't believe me when I said I arranged for a safety signal. He was emotional, frightened—which was atypical for him and made me wonder what was going on. That's when I found out he was sleeping with her. He had seduced a nineteen-year-old college student, his asset, and through his oversight, he cost her everything."

"You were angry."

"I was furious! He did everything he shouldn't have. Every damn thing."

"And then?"

"After that, he and I had no choice but to flee Czechoslovakia. She was most likely being interrogated, possibly tortured, and I had no idea how long such a young person could hold out under those circumstances. She still didn't know me by sight, but Wickham had told her I worked in the State Department, so it wouldn't have been that much of a stretch to figure out who I was."

The image faded. There had been two more interviews over the next week, detailing Darcy's frustration with Wickham: appointments with assets that weren't kept, money that he squandered, and women that he entertained on the agency's dime. Darcy had gone to bat for him on the money issue more than once, but now he was convinced the man was an incorrigible spendthrift. He wasn't fit for fieldwork. If he stayed in the agency at all, he needed to be behind a desk at Langley where he could be watched. A man with that kind of financial history was a prime target for the KGB's stable of double agents.

The last entry was dated February 4, 1982, the day before Darcy left for Budapest. He looked better physically; he'd cut his hair, filled out some. He was tan, Elizabeth noted, and filed that detail away. He looked...good. But then he began to talk, and the agony in his face erased any notice of his improved physical condition.

"You've had additional information in the Ramsgate op."

"Yes. They've found her."

"Jirina Sobota?"

"MI6 got wind of the KGB holding an American asset outside Prague in preparation for transport to the USSR. They, in coordination with our military-trained agents, infiltrated the compound and pulled Jirina Sobota out of KGB hands."

"Where is she now?"

"In a place where she will be safe, physically, and where her emotional trauma will be addressed."

"And where is that?"

Darcy smirked. "Above your clearance level, sir."

"I'll take that up with the director."

"You do that. Sir." He pushed a paper toward the interviewer. "Her whereabouts are sensitive compartmentalized information."

"And yet you know where she is."

"I do."

"Does Wickham know she's been found?"

Darcy's expression hardened. "No, nor will he. His security clearance has been downgraded since we returned. This mismanagement has cost him his career in the field and several opportunities here at home."

"Harsh."

"It will never be enough punishment for what he did to Jirina." Darcy stood. "Interview over."

"I beg your pardon?"

"I've got to pack. I'm leaving tomorrow on assignment."

"Where can we contact you if we need additional information to close the Ramsgate investigation?"

"Budapest. Through appropriate secure channels, of course."

"They're sending you back out there? Even after the incident in Prague?"

"Neither the other side nor the compromised asset ever laid eyes on me. I'll be fine."

"Still..."

"My career might suffer in the short term because of Ramsgate, but I'll recover. I'll be station chief again, somewhere. Mark my words." Darcy turned to the door. "Good day, sir."

For several seconds after Darcy left the room, the interviewer sat. Elizabeth sat as well, watching as the gray suit sleeve reached over and shut off the camera. She spent the next two hours combing through the paper files and reading reports that confirmed it all. Wickham was sloppy, unorganized—took unnecessary chances with information and assets. Darcy had gotten Wickham out of his predicaments before, but there was no cleaning up the Ramsgate mess. Wickham must have somehow persuaded the director to suspect Darcy, though how he had done so, with this kind of record, was a mystery.

Quietly, she gathered the materials and placed them back in their packaging marked "Top Secret: Sensitive Compartmentalized Information." She called up to her own department and informed the secretary she was taking the afternoon off. She drove without the radio all the way back to Fredericksburg, needing the silence to think. There was a letter in the mailbox, asking her to vacate the Fredericksburg property within forty-eight hours. She would be moving back to her apartment near McLean, awaiting her next assignment. When she got inside, she saw Darcy's closet was empty and his things were gone. He'd either had someone clean it out, or he'd done it himself while she was gone. Either way, it seemed that he had no interest in discussing anything with her.

Finally, she remembered that there was more on Darcy's tape. She pulled out the Walkman.

"...as for Wickham...

I hope that after considering all the information from the archived files, you'll realize I didn't ruin him. He did that pretty much on his own. I can only imagine what half-truths he told you and what omissions he made when he told his sob story to the director. But if they kept you in the dark, perhaps it's no wonder he was successful in convincing you I was playing favorites. There was really no way for you to detect any deception on his part, and perhaps you aren't suspicious of your colleagues without provocation."

A chuckle rumbled in his throat.

"A stint in counterintelligence should cure you of that. I should have told you all this last night, perhaps. I have a tendency to lose my heart and my head around you, Elizabeth, and that can be my only excuse for not immediately telling you what you deserved to know. If you have any additional questions, you can ask Fitz. He was part of the team that rescued Jirina. You won't be able to ask me because I will be gone soon. I have another assignment, in the Caribbean, and will be out of touch for some time.

"I'll close by saying that I never meant to offend you or impose on you in any way. You have my professional respect as well as my gratitude for the two times you've saved my life. In spite of everything that has transpired between us, I wish you the very best.

"Goodbye, Elizabeth, and good luck."

Elizabeth rewound the tape and played it over and over. Finally, after about the fourth go-around, she fell asleep to the sound of his voice in her ear.

PART III

22

CIA Headquarters, Langley, Virginia
May 1983

"BENNET, you're turning into a workaholic! Why are you here on a Friday night?"

Elizabeth looked up from her file, annoyed with the interruption. Wickham and Collins were standing in the doorway. Wickham seemed more interested in her chest; Collins was checking out the chart on her wall.

Typical. Ogler and Meddler.

"You know, I might ask the same of you. Why are you two here on a Friday night?"

Wickham grinned. "We're still here, but we're knocking off for the weekend. From what the receptionist downstairs said, you'll be here tomorrow *and* Sunday."

"I'm busy these days."

"You're just not the same fun girl you were before you went abroad."

"Hmm?" Perhaps if he saw she was uninterested, he'd leave her alone.

He put his hip on the corner of her desk. "What are you working on so hot and heavy?"

"Just finishing up some reports."

"On Darcy?"

Annoyance tipped over into temper. "Nope. I'm done with Darcy. Now I'm looking for an *actual* mole!"

Bill Collins startled at her sharp tone, tearing his eyes away from the wall chart—a cloud-like diagram with one oval at the center and lines connecting many ovals with code numbers across the paper.

Wickham eased off the desk. "No need to get testy, Bennet. Just wanted to know if you'd like to go out and get a drink with us."

Elizabeth leaned back in her chair, rubbing fingers across her over-tired eyes. She took a deep breath, observing the man before her with a shrewd eye. Looking at Wickham now, any trace of appeal he ever held was buried beneath the impulsive, financially strapped schmoozer she now knew him to be. And she knew it all, thanks to Darcy—and to Charlotte and the FBI file the two women had compiled on him. Oh yes, she knew all about Oval Number 75-13 on her chart. She got up and drew a green line between Wickham's oval and one of the banks listed in the margin.

She glanced back and saw Collins still staring at her.

"What, Bill?!"

"Hmm? Oh, it's nothing, Ms. Bennet," he stammered. "The director still has you looking for a mole?"

"Not actively," she admitted. "But I like to be thorough."

"So you don't have an actual assignment at the moment?" Wickham asked.

"I have assignments. I'm working on this between assignments."

"For six months?"

"Yeah. So?"

"Well, Darcy's tucked away safe and sound in the Caribbean. So, in my opinion, we got rid of the *actual* mole."

"Where in the Caribbean?" Collins asked.

Elizabeth and Wickham exchanged looks.

Wickham shrugged. "It's no secret. The director sent his ass to

Port of Spain, Trinidad—and good riddance." He turned back to Elizabeth. "Once upon a time, we were a fine team, Bennet. We should go back into the field and work together again."

"I'm sure they will send me into the field when there's something for me to do." Based on the counterintelligence dossier she was compiling on Wickham, however, she doubted they'd send him anywhere in the future.

Collins piped up. "I agree completely. Ms. Bennet does excellent field work."

"I don't know about that," she said. "I haven't been part of an op yet that wasn't a complete disaster."

"Well, there was Budapest...no, wait. East Ber—"

"Thanks, Bill."

"I'm...sure the next one will be...good." His voice faded, but then he plastered on a too-bright smile. "Does she know about the Viceroy?"

"The who?" Elizabeth asked.

"Yeah, Collins, that's a thought. Lizzy, if you're really still interested in this mole business, I could use your insight. Collins has some information on a new asset who reportedly has intelligence regarding a double agent."

Elizabeth considered. Wickham took her silence as encouragement.

"Ironically, the asset wants to meet on Tobago." Wickham held a hand to his ear. "What's that you say? The asset's near Trinidad? And who is the COS on Trinidad?" He looked straight at her with hard eyes. "That's right. The London Fog."

Collins snickered.

"Thing is, the director just gave me a new assignment, and Collins is in the middle of a project too. We wondered who we could get to meet up with Viceroy. You interested?"

"Darcy and I didn't part on the best of terms. I wouldn't want to meet up with him by accident."

"Darcy's in Port of Spain. The asset's on Tobago. You'll probably never run into him."

"He's not being informed about the new asset?"

Wickham shrugged. "It's a counterintelligence matter right now. We don't even know if the new asset will pan out."

"Oh, it's a good lead," Collins said, picking up a file.

"Yeah, all right. I'll think about it." *If Wickham handpicks the officer, he can fill the newbie's head with his Darcy-Is-Poison propaganda. And the Caribbean sounds good. I could use the change of scene.* "No, wait. I'll do it if the director clears me for the assignment." She snatched the file out of Collins's hand. "Give me that! That's sensitive personal and financial information you've got your grubby paws on! You might even know the person."

"Me? I don't know anyone like that."

"You never *really* know anyone, do you?" She slammed the file on the desk.

"So the ovals correspond to people and files?" he asked.

"Yes. Now, go away. Go have a drink and toast my absence."

"What are the red and blue and green arrows for?"

"It's just my note-taking system, Bill."

"Come on, Collins. Let's let the career girl do her job. I'll buy you a beer."

"I prefer gin and tonic."

"Fine. Gin and tonic for you." Wickham banged an accented rhythm on the door frame with his fingers as he strutted out. "Night, Busy Lizzy."

Collins stared between the chart and Wickham's retreating back.

Elizabeth smirked. *Snooping or bootlicking. What will it be, Bill?*

He pursed his lips and then decided. "Okay. Night, Ms. Bennet."

"See you Monday." Elizabeth sat back down behind her desk and opened the file Collins had in his hand. At least he hadn't gotten hold of 78-20.

That file was his.

"HEY." Charlotte picked up a French fry, doused it in ketchup, and then talked around it as she chewed. "Did you know Darcy Sr. was a civilian contractor for the CIA?"

"Nope."

"Long time ago—'57 to '62."

"Interesting. I wonder if that's where Darcy got the idea to go into intelligence."

"Sources say Dad wanted the CIA from the beginning, but Darcy took a shine to the Air Force for a while. Did a tour during Vietnam as a supply pilot."

"But he didn't make a career out of it."

"It wasn't a great time to be career military. Things were discombobulated."

"To say the least."

"Then Saigon fell in '75. Darcy was employed by the CIA by then."

"Why did George Darcy stop contracting with the government?"

"He didn't entirely—Darcy Shipping still has a few government contracts—but the CIA dropped him like a hot potato. After the Bay of Pigs incident."

Elizabeth stopped mid-bite. "Bay of Pigs?"

"Yep. One of his ships was grounded on Playa Girón, and another turned tail and left after President Kennedy called off air support for the invasion."

"My father was at Playa Girón, and I told Darcy that once. He never mentioned his father was a civilian supplier."

"Maybe he didn't know."

"Maybe," she said carefully. "You'd think Darcy Sr. would have steered his son clear of the agency after that."

"You'd think."

"If he did know, maybe our Darcy wanted to be his own man. He could have led a pampered, easy life as a shipping magnate, and yet he chose to serve his country instead."

Charlotte tried to hide a smile. "I sense some softening toward the London Fog since you came back from East Berlin."

"I guess I have softened a little. I've developed some respect for the guy. He's arrogant at times, condescending at others, but he's..." A dozen images scrolled through her mind like a slide show: Darcy grinning, his eyes hidden behind sunglasses on Lake Balaton. Darcy kissing her hand when he woke in the hospital. The shock and hurt on his face when she told him about her real mission in Hungary and East Germany.

"For someone trained in observation, I sure was unobservant," she muttered.

"What are you talking about?"

Elizabeth paused. "While we were in Virginia, Darcy made a move on me."

Charlotte's eyes popped open. "Real-ly?"

"Not a move like a casual, let's-jump-in-the-sack-and-screw move. He wanted..." What had he wanted, exactly? "He thought they were sending him to the USSR. He wanted me to transfer and go with him."

"And here I thought the man was an island. You turned him down, obviously."

"With extreme prejudice."

"And now you wish you hadn't?"

"Not exactly. I'd always thought of him as the target of an investigation, not a guy to get cozy with. Sure, there was some physical attraction because, let's face it—"

"He's hot."

"Yeah, and I've been without for a long time now. A long time."

"You could look somewhere else."

"I know, but every time I go out and look at someone else, I see stupid Darcy instead." She shook her head. "I don't regret not getting involved with him because it's complicated, and I don't need any more complications. But I wish I hadn't been so harsh. I wonder if it might have worked if circumstances had been different. I wish..."

"You wish what, E?"

"I don't know. It bothers me that he's down there in Trinidad, or wherever life may take him in the future, and thinking poorly of me." She squirmed. "Nothing makes you madder or hurts more than when another person says or does something that violates your self-concept, realigns how you see yourself. Through a thousand little comments and actions, even though he didn't always intend to, Darcy did that for me. A lot of the time, it pissed me off, but in the end, I have to admit, it forced me to know myself better."

"A gift—from one of the few people capable of giving it to you."

"Yes, I suppose you're right. I thought I had great intuition. That I was smarter than everyone around me. That I was sharp-eyed and perceptive. In truth, I was what I accused Darcy of over and over again: arrogant, prideful. I swallowed the company line about him, and that made me prejudiced. If there's anything a counterintelligence officer *can't* be, it's prejudiced. It's unwise to only see what I want to see; I have to see what truly is."

"And what *is*, in regards to your feelings about William Darcy?"

"I feel like a fool—which I really hate—and, god help me, I miss him."

My handler still wants me keeping tabs on you. He thinks there's some way to persuade you to join our little team. Especially now that you have been shunted aside by your own agency. Under his direction, I made a plan to lure you—a brilliant plan—but I have a bigger problem on my hands now. They're on my trail. Building a case, a network of possibilities. It's only a matter of time before they put together enough information to sink me. I've got to disrupt the process and get the ringleader out of here somehow.

23

Port of Spain, Trinidad
June 1983

DARCY HELD UP TWO FINGERS, and after exchanging some bills with the bartender, he pulled two Stag beer bottles through the metal bars protecting the pub's gleaming wood and stainless bar. After being in Trinidad through a Carnival, he could see the reason for the "bars on the bars." Sometimes Carnival got rowdy. A few regulars leaned against sunny yellow walls or perched on bar stools, but he took his two ice-cold bottles to a high top several feet away. A welcome breeze blew through the pub from one open end to the other. He handed one bottle to the young man sitting across from him and pushed his sunglasses up on top of his head. The two men clinked bottles.

"Tell me again why you're leaving Port of Spain, Darcy."

He lifted his beer and eyed the younger of his two case officers. There were only two officers here in Trinidad, and the older one was leaving with him tomorrow. "I want out of the city before the rainy season really hits."

"That's bullshit, man. What have you got going on?"

"You just keep your eyes and ears open when you're on the docks this summer."

"Aw," the young man grumbled under his breath.

"And I want regular reports on anything you hear from Grenada."

Henry grinned, teeth gleaming in his handsome, dark face. "You keep the money coming, and I'll keep the reports coming."

"Deal."

"Still don't know why you're taking Rita with you to Tobago instead of me. How's an old lady gonna help you out if you get in a jam?"

"A woman has helped me out of a jam more than once. Besides, what are the chances I'll have trouble on Tobago?"

"That's a good point."

"Besides, I like Rita, and I like her curried chicken."

"Still, you should stick around. That cute little embassy secretary with the blue bikini has the hots for you."

"Only because she doesn't know me too well."

"You haven't been out and about since you got here in January. Sworn off women, have you?"

"Yep—at least for the near future."

Henry shook his head. "That ain't right. Make you crazy before too long."

"Women made me crazy in the first place. In fact, I'm saner now than I've been for over a year."

Henry narrowed his eyes and gestured toward Darcy with his beer bottle. "Then it ain't women that made you crazy, it was *a woman*."

Darcy only smirked and drained his beer bottle. "I'll check in each Thursday evening, so stay available between sundown and bedtime. And, more than likely, I'll be back in Port of Spain before the end of the year. If you need to reach me in between times though, call the number I gave you with a coded message."

They chatted on and off while they finished the Stags as the sun sank lower in the sky and the breeze kicked up, stirring the thick tropical heat. Darcy set his bottle on the table and pushed to stand up.

"Keep your ear to the ground, my friend." Darcy reached over and shook his young officer's hand.

"What's your hurry?"

"I gotta pack my bag. You take care, Henry."

"Will do, man. Will do. I'll see you around."

DARCY MOVED AROUND HIS APARTMENT, putting clothes and other items into his duffel. The windows were open, and he could hear the sound of the street life below even over the hum of the fan he'd come to depend on. Life moved slower in the tropics. He was learning to accept that and even enjoy it some. Perhaps Bingley had been right: Darcy had slept more, considered more, waited more, and learned more, both about the station and himself than he had at any other post he'd been assigned. Odd how he hadn't realized how tired he was until suddenly, after about six weeks in Port of Spain, he wasn't tired anymore.

And Tobago would move even slower than the capital on Trinidad. Oh, he *could* stay in Port of Spain. Could have an affair with the brunette in the blue bikini, maybe get a look inside the embassy. Maybe get a line on current agency activities. But why?

Why?

There had been many times over the last few months he'd asked some form of that question. Why Trinidad and Tobago? Why did the agency want him away from Langley if he'd been cleared? Why was he really under suspicion in the first place? And perhaps more importantly, why should he care what happened to his career now? Trinidad wasn't a bad place. He had a couple friends here, good colleagues. His job was easy, so very easy. He could bide his time here in the tropics, maybe finish out his years in the agency and fade away into anonymity. The London Fog—dissipated and burned away in the hot Caribbean sun.

Or he could leave the agency altogether. He'd considered resigning when he was denied the USSR assignment. He entertained the thought of going home to Baltimore and acting the playboy bachelor before settling down with some newfangled, eighties version of a Southern belle. He could take an active role in the business his father left him instead of being an absentee board member voting on company decisions from an ocean away.

If he left the agency now, though, he would leave with a stain on his reputation, a blemish that would last forever. It would be almost impossible to clear his name from outside the agency. With no security clearance and no contacts, he'd lose any advantage he possessed that might help him find the truth. The upper echelon had technically cleared him, but then they shoved him aside like a bad apple with a bruise. If they only knew how easy untraceable treason could be. They treated him, a stellar officer, as if he were an embarrassment, a reminder of screw-ups from the past. In their minds, it was better to just start over with a new agent, a fresh face.

A fresh face like Elizabeth Bennet, perhaps. Wasn't that what she was to counterintelligence, to the director? An unsuspecting young woman, easily led? He considered that. Well, maybe she was at the beginning. But she'd been out in the field now for over a year, had seen how Europe worked. Hopefully, she'd read the reports on Wickham, and wherever she was now, she was away from his subtle, toxic manipulation.

He wondered where she was now.

Wickham might have misled Elizabeth early on, but Darcy knew she could think for herself. No greenhorn would stay green forever. So she'd learn her lesson like everyone else. And she'd appreciate the guidance Darcy had given her once she experienced how the agency chewed people up and spit them out. His anger banked, sharp and fast, but then faded into a gentle regret.

The truth was—he missed her. Plain and simple. He missed her snarky comments, her sense of adventure, and her open, engaging smile. She was one of the very few people he'd ever met who had the innate ability to live out a cover story yet keep her soul intact. She was like Bingley in that regard and unlike Darcy, who used disguise of every sort to hide from the world and, in so doing, hide from himself.

She was a woman with integrity, anchored to her mission, and persistent in achieving her objectives. He admired her for it. And he wanted her, even now. It was humbling to admit that fact. His chest ached when he thought of her, which was often. He wanted that levelheaded, blunt, brave beauty to buoy his own cynicism. She entered his imagination ten times during the day and invaded his dreams at night. It wasn't surprising, really, when he considered he'd looked at her face more days than not for over a year.

Not that he couldn't be without her. He was living without her now, wasn't he? And had been these seven months. But he knew, whatever Fate brought him on the other side of Trinidad, either in the agency or outside of it, he'd still want her. He was realistic enough to admit she might not want to be part of his complicated, crazy existence, but that didn't eliminate the hole that yawned wider and wider each month he remained in this paradise alone.

Perhaps he couldn't show her the real William Darcy, whoever that man was down deep, but he wanted Elizabeth Bennet to see how he truly felt about her. What happened from there, he had no idea, no angle to play. It was uncharted territory for a man in his position, a man who planned everything. He was reminded of the old Hunt-Lenox globe his father had shown him on a trip through the New York Public Library. Off the coast of Asia, a then-unknown land, were written the words "Here are dragons." For a man burned by unrequited love, dragons lurked around every bend in the road.

Right now, though, he had more immediate concerns. He'd never been a particularly paranoid man, considering his line of work, but he was convinced there was a betrayer in their midst, a wolf in sheep's clothing—someone who wanted him away from the center of things. Although there were certainly other possibilities, Wickham seemed the most likely suspect. He'd betrayed Jirina, he'd manipulated Elizabeth, and bamboozled the director. He was probably behind the decision that resulted in Darcy being virtually expelled from Langley. Wickham apparently rid himself of the only officer who knew what he was capable of.

But Darcy wasn't down for the count yet. He'd bide his time, keep his options open, and when the gears snapped into place, he'd make his move, lay his cards on the table, and play his hand. He chuckled at the trite analogies. He had lived his whole adult life as a stale spy cliché with his cover stories and his silly spy rules. There was nothing smooth or sophisticated about him, not now, not here. Maybe not ever again. He was a man whose career had been buried alive, but by god, he'd claw through the dirt to the surface. Somehow, he'd breathe in the clear air of innocence.

And he was thinking in trite analogies again.

The time in Tobago would be a respite of sorts, but there was still a tiny bit of intelligence work to do. With Henry in Port of Spain, and he and Rita Gardiner on Tobago, they planned to listen to the rumblings from Grenada, which was about the only real intelligence that came out of the region.

A few hours and a plane ride later, he pulled his Jeep into the drive of his rented villa on the northeast shore of Tobago. It was almost the exact opposite point from the airport, an hour's drive, but he'd done that on purpose. The quiet fishing village on the windward side of the island gave him exactly what he wanted—sailing, fresh catch for dinner, and quiet, brooding space. Rita was close by, and after he let himself in, he saw she had already dropped by to make the house livable, including laying in a stock of Bug-Mat repellent and vaporizers, accompanied by a note: "For your room at night. It's rainy season, so don't forget."

He smiled at the brusque tone and made a mental note to clear the bedroom of mosquitoes before bedtime.

24

The island of Tobago
July 1983

"You been into town this week?" Rita glanced up at him as she wiped down the counter.

"No, ma'am."

"I think you need some time away from this house."

"I've been down to the fishing dock. Every morning and evening."

"I meant to engage people in real conversations, not gathering intel. Why don't you take that fancy boat of yours around to Scarborough? Spend the day down there, see what there is to see in port."

"As a matter of fact, I planned to do just that. I've got to check in with Henry, and the weather's favorable today."

"Mm-hmm. I think that's a fine idea. And while you're gone, I'll whip up some meals to last you through the next few days."

"Going somewhere?"

"Got to see my sister in Castara. I'll be back on Tuesday though."

"I think I can make it that long without starving."

"Pfft." She smacked him gently on the arm with her cleaning cloth. "You ain't lookin' like you miss too many meals."

"Thanks to you. You don't have to watch over me, you know. You're an intelligence officer, not a housekeeper."

"Maybe they pay me to watch over you too." She had her back to him and missed the resigned expression that crossed his face.

"Et tu, Brute?" he mumbled.

She whipped back around. "Oh, don't give me that wounded look. They don't pay me for that, but I don't mind cooking a few meals, using a mop now and then. Gives me something to do. This snooping business can be mighty dull."

She patted his cheek as she passed him on the way to the stove and gave him an appraising look. "You are looking better than when you came here." She poked him good-naturedly in the belly. "Fillin' out. Got some sun too. Reminds me, don't forget a little sun lotion on your trip today."

THE WIND WAS gentle for the time of year, and Darcy took his boat all the way down past Scarborough to a little port just beyond Rockley Bay. He wandered through the village fresh air market, absorbing the sounds and sights—laughter, bargaining, splashes of color on the fruit and vegetable stands, the feel of the crowd pressing in and passing by in waves.

"I've forgotten what it's like to be one of the living," he thought.

A swish of white linen caught his eye. A woman—tourist by the look of her—stopped to peruse the fruit from one of the local vendors. Although her back was to him, he stopped, compelled to watch as she reached out to pick up a mango, the pale skin of her arm striking against the varied shades of tan and brown in the crowd. She wore a straw hat, and the white dress showed the outline of her legs as the sun shone from behind her. She paid the vendor and moved on. Intrigued, he made a move to tail her. He sometimes tailed visitors until he could ascertain their reasons for being on the island: vacation, business, etc. He was close, maybe ten feet behind her, when she turned, and he nearly stumbled.

Hallucinating. Elizabeth. In Tobago. Unbelievable.

She saw him as well and was nearly as startled, although not really shocked, he observed. More...embarrassed. Blood pounded in his veins as he lifted a hand in greeting. She smiled, nervously, and he felt his own grin beaming and his feet hurrying toward her. A quick glance around revealed no other interlopers in the marketplace. As far as he could tell, they were truly alone.

"Well, hello."

"Hi." Her voice was soft, unsure.

Not knowing her cover, or anything else about her reasons for being in Tobago, he began with an introduction. "Have we met before? You seem familiar."

She stifled a chuckle, and shook her head, her nervous demeanor replaced by that warm, intelligent smile that reached her eyes. "Perhaps. I'm Elizabeth."

He reached out a hand, took hers. The little tingle was still there and raced up his arm and into his heart. "William Darcy."

"I believe I do remember you. Nice to see you again, William Darcy."

"What brings you to Tobago?"

The smile faded a bit. "Business, I suppose. I'm awaiting a colleague."

"Oh." His expression darkened.

"It's no one I've met before, so I'm not sure what to expect."

"Ah." He relaxed. *Not Wickham, then.*

"What brings *you* to Tobago?" She seemed genuinely surprised. "Most people coming to Trinidad and Tobago flock to Port of Spain."

So she wasn't expecting to find him here. Intriguing. An intelligence officer hoping to sneak in and out of the country without alerting the station chief? Or maybe she was sent to keep tabs on him again and was using Tobago as a base? He'd left Trinidad without any official permission. Either scenario suggested she was still working in counterintelligence.

"I came here for the peace and quiet, to be honest."

They stared at each other a moment.

"Would you like a drink?" he asked suddenly. "There's a nice little waterfront bar not too far from here."

"Umm...sure. That would be nice."

He gestured with his arm, resisting the urge to touch her. "Carry your basket for you?"

"What? Oh..." She handed it to him. "Thanks. I was looking for fresh bananas."

"Looks like you found some."

"I get a craving for them now and again, ever since East Germany, when I couldn't find one to save my life."

Not hiding their history together. He vaguely wondered if she was wearing a wire. No skin off his nose. He had nothing to hide either. He led her outside the market and down toward the water.

"Ever had a Dirty Banana?"

"A what?"

He caught her expression and smiled. "And that wasn't some kind of lame innuendo. It's a Jamaican drink with coffee liqueur and rum."

"Oh." She grinned.

"I'll make you one sometime."

"I've never been to Jamaica. I suppose you have."

"Yes."

"Is it beautiful?"

"Parts of it. There's poverty there. There's suffering, like most parts of the world."

"I've seen that, too, in the places we've been."

"That's one of our job perks."

"Seeing the hardship and privation—that's a perk?"

"In a way, I think it is. Seeing the world—really seeing it, not just the tourist's bird's eye view of a place—gives us truth. Not even the wealthy travelers genuinely experience a locale the way you and I do. And that experience is a direct result of our work."

"It's one way to look at things, I guess."

"Where are you staying, Elizabeth?"

"A little villa about three miles down the beach here."

"You walked?"

"Sure, I walked."

"Just to shop for fresh bananas?"

"I like walking."

"I remember."

She looked at him, unbelieving.

"From our time in East Berlin. I also remember waiting outside the theater for you. I followed you home several times to make sure you made it safe and sound."

"I had no idea. You didn't have to do that. I can take care of myself."

"No doubt you can. I know you saved my skin more than once. No, following you home was more for my benefit, so I could have some peace, knowing you were okay."

Elizabeth's expression softened. "I always thought you were waiting outside the theatre for Anneliese."

His face clouded.

"Sorry," she replied, touching his arm. "I didn't mean to bring up unpleasant memories."

He slid his hand into hers and rejoiced when she didn't look uncomfortable or yank it away. "You know, I've not always been the man I wanted to be. I've used people—we do that in this business of ours."

"We do."

"It disturbs me, deeply, what happened to Anneliese. Saddens me. I judged that I had to defend myself, prevent my capture above all for the sake of many other officers, and I did what I had to do. Over the years, I've been forced into a few of those decisions where there were no good choices."

"It goes with the territory."

"But some things I did do right. When we were in East Berlin, Anneliese pursued me, but I didn't sleep with her—on that trip we made to West Berlin or any other time. It was one of those times when I made a decision to act, or in her case, not to act on an opportunity because it was the honorable route, and it didn't seem wise. I'm grateful now I made the decision not to use her that way. Some crises of conscience are gray and muddled, but there are times when—well, the right course of action stares you in the face."

Darcy stopped, tugged on Elizabeth's hand, and under a palm tree on an almost deserted seashore, he kissed her—a delicate, tentative brushing of lips. When he pulled away, she stumbled toward him, eyes closed, cheeks and lips flushed. She opened those fine eyes and stared at him in wonder.

"I'd almost forgotten how beautiful your eyes are," he remarked, stroking her cheek with the backs of his fingers and running his thumb over her bottom lip. "Elizabeth. Beth. Liz. *She*. By any name, you are the most amazing woman I know."

"Darcy, I..."

He picked up her market basket and began walking again. "There's a top-notch local restaurant between here and your place. We'll spend the afternoon, nestled at the Lambton with two Carib beers and a plate of roti stuffed with some kind of spicy chicken— unless you already have plans, of course."

"I don't, but..."

"And we won't talk shop, not here, not now. I won't ask why you're here—mostly because I don't really care why. I only care that I can see you and talk to you again."

"I'm not here to watch you."

"Like I said, it doesn't matter."

"I didn't want you to think..."

"I don't."

"You've been cleared of any suspicion."

"And you are the person mostly responsible for that, according to Bingley. Thank you."

"You're welcome."

"Now there's just one more thing to get straight." It was high time Darcy began the intricate dance of reconnecting with the woman he was now convinced he'd fallen for, hook, line, and sinker.

"What's that?"

"Beer or mixed drink with your roti?"

She smiled. "Okay, you win. Let's eat."

25

ELIZABETH'S villa shone pink with the light of the setting sun. It sat on a cliff above the ocean, palm trees, and neglected shrubbery adorning the front of the house. A gravel drive led to a carport sheltering her Jeep. Sounds of the approaching evening surrounded them: the distant crash of the waves, a peal of laughter farther down the street. A gentle wind unsettled Darcy's hair, worn just long enough to remind her of the longish queue he'd worn in East Germany.

She pulled a key out of her bag, unlocked the door, and stepped in. She turned when Darcy didn't follow her and found him waiting patiently outside the stoop.

They stared at each other. A moment fraught with possibilities passed between them.

"Ask me in?"

She reached out a hand. "Come in." And closed the door behind him.

"Nice house."

"Yeah, not too bad for a NOC. It's not luxury, but it will do—and probably cheaper than a hotel. I'll be here for at least a month, I gather." She reached for the refrigerator door, and light spilled into the darkening room. "I don't have any beer, but I've got a bottle of wine."

"Sounds good." He pulled out a chair and sat at the little kitchen table.

"I know we said we wouldn't talk shop, but..."

"We can, if you want. I am the station chief here after all."

"I just feel like I need to get this out of the way. You're not under suspicion, but at the risk of sounding obsessive and paranoid, I believe there is, in fact, a mole in the CIA."

"It's not obsessive or paranoid. Actually, I believe you're right."

"You do?"

"And I can see why maybe it looked to some people like it was me."

"But it's not you, so..."

"Who is it?"

"Exactly." She gave the corkscrew one more vicious twist and then tried to tug the cork free.

"Here." He got up and went to her, covering her hands with his.

"Thanks." Little currents of lustful awareness ran up her arm and into her belly.

"You're welcome."

She reached into the cabinet for glasses. "So I've been working on the 'mole issue' in between the ratty, little assignments they send over from the State Department."

"Any luck?"

"Not great luck."

"Investigations like these can take years."

"And I'm not always a patient woman." She smiled. "I am less likely to jump to conclusions than I was a year ago. And I've learned more about my colleagues than I ever wanted to know."

"Counterintelligence woes."

"Most definitely."

"So, how did you end up here on Tobago?" He stopped, shook his head. "I said I wouldn't ask that."

"No, I want you to know. I wouldn't want you to think you're in any kind of trouble. Or that I put myself in your way."

He took a step toward her. "I'd have no problem with you putting yourself in my way. None whatsoever."

Blood beat under her skin and warmed her face. Thank goodness for the cover of twilight!

"Um..." She paused, trying to formulate an intelligent sentence. Why couldn't she even *think* straight?

"Yes? Go on."

"So, when Wickham told me about a new asset down here, someone with counterintelligence information, I volunteered to run him. I didn't want George to spin it as another 'Darcy is the root of all evil' story. I wanted my own eyes on it."

"Sounds reasonable."

"I'm waiting for the asset to contact me through secure channels here on the island."

"Which, in this case, is probably a post office box?"

"Any advice?"

"Just watch your back. Use your tradecraft, and—what am I saying? You know what to do."

"No Spy Rules to quote?"

He chuckled. "Ah...no."

"That's a shame. Believe it or not, I've sort of missed those." She handed him a glass and held hers up. "Here's to the irony of first impressions."

He clinked his glass with hers. "And the good fortune to overcome them."

He took a step back and looked around the kitchen. "Show me around the place?"

"Sure." She stepped around him and led him into the living area where a wicker couch and a couple of chairs were grouped. The table was strewn with newspapers and magazines.

"There's a bedroom, a bath over there." She halted and cleared her throat. "A deck." She stepped through the screen door. "A view of the ocean, which was an unexpected and pleasant surprise." She laid her free hand on the railing and sipped as she gazed out into the darkness, acutely aware of him moving up behind her.

He glanced up. "And a view of the stars."

"I hadn't noticed."

He took her hand from the rail and holding it in his own, pointed up to the sky. His breath stirred her hair and made her shiver. He smelled like spices and ocean.

"Are you chilled?" He rubbed a hand up and down her arm to warm her.

Was he smiling? She thought she heard the warmth of a smile in the darkness.

"I'm fine."

Darcy stepped away again. He seemed to follow a pattern of approach and retreat, approach and retreat, almost as if—her mind whirled—was he wooing her? Raw, exposed nerves sent out frissons of danger and thrill along her spine. Moonlight spilled over the line of trees, illuminating her face and leaving his in shadow. "Are you pleased with Tobago?"

"Yes, how could I not be pleased?"

"Your good opinion is rarely bestowed and therefore, is more worth earning."

"How about you? Do you like it here?"

"At first, I was disappointed to be sent to Trinidad instead of Moscow, but now I can honestly say I'm glad to be here. That surprises me as much as it does you."

"I'm not surprised."

Darcy laughed. "Your expression says otherwise."

"You just seemed like a fast-track company man."

"I was when we met. A lot has changed."

"Meaning my investigation changed a lot of things. I'm so sorry."

"No. Well, not just that. Perhaps the investigation brought things to a head, but I've been overdue to step back and take a look at my life for some time now. Several events conspired to force my hand. Don't be sorry. I'm certainly not—because that investigation was the reason I met you."

She downed her wine in three successive gulps. "More wine?" she asked, beginning to turn back inside.

He set the glass aside. "No. I'm going to need to have all my wits about me tonight."

Her "why" was muffled when he moved in—his hands on her hips, lips brushing hers—softly at first, and then with more command as he pulled her closer.

She let him—that was what would amaze her later on. She let him because he was warm and familiar yet exciting and mysterious. She let him because, whatever else she didn't know about him—and there was a lot she didn't know—she knew him in essentials. Down deep, she saw him so clearly: brave, clever, strong, confident, passionate. And hot.

His hands slid up her sides so his palms brushed her breasts. She gasped, and he plundered her opened mouth.

HEAT SHOT through him when that little whimper escaped her throat.

His hands moved from her sides around to her back—one hand grasped the back of her blouse, one hand tangled in her hair. Always acutely aware of her, he watched her eyes slide shut, felt her hands outline his shoulders, and clasp around his neck. He didn't need the wine; he was drunk with her. She reached behind her, fumbling for the door handle, and he nudged her back inside. Control—he had to keep control even though his mind and body wrestled each other in a desperate struggle for restraint.

She backed away, clinging to his hand as she meandered toward the bedroom.

"Are you sure?" he asked.

"I...I'm sure about tonight. I can't think any farther ahead than that."

"Then that's what I'll take." He ran a finger down the line of her breastbone. "And then, perhaps, you'll let me take a little more." He undid the top two buttons of her linen blouse and flipped open the catch on the front of her bra, slipping his fingers inside to cup her breast. He thrilled to the sound of her sigh when he rubbed a thumb across her nipple and marveled at the contrast between his tanned arm and the ivory of her chest. How different they were, and yet how right they seemed together. He backed her to the bed as he pushed her top over her shoulders and down, and laid her in front of him, one knee on the bed between her legs. The linen bound her arms to her side. Fortunate that, as it let him look and touch as much as he liked. He spread the blouse and bra apart then traced her body with his fingers before leaning over her to trace the same path with his lips. She squirmed, trying to get her arms free, but he shook his head. "If you touch me now, Elizabeth, I'm liable to take you apart. I want you that badly, and I've wanted you for that long."

"Since Virginia?"

"Since the first moment I held you in my arms on a dance floor in Budapest."

"I...I didn't know."

"You know now." He stood, rucked up her skirt, and smoothed his hands from her ankles to her knees and beyond. His hands wandered over her inner thighs and up to her hips before drawing down her panties. He stared down at her, his icy blue gaze intense. Then he knelt down, drew her toward him and with great tenderness, he used his mouth on her.

THE ROOM SPUN as she cried out in surprise. He kept on, bringing heat and the temporary insanity of desire, murmuring unintelligible words against her skin. Her body arched involuntarily, and she almost sobbed when he took his mouth away.

"You're as slippery as dew on the grass," he said as he replaced lips and tongue with fingers. He ran his nose over where the heat and urgency coalesced under her skin. He smiled up at her, a wicked, fiery smile. "And you smell just as sweet."

Her breath burst from her in a groan.

"Yes, darling, call to me." He kissed the juncture of her hip and her leg as his hands worked some kind of dark magic in her. "Come to me." He rubbed a stubbly cheek against her hipbone. Then, almost delicately, he bit it.

She erupted under him.

When she was able to open her eyes, he was staring at her in fascination. "Beautiful," he whispered.

He stood, drawing her skirt down until it made a puddle of linen on the floor. She watched him simply because she couldn't tear her eyes away. He stared back, absolutely still, watching her, like a panther watching its prey.

"Take your clothes off," she commanded, still gasping. "I want…"

He complied, pulling his polo shirt over his head and doffing the khaki shorts, before leaning over her on the bed. "You want…?"

"I want…"

"I want, too." He levered her hips up, a guiding arm underneath her, and entered in one swift stroke.

ANOTHER CRY FROM HER, and he closed his eyes, forcing himself to stop. Months of physical deprivation and longing threatened to overwhelm him. "Elizabeth, dear god. Elizabeth."

She reached up to draw him close. "Now, you come to me."

He rode her in blind delight, roused still further by her ability to keep pace. The world narrowed to the two of them, and as he went over the threshold into oblivion, he pulled her over with him.

I'm not pleased with this turn of events. This isn't what I wanted, but all these things you set in motion, starting way back in Prague, have led us to this point. You've forced me into this. You've brought Elizabeth into this mess. Can't you see what you've done? I don't want to kill her, but I have to. She knows, she knows. And if she puts her head together with the FBI, she'll know it's me. I had to get her away from her notes and her files, and that bitch she pals around with at the Hoover Building. Keep her busy, keep her occupied. Keep her thinking that the answer is out there, not here inside the walls of Langley. I needed a decoy. And I found one—you.

26

"ARISE, SLEEPING BEAUTY." Darcy leaned across the bed, brushing her hair from her face. Her eyes opened suddenly, full wakefulness—a quirk he'd learned about her over the last several days. It charmed him. No lazy, sleepy-eyed mornings for his Elizabeth. She woke instantly, ready to face the day.

"Is that coffee I smell?" She rolled over and stretched her arms to the ceiling.

"Yes, ma'am. I brought you a cup."

Pushing up on elbows, she grinned at him. "My hero." The smile turned sultry.

His heart started pounding, but he squelched desire beneath a laugh. "Don't tempt me, darling. We can't spend all day in bed. I've got a mission for us today."

"A mission? You're kidding!" She flopped back on her pillow. "I don't want to think about work. I'm on vacation. Sort of."

"It's not an agency mission."

"Then what is it?" She sat up and took the coffee cup he offered her. Sipped. "God, this is good."

"Nothing like the fresh-roasted, local stuff."

"I agree." She set the cup aside and crossed her arms over her knees. "So what's the mission?"

"It's not what. It's where."

"Huh?"

"Let's a take a run. I'll fill you in." He jerked back the covers and took her hand to pull her to her feet.

"Here's your hat, what's your hurry?"

Laughing, he turned to the door. "See you downstairs."

They set a leisurely pace, barely making indentations on the hard sand under their feet. Although it was right at dawn, they'd each worked up a sweat in the tropical morning air.

"Okay," Elizabeth reminded him, "so, what—no, where are we going?"

"Barbados."

"Barbados? How long will we be gone? I can't just pick up and go away with you, Darcy. I have to be here to—"

"Just 'til tomorrow, maybe the next day."

"What's there?"

"It isn't what's there...it's who."

"First it was where and now it's who."

He broke stride. "I'm not saying this right."

When they slowed, she took his hand. That one gesture brought him such joy. He squeezed her hand and smiled at her. *She.* Just her presence gave him hope, gave him courage.

"Did you watch the Ramsgate debriefing interviews? Read the reports?"

"I did."

"So you know MI6 found Jirina Sobota. Alive."

She nodded.

"We're going to see her today."

"She's on Barbados?"

"Yes."

"Mm, okay."

"There's more..." He dropped her hand and looked out to sea.

She took a moment to catch her breath, arms akimbo, watching him while he watched the horizon and concentrated on something beyond the sea and sky. "William Darcy," she said in a gentle voice. "You can trust me."

He turned back. "I know I can. That's why we're doing this." He led her to a rock and sat down with a weary sigh.

"You have to understand: Jirina isn't just an asset. Not to me."

"Yes, I know. You feel responsible."

"I do, even more so because..."

"There's something else to this, isn't there? Something besides a professional relationship."

"Yes, but not the way you're probably thinking. She and I weren't romantically involved—ever. We never even met before the Brits rescued her. She was Wickham's lover, and that's still a hard thing to articulate even after all this time because..." He blew out a breath. "Jirina Sobota is my half sister."

Elizabeth's eyes widened. Finally, in a whisper because her voice failed her, she spoke. "I see."

"I sure didn't. Not until it was way too late."

"How *did* you find out?"

"It's a long, convoluted story."

"I've got nothing but time today."

His face broke into a quick, sad smile. He kissed her to fortify his own resolve.

"When I came back from Prague, I spent all that time being debriefed. While they had me captive at Langley, I got roped into some of those lectures at The Farm, like the one where you saw me for the first time."

"I remember."

"I bet. I wasn't myself really during that period. I'm sorry I was rude to you."

"You were rude, and not just to me. But there were extenuating circumstances, and I realize that now. In essentials, where it counts, I believe you are pretty much the way you've always been."

"That's a kind way to say it." He rested his arms on his knees. "The debriefing was arduous, and afterward, I went back to my parents' house in Baltimore to recuperate, rest a little, get away from Langley.

My mother was gone, spending the winter in Florida the way she does, and I had the house to myself. I rumbled around, searching through boxes in the attic, old things Mom had packed away. It was just past the holidays, and I was missing my father."

"When did he pass away?"

"It's been almost seven years ago now. He had a heart attack. It was unexpected. I was actually in the States when it happened, but there was no time to say goodbye. I guess I was trying to do that by going through his things. He and I, we had a...tumultuous relationship."

"Why?"

"He never wanted me to join the military, but I was set on the Air Force. Before I went in, he wanted me to join the CIA, but afterward, he suggested I go into the family business. I considered it for all of half a second. It wasn't for me, even though a part of me wanted to please him. In the end, I opted for the CIA as a compromise of sorts. They recruited me pretty hard, and I felt the need to...break away, be my own man."

"I know what it's like to live in the shadow of a parent. My dad was larger than life to me—more an idea than a person."

"We all want to make our own mark."

"True."

"Anyway, I knew he had traveled a lot in his career. Darcy Shipping conveys, among other things, glass for automobiles, airplanes, and the like, so he'd been all over the world. If you've done your research, you know he lost his CIA contracts after Playa de Girón."

She nodded.

"And in 1962, he was in Czechoslovakia for a time. If you watched the Ramsgate tapes back at Langley, you know the rest of his story while he was there. It's Jirina's story."

"But on the tapes you said Jirina's father found out about her when she was fourteen. Why didn't he tell you about her right after he found out himself?"

"I think perhaps he planned to after he got her to the West, but he died before he could make that happen."

"Does your mother know?"

"No, I don't believe so. Their marriage wasn't the best, especially in those last years. They were separated off and on, so he wouldn't have confided in her, and I doubt she's found out on her own."

"So if he was gone and she didn't know, how did you get wind of it? How did you even begin to suspect?"

"When I was home, those weeks after the Prague debriefing, I found a safe deposit key in his things. As you know, no intelligence officer can resist a mystery like a key with no lock. It took some doing, but I found the bank, and as his heir, I had access to the safe deposit box. Inside was a letter from Jirina's uncle; he wanted her off his hands. Her mother had always been trouble for him, ensconced in the government as he was. And Jirina, the rebellious artist's daughter, wasn't an asset to a man who was trying to climb the ladder of the political elite."

"Poor Jirina."

"Yes, she was telling us the truth. We knew that her father was American from our intelligence sources. We just didn't know he was my father too."

"How did you confirm?"

"Our ambassador showed Jirina's family a picture of my dad. Jirina also had a picture Dad had given her when he'd visited—a picture of him and her mother together. When he returned from Czechoslovakia that last time, he had been gathering evidence of paternity, including tissue, blood, and serology typing. All the results were in the safe deposit box with the letter. He was trying to build a case so the government would be more likely to give her exit papers. After comparing the photos, we compared his blood and tissue test results with Jirina's, and voila—instant sibling.

"I was prepared to squawk until the agency agreed to keep her parentage compartmentalized information, but it wasn't much of a fight. It must have been an awkward situation for them—a young woman, daughter of a disgraced civilian contractor, former asset, sister to a current agent, placed in a Communist government official's household? Yeah, awkward at the very least. As for me, I was adamant

Wickham not find out. I wanted him as far away from her as possible. So, I brought her to a private villa my father owned on Barbados. She has round-the-clock nursing and supervision and an agency-vetted psychiatrist. I sneak away to visit her when I can."

"That's why you were off the grid before Budapest," Elizabeth muttered to herself.

"Found out about that, did you?" He tugged her up by the hand and began the walk back to his villa. "I have to warn you, Elizabeth, she still isn't well. The KGB broke her. She's docile and sweet, but she coped by dissociating. As her brother, I'm her anchor to reality. She's fixated on me as her rescuer even though, to my shame, I had precious little to do with it."

"You're making sure she's cared for. That counts as rescuing in my book."

"I'd like very much to introduce the two of you. For a couple of reasons. One, I've seen how you were with Johanna Bodnar, how she came out of her shell. I know it's not the same kind of illness, but I hope that, over time, maybe you could help Jirina too, even if it's just a little bit. And two, I want to share this part of my life with you. It's a painful piece of my history to be sure, but Jirina's important to me. She's my only sibling. I've spoken with her, and she wants to meet you."

"I'm honored, Darcy. Truly. I'd love to meet her."

"One more thing—when we get there, you should call her by the English form of her name. She wanted to change it, to embrace her new life—or so the psychiatrist said. I thought it was a good idea because her English name would help safeguard her anonymity on Barbados."

"Oh, okay."

"Her mother named her after our father."

"So I should call her..."

"Georgina."

27

Darcy helped Elizabeth into the small plane and turned to speak to the mechanic on the ground. They were on an isolated runway, miles from the small airport in Scarborough. Elizabeth saw a bill exchange hands and a handshake before Darcy climbed into the cockpit and began flipping switches in preparation for takeoff.

"Off the grid again?"

"I paid him extra. If I don't call in, he'll give the authorities a flight plan so they'll come looking for us." He grinned. "But don't worry, darling, I'm an excellent pilot."

"Good to know."

A short time later, they touched down on an airstrip much like the one they left on Tobago. An abandoned Jeep was waiting with the keys inside. Darcy certainly had the connections to get what he wanted, when he wanted it. After several minutes on a gravel road, they turned up little more than a well-worn path of tire tracks. After a steep uphill climb, they broke through the trees, and Elizabeth had to swallow a gasp.

The house—no, the mansion—was beautifully nestled within a grove of trees. She could barely glimpse its columns and verandas. The roofline was gently sloped with red clay tiles, and the gardens were lush with poinciana, palm, and various flowering shrubs. Darcy rumbled to a stop beside a guard shack, and a burly man in sunglasses and a uniform of khaki shorts and camp shirt stepped out.

"Mr. Darcy, good to see you, sir."

"And you, Barrett. What's the news?"

"Been pretty quiet around here."

"How's Georgina?"

The guard spared Elizabeth a surreptitious glance then turned his attention back to Darcy. "Okay. Think Mrs. Reynolds wants to talk to you about a fence though."

"Fence?"

"Yeah. Little gal was found swimming before dawn one morning last week—alone."

"Hmm. That *is* a problem."

"Yes, sir."

"I'm not sure a fence is the best option. It might scare her, and I don't want her to avoid the pool. Maybe we can just beef up the alarm system? Set it up so Ms. R knows when she leaves the house? Or float some kind of alarm in the pool itself perhaps?"

"I'll look into it."

"I'll speak to Dr. Reynolds as well. Get his take. Thank you, Barrett."

Elizabeth marveled at the beauty and serenity of the place as the Jeep rolled toward the house. Palms lined the driveway. The heady scent of hibiscus spilled from containers on either side of the front door. A porch swing barely shifted in the breeze that intermittently stirred the thick, tropical air. Darcy pulled the vehicle in front of the house and turned to her with a smile. He leaned over and kissed her mouth. "Welcome to Pemberley."

He took her hand as they ascended the steps. He turned the doorknob and walked right in.

"No lock?"

"Pemberley is more than just a house; it's a compound. A door lock isn't necessary. My father built the original structures: the villa, the boathouse, the guesthouse. I added to the property when I moved

Georgina here. There's fencing around the perimeter, electronically monitored and well hidden for her sake. Since her captivity, she's frightened of being confined." He tossed his keys on the counter. "Ina? Where are you, sweetheart?"

Elizabeth had been expecting a Spartan, modern sort of place, so the Victorian Laura Ashley look surprised her until she remembered that, currently, this was a woman's house.

They ambled through tastefully decorated but ornate rooms, each open to a veranda by a set of French doors. The sound of piano music drifted from another part of the house.

"She's in the library." He beamed with pride. "It's good to hear her practicing again." He took Elizabeth's hand and paused when they reached the library doorway. The music halted, the performer stared in momentary confusion, and then a smile bloomed across her features.

"William!" The piano stool scraped across the bamboo floor as the young woman formerly known as Jirina Sobota stood and raced toward her brother. "I forgot you were coming!"

"Remember, Georgina? We discussed it yesterday."

Elizabeth turned toward the voice and saw an older woman dressed in bright colors that made a stunning contrast with her dark complexion.

"Mrs. Reynolds." Darcy greeted her with a warm two-handed handshake. He turned to his guest. "This is Elizabeth. She's a colleague and a friend. Elizabeth, this is Gabrielle Reynolds, who manages Pemberley. And this"—he paused, placing a hand on the younger woman's shoulder—"is my sister, Georgina."

Mrs. Reynolds gave Elizabeth a considering look and then slipped into gracious hostess mode. "Welcome."

"Elizabeth, Liz, Beth..." That same look of momentary confusion crossed her expression. "Which one is the real you?" Her English still had an Eastern European lilt to it.

"Now, there's a question." She smiled at Georgina. "William calls me Elizabeth."

"Then I will as well. My brother has told me much of you."

"Oh, really? I'm sure that was an interesting conversation."

She smiled. "He says you're an excellent intelligence officer and that you speak many languages."

"Not so many."

"Czech?"

"Not very well, I'm afraid—just enough to get myself in trouble."

"I've been in trouble."

Elizabeth mentally kicked herself. She was trying too hard to be witty, to make a good impression, and had forgotten what the young woman in front of her had endured at the hands of the KGB. She took a deep breath and forced herself to relax. The overwhelming resplendence of the house, the scrutiny of the housekeeper, the burden of trying to connect with a shy and emotionally wounded girl—all these things made it easy to lose sight of what was important and real: the new and fragile bond between siblings.

Georgina turned a glowing smile on Darcy. "But I'm not in trouble now. My brother rescued me and brought me here so I could get well. I wish he could stay with us, but he has his work. He comes when he can." The last part sounded like it had been parroted straight from a counselor's mouth.

Darcy gently turned the topic from himself. "Dr. Reynolds said you've been working on something, a new project of some kind."

"Oh yes!" Her eyes shone. "I've been working on surveillance equipment. Listening devices mostly, but I just finished the prototype of one that reads electronic banking entries. I'll show you."

"I'd like to see that."

She seemed to register Mrs. Reynolds' hand at her elbow and stopped, peering into her brother's face. "But first, we eat, yes? Forgive me; I've forgotten my duties as hostess."

"And I've forgotten mine as host. Elizabeth, would you like to rest? Or have some lunch?"

The considerate, lord-of-the-manor persona gave her whiplash. Who was this man? Suave, debonair spy about town? Moody theater man? Grumpy agent? Laid back civil servant marking time in paradise? She wasn't sure she knew the real William Darcy, but she had to admit she liked this version very much.

"Lunch sounds great."

Mrs. Reynolds chimed in. "I'll have the kitchen serve up something, say in about a half hour?"

"Thank you, Gabrielle." Darcy turned back to Georgina, who had a mischievous twinkle in her eye.

"William, why don't you show Elizabeth around? I'll see you at lunch."

28

DARCY STUMBLED into the kitchen the next morning after waking up, bleary and alone. "*Dobrý den, bratř.*"

"Good day to you too, little sis." He leaned over and kissed the top of her head as she peeled an orange. "Where is Elizabeth?"

"She said something about using the studio this morning."

"She's a dancer in addition to her medical training and knowledge of languages and tradecraft..."

Georgina smiled indulgently. "You don't have to convince me of her accomplishments, William." She shooed him toward the door. "Go find her. Go!"

He found her in the studio, heavy-rhythmed music pumping from the stereo speakers at the end of the room. She wasn't dancing as he expected, but instead, she was posed in a graceful lunge, facing the window overlooking the bay. Her arms reached over her head, parallel to each other, fingers pointed toward the ceiling. He watched as she straightened the bent leg and brought her body forward, straight back, facing the ground, delicately balanced on that front foot, the other leg straight out behind her, arms now parallel with the floor. Finally, she brought the back leg forward to meet the front, her body swinging upright. Sweeping her arms overhead, she bent forward, placing hands outside her feet, head almost to the ground.

He pushed off the door frame and slowly approached her from behind, appreciating the view. Thinking to surprise her, he reached out a hand to her well-rounded buttock.

So, he plans a sneak attack. Elizabeth bent her knees, reached back, and grabbed both his ankles. With a mighty yank forward, she dumped him on his very fine ass.

"Ha!" She whirled around to face him, hands on her hips. "Don't sneak up on a woman with hand-to-hand combat training, Darcy!"

He pushed himself up to sitting. "Don't be silly! You just caught me off guard. I was distracted. By your ass...ets."

"Mm-hmm."

"That rudimentary training you get at The Farm is nothing compared to mine." He tapped his thumb against his chest. "Military man. I should probably show you some techniques in case you—"

She pounced, landing with her inner thighs on either side of his ears.

"Ow! That was my head that just hit the floor!" He stopped. "Intriguing position though."

Elizabeth laughed. "Okay, military man, let's get a mat, and then you show me what you got." She pulled a large mat and spread it out on the floor. As she stood, he got her from behind—one arm across her neck, pinning her arms back against his body.

"You understand the element of surprise, darling, I'll give you that. But the fact is, I'm bigger than you, and bigger usually wins."

She reared back and missed head butting his nose by an inch or two, but it put enough space between them that she got him in the solar plexus with her elbow—just hard enough to get away.

"In real life, this is where I'd run like hell." She bounced on her toes and held her arms up, boxing style. "But I'm having fun." She landed a playful kick on his side then threw a punch toward his jaw, which he blocked with his open hand. Keeping hold of her fist, he twisted her arm behind her and slammed her back against him. His free hand drifted down her abdomen to her hip. "Gotcha," he whispered into her hair.

She roared in frustration and tried to bend down, to throw him over her head. He barely moved.

"You gotta mean it, Beautiful."

They grappled as she tried to bring him to the mat once again. "Oh, I mean it, tough guy."

"If only you had a blunt object within reach."

"I'd crack it over your thick skull."

"That's exactly right. Use whatever's handy." He pushed her face down on the mat, holding the squirming mass of her with his torso.

She tried to kick him in the crotch, but her heel bounced helplessly off his buttock.

"Vicious little thing, aren't you?"

"Truce?" She turned her head to the side.

He leaned down and kissed the up-turned check. "Truce."

He rose onto all fours, and she caught him with the back of her hand as she rolled over and tried to scramble away. He pinned her to the mat so they were face-to-face, center-to-center.

"You said truce," he growled.

She bucked and writhed under him. "No truce!"

"Yes truce!" He ground himself against her.

A harsh groan escaped her, sending heat straight to his loins. He took her mouth, demanding entrance. She gave in, her body limp at first then undulating under him. He drew back, taking in her disheveled appearance—hair in disarray, face flushed—and grinned. "I like fighting as foreplay."

She pushed him off her and sat up. "You, Darcy, are a perv."

He laughed. "Apparently. Who knew?"

"Oh, I did." She grinned back at him, fine eyes sparkling with dark delight.

"Good lord, woman. I want you more every day."

"Then you're going to have to"—she crawled toward him and

kissed him, licking his lips as she did so—"catch me!" She leapt forward, her feet hitting the ground at a run. He caught her almost at the studio door, and they embraced with a feverish intensity, lips and hands roaming and grabbing everywhere as he backed her through the doorway and into the hall. Looking around, he spied a changing room. "In here," he panted.

"We can't. Not here."

"It's my damn house. We sure as hell can." He pushed her back against the changing room door, pushed up her shirt, and rubbed his thumbs over her bra. The back of her head made contact with the door, a gentle thud. Hands pushed down shorts simultaneously. He lifted her with one arm, so she wrapped her legs around him and held on as he took her against the door. She was lost—in him, in the moment—a bundle of light and heat being batted around without form, without purpose. He groaned, louder with each thrust. At one point, her gaze landed on an arousing view from the mirror on the opposite wall. She watched them move together, filled her hands with the damp waves of his hair, and let his voice fill her ears as he lost control. She stared at the mirror, into her own eyes, and let herself fall after him.

GABRIELLE REYNOLDS LOOKED up from her paper at the sound of squealing and laughter overhead. There was a flurry of running footsteps, and then a door closed with a mighty slam.

Georgina sipped her last bit of tea. "I guess he found her."

The elegant, reserved housekeeper raised an eyebrow and looked across the table at her charge. "Seems so."

"I will go practice piano now." Georgina stood, lips twitching in amusement. "At the other end of the house."

Gabrielle watched Georgina leave. Then she picked up her newspaper and her coffee and stepped out to the table on the back terrace.

Well, look at you two! I have to say, I'm surprised. I never saw that one coming. Oh, I knew how you felt; having been a man in love myself, I could read the signs. But her? She surprised me. And what a surprise she was! Never knew she had it in her.

I don't like surprises.

And while my surveillance gave me a little prurient thrill at first, a couple of days was enough. To be honest, you two bore me. Yawn. Holding hands. Running up and down the beach. Salsa dancing in the Chestnut Tree Lounge. Canoodling in the Lambton Restaurant. How pedantic. How predictable. How pathetic.

So, enjoy her. The happiness of these days in paradise will torture you for years after she's gone. Welcome to the Seventh Level of Hell, Darcy.

29

Darcy pulled his Jeep onto the gravel drive at Elizabeth's villa on Tobago. Putting the vehicle in park, he turned to her, one arm across the back of her seat, the other hand on the steering wheel. "How about you ask me in?"

She laughed and shook her head. "No! Haven't you had enough to last you a while?"

"Darling, I'll never have enough, not of you anyway." He leaned forward and the kiss he gave her was gentle, tender. He skimmed a finger across her jaw. Her heart shimmered and melted a little more.

"Elizabeth. Let me stay with you."

"I can't. First contact with my asset tomorrow."

"I'll go with you. I know the area you told me about. Mrs. G's sister lives in Castara, and the cove is just north of there."

She shook her head. "Not necessary. Besides, this may be my last assignment for counterintelligence, and I want to do a good job."

"Training your replacement?"

"No. Well, maybe. And I'm not doing an end run around you either, Station Chief."

"Meeting the asset on Tobago is an odd coincidence, which makes me think it's not a coincidence at all."

"Don't worry. I can take care of myself. I'm not sure why Wickham's asset chose this locale, but most likely so he would have some neutral ground to give information."

"Makes me uneasy, having an unknown prowling around here."

"I do know that, Darcy. I'm being careful. I'm just the courier. Since this is the first contact, I only check the drop. He won't even lay eyes on me."

"I wish you'd let me come along."

"You need to maintain your anonymity on Tobago. I, on the other hand, will be gone in a matter of days."

"I still don't like this." He sighed. "But I know I can't talk you out of it. Call me as soon as you get back."

"Sure thing."

He kissed her again. "The minute you walk in the door."

"I promise."

"Goodbye, darling."

"See you soon."

Elizabeth turned and watched the Jeep disappear down the street, holding up her hand as Darcy sent her one last wave. She turned back to the door and fished out her keys. With a sigh, she shoved her way inside and set her bag on the table.

"Doing the walk of shame?"

She whirled around, caught off guard without a weapon or any way to defend herself.

The light blinked on, and there on a bar stool in the corner of the kitchen sat George Wickham.

"George!" She covered her heart with her hand. "You scared the shit out of me! What are you doing here? I thought you were in Washington."

"Where the hell have you been? I've been trying to reach you for four days."

"I took a couple days off."

"You're not here to take vacation. You're here to retrieve information from an asset."

"Back off, Wickham. You're not my boss."

"I sense some hostility here."

"Why are you even on Tobago?"

"Definite hostility."

"Answer the question."

"The director wants another set of eyes on the situation. He was concerned about you when my attempts to contact you came up empty. Looks like he was right to be worried, given the company you've been keeping."

"I don't have to justify my actions to you."

"Perhaps not, but you might have to justify them to the director."

"Look, I don't want to argue. I just want to make this meeting and move on with my life. I've decided to leave the CI department. You were wrong about me all those months ago, George. I'm not cut out for counterintelligence, and I don't want to do it anymore."

"Never thought this would happen to you."

"What?"

"Never thought you were the type to fall for the Darcy mystique."

"I don't know what you're talking about."

"I saw who brought you home. Nice little romantic scene in the driveway."

"No one likes a voyeur." Elizabeth's cheeks burned with anger and embarrassment. "Darcy and I have gotten to know each other over the last several months."

"Looks that way."

"Let's just say, I've discovered he improves on acquaintance."

"Does he now? Has he stopped massaging the facts to cast himself in the best light? Does he no longer treat everyone he considers beneath him with contempt? Is he no longer a pompous ass?"

"You misunderstand me. When I say he improves on acquaintance, I don't mean that *he* has really changed all that much, but rather that my opinion of him improved the longer I knew him."

"Best watch yourself. He'll bury you to suit his own agenda—just like he did me."

"You would have liked to stay in the field?"

"Very much. I was a good field officer."

An image of Georgina swam before her eyes, and anger shot through her. "Bullshit. Just bullshit! I've seen the tapes. I've read the reports. I've got a damned file on you. I know now you weren't quite the field officer you claimed to be. I learned your screw-ups led to Jirina's capture, despite Darcy's attempts to protect her, and that you somehow bamboozled the director into investigating Darcy because he reported you." She reached inside her bag and put her hands on her revolver, just in case she needed it. "I know the story, and now I'm wondering if Jirina's capture was only the result of your incompetence or there was more to it than you led me to believe."

"I'm not sure I like what you're suggesting." His voice was cool, but she saw the flush of temper on his face.

"Did you set Jirina up to betray her to the Czechoslovakian secret police? Are you setting me up tomorrow too? Are you on the Soviets' payroll to solve your financial woes?"

He pulled a cigarette out of the pack in his shirt pocket, lit it, and studied her. "You really think I'm capable of that?"

"I'm curious as to why, instead of answering me directly, your default response is to answer a question with a question."

He bolted upright in his chair, making her jump. "Damn it, Lizzy! What do you expect me to say? You've got your damn information from the FBI and think you know it all. What answer could I give that you would even believe at this point?"

She didn't respond, not knowing what answer would possibly convince her.

"That's what I thought." He scanned the room for an ashtray and, not finding one, stepped over to the sink to tap the ashes off his smoke. He took another drag off of it then stubbed it out.

"Tell you what, Officer Bennet. *I'll* check the drop tomorrow. You can just go along for the ride. You'll see that, not only am I on the up and up, but this new asset is everything I said he'd be."

"You'll check the drop?"

"Of course. I know there's nothing to be afraid of."

"It's *my* job to check the drop, and I always do my job."

"I said *I'll* do it." His voice was tinged with irritation. "You can still send the message to Langley and 'do your job.' And I will get my job back. This mission will show that I'm still good enough for fieldwork. No one can argue with me after I bring in a big fish like Viceroy."

"That's a stupid code name," Elizabeth muttered under her breath.

"You think? The director came up with it." He grinned, a shadow of his old charm, but it was unsubstantial, fleeting, like the man himself. "You're one to talk about stupid code names, Fine Eyes. The eyes aren't your best feature, by the way." His gaze roamed her figure.

She watched his every move as he made his way to the door and turned back to face her.

"So yeah, I'll check the drop. You come along to play witness and take my triumph back to Langley and to Darcy since you and he are"—he air quoted with a smirk—"*close* now. Let him gnaw on my success awhile. He can't stop me forever. I'll be back in the field in no time."

"Fine then. Suit yourself. You can check the drop." Elizabeth crossed her arms and stared him down. "Now, if you don't mind, tomorrow's an early day, and I need some sleep. My vacation wore me out."

"Sad. Not so much a woman of the eighties now, are we? Just like every other female agent since the OSS: dangle a man in front of her and her brain goes to mush. And they say men think with their dicks."

"I won't remind you what a hypocrite you are. Poor Lidia."

"Who?" He chuckled. "Just kidding. I remember her. I remember all of them. Pick you up at 5:30 a.m. Drop is right after dawn, but we'll surprise him. I want you to actually lay eyes on the son-of-a-bitch. That should prove it to you. Good night, Ms. Bennet. I'll show myself out."

"Asshole," she said as she locked the door after him. "Just get through tomorrow, Elizabeth. After that, you'll never have to see George Wickham again."

HE WAS LATE. No surprise there. His horn blared in the pre-dawn light, and she climbed into his rented Jeep without a word. They rode in silence down to the secluded cove on the leeward side of Tobago. Elizabeth could hear the ocean as they approached the predetermined drop point. She'd agreed to it, but now that she was here, she didn't like it. Left to her own devices, she would have bolted.

"This is sketchy, George. I don't like the isolation, the time of day. I've got a bad feeling about this."

"Viceroy wants privacy. He says the intel he has will shake up the agency, and he's nervous about being identified. He doesn't want the local CIA involved."

She pulled out her pistol, checked it.

"Glad to see you're armed. Try not to shoot me in the dark though."

"And you do the same."

He cut the engine and rolled to a stop beside the path. "We'll walk in from here."

"The message said the drop is beside a rock formation down next to the water."

As they approached the knoll above the meeting place, the crashing of the waves grew louder. Looking down on the beach, Elizabeth saw a lone figure approach. Asset looked male, about five foot ten, she observed. Short hair, but it was still too dark to see his face.

"There he is. See: real person, real asset. No funny stuff. No KGB. We're all alone—just the three of us."

"Yeah." She folded her arms across her chest, rubbing them to shake the sudden chill. The man knelt down beside the rocks, fumbled in the dark for a minute, then walked away, scanning all around him before he disappeared into the trees.

"Okay, I'm going down there. Wait. Shit."

"What's the matter?"

"I don't have my flashlight. It's darker than I thought it would be. I'm gonna have trouble finding the drop among those rocks."

"Maybe you should have waited until the appointed time like he said. Then you'd have sunlight."

"Run back and get the flashlight for me, would you? It's in the glove box."

Elizabeth sighed, exasperated. "I'm not your flunky."

"Just get the damn light, Lizzy. I'll meet you down there."

She trudged back to the Jeep and began digging through the papers, wrappers, and junk. She found the flashlight and closed her hand around it. That's when she heard the gunshot.

Her heart leaped into her throat, preventing her scream from escaping. At the same instant, she rose up and hit her head on the roll bar. Still seeing stars before her eyes, she reached for her pistol as she stumbled down the path toward the beach. She'd gotten maybe fifty feet when someone took her to the ground. Fighting, she wiggled away, but he caught her legs and held her down. Her gun had been knocked out of her hand, and it was lying on the sand just out of reach. She made a sound of terror, of desperation, and fought even harder when he covered her mouth.

"Shh, shh, darling. Elizabeth. Shh, now. The shooter hasn't left yet."

She froze.

"You're okay. It's me. It's William." He stroked her hair, brought her head to his shoulder as they lay on the sand.

"What are you doing here?"

"Shh. I'll explain later. Are you hurt?" With shaking hands, he cataloged her limbs, her torso, her face, checking for injuries.

"No." She wanted to sob, to babble, so she pressed her lips together firmly to keep any sound to herself.

Staying low to the ground, he led her by the hand toward the knoll overlooking the beach. Right before they reached the crest, he dropped to his belly and commando crawled up to peek over the ridge. He pulled small night-vision binoculars out of his shirt pocket and adjusted them.

Elizabeth had calmed enough to stop perceiving time as if it were stretched and distorted. She lay beside Darcy as he watched the scene below. In the predawn, she could see the shooter, a dark form running toward the rocks. She saw him crouch, roll his victim over, and sit back suddenly. Then he stood, running fingers through his hair as he paced back and forth a few times before picking up something and flinging it into the sea. She heard a roar of frustration, and then he turned, heading back to the other side of the beach.

"Got the wrong officer, didn't ya, asshole?" Darcy muttered.

Elizabeth heard an engine roar to life then fade off into the distance.

"I bet he doesn't know you're here. He thinks Wickham came alone, last minute change of plans. He might double around to Wickham's Jeep to make sure, though. We need to get out of here."

"We can't just leave George down there."

"We won't if we can help it." He cradled the side of her face, forcing her to look at him. "You didn't bring anything with you, did you?"

"Nothing except my weapon." She crawled forward to grab it.

"No papers, no keys still in the Jeep?"

"No. Spy Rule Number Five, remember? When sneaking around and worried you might get caught, leave your ID at home. And I hid my key outside the villa."

"Good girl. Now we don't have to risk going back."

"How will we get out of here?"

"I have a way. Come on." He led her down to the beach, using the foliage to mask their approach until they had to step out into the open. "Cover me," he whispered and took off toward the rocks where Wickham lay in the sand. She moved toward the two men, the ocean at her back as she scanned back and forth, pistol at the ready.

"I think we're in the clear." She squatted down next to Wickham's head. "Surely he would have taken a shot at us by now if he was still around. How's Wickham?"

Darcy looked at her, his mouth set in a grim line and shook his head. The heavy presence of Death lurked at the edges of the scene as the red light of dawn crept toward them over the sand. "Oh, surely not, Darcy. He can't die." She began to inspect the wound. "At least he's not conscious."

"Not at the moment. He was a second ago."

"Did he know who shot him?"

"I don't know. He only said, 'Should've known. Wilhelm.'"

"That's the name—"

"Anneliese gave me before she died, I remember." Darcy yanked off his shirt as he talked, and used it to cover Wickham's wound. "Help me take him down to the water. Mrs. G brought a boat down here yesterday. It's anchored just beyond that grove of trees."

"You followed me?"

"Yes." His reply was terse, without apology.

Moving Wickham was a risky business, but with Elizabeth's help, Darcy managed to heave him over his shoulder. She covered them while they made their way to Darcy's Zodiac. While Darcy pulled up the anchor, Elizabeth found the first aid kit and rifled through it, but there was little besides clean gauze. The two of them said nothing but became more somber by the minute. Wickham's wound was serious, more so than Darcy's gunshot in East Berlin. It was becoming clear there was little she could do.

Darcy's hands flew over the console as he started the boat, steered out of the bay with a terrific spray of water, and picked up the radio mouthpiece. "Henry? I've got a medical emergency here. No, it isn't me. Have a team standing by. If he makes it, they'll probably air-vac him to San Juan or Miami."

Elizabeth startled at the movement beside her. "He's coming to."

"You?" George gasped.

"I'm fine. You will be too after they fix you up."

He croaked something unintelligible.

"Hurry, William." But she knew he was going as fast as he could.

"Tell Darcy..." He grimaced and tried to bend his torso.

"Shh, lie still, George."

"Sorry. About Jirina."

"You can tell him."

"No. I can't." And he was gone.

The boat bounced and swayed, throwing the occasional sea spray over them. The bright morning sun lent a surreal quality to the trip— a boat ride with a dead man's head in her lap. A part of her wanted to scramble as far from him as she could, but she sat there, unable to move, and for a moment, unable to breathe.

Darcy seemed to understand the shock and her need for silence. Finally, he broke the quiet with another call on his radio.

"Henry? Change of plans. Have the coroner meet us at the dock. And I'll need secure transport back to my office." He glanced at Elizabeth. "For two."

Within hours, George's body was on a US government jet to the States, the local police were satisfied and/or bribed with the story of two lovers finding a dead body on a deserted beach, and Elizabeth was sitting in Darcy's office in Port of Spain, chewing on her thumb and trying to place a call to Charlotte Lucas at the FBI.

"Ms. Lucas is out of the office until next week. Is there someone else who can help you, Ms. Bennet?"

"When did she leave?" It was unlikely that Charlotte would take a vacation, not when they were in the middle of designing a trap to use on the mole.

"Two—no, three days ago."

"Did she tell you exactly when she'd be back?"

"Actually, I didn't talk to her myself. Someone else took the message. Said she and her boyfriend took a trip."

Charlotte's not seeing anyone. "Can someone just please call and check on her?"

"We can go by her place, but if she isn't there, there's not much we can do. If she doesn't turn up at the time she said she would, you can file a missing person's report."

"This is ridiculous! She's an FBI agent. Somebody over there can bloody well find her!"

The voice stiffened. "Yes, ma'am. I'll report your concern."

She slammed the receiver onto the cradle with a satisfying thud.

Darcy came in behind her and put a hand on her shoulder. "I've got some instructions from headquarters."

Elizabeth's voice shook. "What is going on?"

"Somebody tried to kill you today."

"I know that! Don't patronize me, Darcy. I want to know why."

"My guess is you've hit awfully close to a nerve. You've found something that has made you dangerous to a well-buried double agent."

"But what, specifically, would that be?"

"Tell me what you've been working on."

"Translations, mostly. From various departments."

"That's all?"

She started to open her mouth and shut it tight.

Darcy swore. "You can't tell me. Damn it!" He paced to the office window and back. When he turned, the famous Darcy scowl was firmly in place.

"Elizabeth, answer me honestly: Am I still under suspicion?"

"No. At least not as far as I know."

"As chief of station here, I should have been informed about this meeting of yours."

"I did inform you."

"I meant through formal channels. The director could have sent a dossier or even just made a damned phone call. Why won't they trust me with intelligence operations going on in my own field office?"

"I don't know."

"Why did the asset want to meet here on my island?"

"I don't know that either. Wickham let me have the assignment after I volunteered. He got permission from the director."

He paced back and forth behind his desk. "This is maddening. You're being flown back to the US in two hours. They're finding you a safe house now. I won't know where or how to find you if you can't tell me anything."

"I can't, Darcy. It could spell trouble for you if you knew—and you don't need any more trouble."

"The director has expressly forbidden me to accompany you back home."

Her chin rose with stubborn defiance although she fought to keep it from trembling.

"I can go alone. I don't need a babysitter or a knight in shining armor."

"Elizabeth." He knelt down on one knee in front of her, a bizarre parallel to a proposal. But instead of declaring his feelings, his eyes bore into hers, trying to read her face. He took both her arms in his hands, slid them down to her hands.

She looked down at their intertwined fingers. "Besides, you have a job here. I won't have you jeopardize that for my sake."

"Do you not understand the grave danger you're in? Someone has penetrated the counterintelligence department. It isn't about your career or mine. Your life is at stake! There is someone out there who knew enough to link you to CI and to Wickham, and was able to use him to try to kill you."

"Don't you think I know that?"

"Can you at least tell me who this Charlotte person is?"

"She's not even CIA, she's..." She shook her head. "I'm afraid for her. I think she's missing." Tears filled her eyes and spilled over. "I started working on this alone because I didn't know who to trust anymore. I still don't, and I'm afraid."

He crushed her to his chest. "I am too, darling. I am too."

"Darcy?"

"Yes?"

"I want to go home. Maybe change my clothes."

"You can't go back to the villa," he said. "It isn't safe. But I think we can find you something to wear without blood on it."

"Thank you."

"If it's any comfort, I don't know who to trust either. And I don't trust any of them to take care of you."

"Your hands are tied. I know this. If you get involved, it will throw suspicion right back on you."

"Perhaps, but—"

"I have to go," she said. "Alone."

Elizabeth wiped her tears with the back of her hand. "Can you find those clothes for me now? I don't think I can wear these much longer."

"Of course." He stood. "Of course." He leaned out the door and spoke in low tones to a woman in the outer room.

He came back and sat behind his desk, fingers steepled, his eyes on her face, watching, contemplating.

She looked down at her blood-covered shirt, holding it away from her body. Her face crumpled.

TWO AND A HALF HOURS LATER, Elizabeth leaned her forehead against the window of the agency's small jet. Darcy had spoken personally with the pilot—knew him from a stint in Paris—and had finally agreed to let her go. She saw Darcy standing on the tarmac as she taxied to the end of the runway. The jet turned, and as it raced back by the airport's gate, she thought she saw him still standing there, hands in the pockets of his khaki pants, his hair tumbled by the rushing air of the jet. She lifted her hand to touch the window.

What if we never see each other again?

Damn it!

I thought he was you. At first, I thought he was you. I was surprised, I have to admit—expecting that silly little whore of yours instead, but then I thought, "The white knight has gone in his lover's place." Sure, I'd have to go back to her villa and kill her too, but this was like a bonus. Convenient... and efficient. Then I rolled him over, and it wasn't even you, you sorry son-of-a-bitch! It was only Wickham! Stupid asshole.

Not that I had anything against him personally. Some men just aren't cut out for covert operations. It takes guts, which he had. It takes brains, which he had to some degree. But it takes control over your impulses most of all. And self-control? He never had that. Not like you and me. It's why we were made for the spy game.

30

ELIZABETH WOKE when she felt the plane's landing gear engage. The sun was sinking behind her, and she saw deep blue ocean below rather than the Chesapeake Bay and the monument-strewn skyline of DC. *What the hell?* Unbuckling her seat belt, she made her way up to the cockpit.

"Where are we?"

"Five miles due west of Bridgetown, Ms. Bennet," he shouted over the roar of the engine.

"Bridgetown? As in Barbados?"

"Yes, ma'am."

"And why are we landing in Bridgetown?"

"'Cause Darcy said we were."

"He didn't tell me."

"Sometimes he does things on his own like that without telling anyone. He radioed me the confirmation from Langley a few minutes ago."

"Hmm. Where am I supposed to go when I get there?"

"Ground transportation will meet the plane."

"How do I know to trust ground transportation—or you, for that matter?"

"He said you'd say that." The pilot grinned. "He said, 'Tell her to check her book.'"

"Book?"

"Your LeCarre book." She stared at the back of his head then turned without a word and went into the cabin to fetch her bag. Sure enough, *The Little Drummer Girl* lay buried in a change of clothes. Inside the cover, she found an envelope addressed to her in his slanted, looping handwriting.

Dearest,

I have made arrangements for you near the estate, at least temporarily. The director thought to hide you in Virginia again, but I was able to persuade him otherwise, or rather, Charles was able to persuade him. I have little to no pull in that quarter any more.

Our friend from the guard shack will meet you on the ground and escort you to your safe house. I chose him because you know his face, and he can be trusted. I'm coming to you as soon as I can, hopefully with some answers. I have some information to round up first.

Destroy this message—it's on water-soluble paper.

Be cautious. Be safe.

—W

Elizabeth disintegrated the message in the lavatory sink and returned to her seat. The pilot seemed content to leave her to her own thoughts. So Darcy had—well, basically he'd abducted her, hadn't he? In his arrogant, I-know-best way. It kind of pissed her off. Did he think to hide her forever? Like he had hidden Georgina? Her life was in turmoil, perhaps, but she certainly wasn't broken. She hadn't endured what Georgina had. He wrote he would be coming to her. So she was just supposed to wait? Do nothing? Of course, hidden away from an assassin was hidden away and doing nothing—whether here or in the States.

And when it came down to it, what choice did she have?

The Park, Washington, DC

BINGLEY FROWNED into his cup as he dumped two packages of sugar in the coffee and stirred it in methodical circles. "I convinced him that we needed to hide her fast, and that's why he relented, but you can't just take her off somewhere indefinitely! The director wants her close to McLean so he can debrief her. Scuttlebutt is she had some office files. Have you heard about those? She used the written order CI gave her to investigate you, and she's been working on her own in between assignments, looking into the records of other officers and assets. The director's pissed she went off and collaborated with the FBI before going through the proper channels."

"And yet, apparently she found something."

"Looks that way."

"But she doesn't know yet what that something is. That's why I'm here in DC. I want to take her files with me when I go back."

Bingley laughed without an ounce of humor. "They'll never let you do that. You can read through the files. You have the clearance to do that much, but taking them out? No way."

"Elizabeth needs to lay eyes on them to continue her investigation."

"No. They can't leave Langley."

Darcy let the topic drop; he had another way to get that information to Elizabeth, thanks to Georgina.

"Elizabeth isn't part of your team anymore. This isn't Budapest or East Berlin. She's the director's responsibility now, not yours."

"She was working in my corner of the world even though I wasn't told beforehand."

"But she was a NOC. Technically, you had no right to do what you did, spiriting her off that way. No right to take her protection into your own hands."

Darcy started to speak then paused as if reconsidering. Then he blurted out. "I'm in love with her."

Bingley stopped stirring. There was a long, uncomfortable pause. "I see," he finally said.

"And yes, I do appreciate the irony. How that must sound to you—coming from me."

"Feels different on this side of the coin, doesn't it?"

"Charles—about Johanna—I've reason to believe I may have—misinterpreted her feelings."

He held up a hand. "You had my best interest at heart. I know that. Doesn't make your interference right. Now I've got to decide what to do to rectify it and whether that's really the best thing for Johanna." He looked miserable for a moment, but then he waved the emotion away. "But the fact is you've overstepped your authority by hiding Elizabeth from everyone, even her own government."

"It's not about authority. It's about responsibility, and, damn it, Charles, it's about safeguarding her life. This was attempted murder of a CIA officer on my turf. How could I just let that stand and do nothing?"

"You can't save her if we're all kept out of the loop."

"Working outside the agency may be the only way we can save her."

Bingley scoffed. "Don't be so dramatic."

"The director wants her here to debrief her. I understand. He wants to know what she was working on, and he thinks she'll be safer in the States. Generally, that would be true. But. Not. This. Time."

"How do you get that?"

"Because this time the danger is from somewhere within Langley."

"What?"

"Elizabeth was in Tobago to meet with Wickham's 'Viceroy'—the same asset who contacted Wickham with information for counterintelligence and insisted on meeting there. I don't think that location was a coincidence. It was meant to cast suspicion on me, but I also think it was an attempt to get Elizabeth away from whatever information she and her friend in the FBI found."

"Where did this 'Viceroy' come from?"

"That's what I want to find out. When I do, I'll have a definite lead on the mole."

"Good god, man! Do you think this goes all the way to the top?"

Darcy's expression was grim. "I don't know, but I can't really eliminate anyone at this point. When she and Wickham went to the rendezvous, the shooter was waiting for her. That tells me inside information—from inside counterintelligence—is in play. Only by a quirk of fate..." He couldn't go on, couldn't articulate what might have happened had Fate not intervened. "So in this case, she won't be safer in the States. I can protect her better using my security, my place, because virtually no one knows about it."

Bingley whistled. "Man, oh man." He shook his head. "It's an idea, I suppose. I'll discuss it with the guys on the seventh floor. Sure looks like the mole was after her. Why else would he single out Elizabeth to meet Wickham's asset?"

"At first, I thought Wickham himself was the leak. And when I discovered her there and that it was his asset she was contacting, I thought he was trying to get her by herself, cull her from the herd so he could take her down. That's why I had Mrs. G put the boat there the night before. And why I followed Elizabeth and Wickham that morning."

"Fortuitous."

"Yes."

"What will you do now?"

"I'm itching to go through Wickham's office and find that order."

"Then you're off to Barbados. What about Trinidad?"

"I'm taking a leave of absence—for personal reasons. Henry's in charge."

He heard throat clearing to his right. "Your check, sir." The proprietor of The Park coffee shop appeared at Darcy's elbow and laid the check between the two men. "How was everything today?"

"Excellent, as always, Mr. Baker. Thank you." Charles reached over and picked the paper off the table.

Mr. Baker looked back at Darcy, a kindly twinkle in his blue eyes. "We aim to please."

Darcy, lost in his own thoughts, looked up and nodded curtly.

"You gentlemen have a nice day." He walked away slowly, a slight limp in his step.

"Nice guy," Charles commented before finishing his coffee in one long gulp. "Good coffee. The man's an institution. I wonder how many government types he's served coffee to over the years? He's been here since I came to work at Langley."

Darcy pushed back from the table and stood. "I've used this place to convey a message or two myself over the years." He thought of the package he'd left Elizabeth after their stay on Hunsford Street. Making that tape hurt like hell, but it sure was a game changer. "You'll persuade the director I'm not kidnapping Elizabeth? I'm trying to save her life— and the lives of countless assets and officers. We have to find this guy."

"You're sure it's a guy?"

"It was predawn when I got that glimpse of him on Tobago, but I'm sure he was male. Men and women move differently."

A shadow of a grin crossed Bingley's face. "Boy, do they ever." He stepped up to the cash register to pay his bill.

"1965," Darcy mumbled.

"Pardon?"

"1965. You wondered how long The Park has been here." He pointed to a plaque on the wall behind the cash register. On the gunmetal gray background, the letters shone in gold: *The Park. Established 1965.*

"Like I said," Charles replied, "an institution."

Darcy devoured pages as fast as his photographic memory and his tiny hidden camera could go. Elizabeth's files were full of biographical, financial, and surveillance information on a couple dozen people. He recognized some of the information as his own. Right down to his father's government contracts back in the fifties and sixties.

"Thorough, aren't you, darling?" He snapped some photos of the next file. Thing was, none of it had names, only code numbers.

"Where would you hide those, Elizabeth, my love?" He opened her desk drawers, checked for false bottoms. Nothing.

The door opened, and a voice rang out. "It all goes, gentlemen. All the contents of this office go to archives." Bill Collins stopped on a dime when he saw Darcy behind the desk.

Darcy saw a flash of temper and contempt quickly smothered with an ingratiating smile. "Mr. Darcy, I didn't expect to see you here. I thought you were on Tobago."

"I brought Wickham's body back. Given that they worked together, I thought there might be something useful in Elizabeth's notes, something that would point to who killed him."

"That was a real shame, wasn't it? I liked Wickham, but it sounds like he was...impulsive. He convinced the director he had to go down there, see what was what, and then he went and got himself killed."

"Somebody shot him in cold blood; that much is certain."

"No way!"

"I was there. I saw it go down."

Collins eyes widened. "You were actually there?"

"No one knows if he was the real target or not."

"Oh."

"In fact, some people—including me—think the bullet wasn't intended for him at all."

"Really? Then it's an even bigger shame. Have you found anything that would help you figure it out?"

"Perhaps. I'm going to confer with a colleague of Elizabeth's."

"Where is Ms. Bennet? I was just told to move her office files to archives."

"Tucked away, safe and sound. For now."

"Sounds serious."

"She had a history of working with Wickham. It seemed prudent to put her under protection."

"She must be abroad then. No one's been moved to the safe houses around here."

"She's safe. That's the important thing."

"Of course. Well, if you're finished here..."

"Sure. These aren't much help."

"Why not?"

Darcy tossed the file on the desk in front of him. "No names. Only code numbers."

"Perhaps the woman at the FBI has them—the one Ms. Bennet was conspiring with."

"I wouldn't call a coordinated investigation 'conspiring,' Collins."

"No, of course not. I'm sure it was all on the up and up. You're right."

"I'm going through Wickham's office next. Trying to find the order that sent Elizabeth Bennet to the Caribbean."

"I can save you the trouble. There was nothing of value in that office. The man kept horrible documentation. There was no signed order."

"No order?"

"Unless he took it with him."

"This just gets weirder and weirder. Elizabeth saw an order. She wouldn't have gone otherwise."

"If we could bring her in—question her—we might find out, but she's incommunicado." Collins eyed Darcy with speculation. "*You're* here though. Since you witnessed the incident, they may want to debrief you. Let me just call and ask."

A frisson of alarm raced up Darcy's spine. He didn't want to delay his departure one second longer than necessary. He couldn't protect Elizabeth from inside Langley, and with a mole burrowing inside the walls, who knew if he'd make it out alive.

"Okay, fine. I'll be in my office." Darcy yanked open the door and left, leaving Collins standing in the middle of a team of employees filling boxes— and frowning.

Instead of his office, Darcy made a beeline for the exit.

He stood in line, waiting to pass his briefcase through the metal detector. It was near the end of the day, and the line inched along, feeding his impatience to get the hell out of Dodge. He glanced up at the mezzanine behind him, saw Collins standing there, hands on the rail and searching the crowd. Darcy turned back, putting a big line-backer of a guy between him and Collins's line of sight. Collins pushed off the rail in frustration, and Darcy stepped up to the scanner.

"Mr. Darcy, sir. How was your day?" The young security guard opened the briefcase and examined the contents. "What's this?" He held up the pen.

"Birthday gift." He lied. "From my father." *Indirectly.*

"Nice. Never seen one like that before."

"My family says it's one of a kind." He stuck the pen in his shirt pocket, took the briefcase, and turned toward the door. The phone behind the guard rang. Darcy kept walking.

Once out of sight, he raced for his BMW. His tires squealed as he made his way out of the parking garage. He flashed his badge at the gate and sped out into the muggy evening.

I'm back. Back in the New York Groove. Back in Black. The Bitch is Back. Actually, the bitch isn't back. Where exactly are you hiding her, asshole? Because I know you're in on it. Somewhere in the Caribbean is my guess. Thought my handler might know, but he was worthless. Wouldn't tell me a thing. All he did was try to talk me back into the fold. He just doesn't get it. I'm not his to command anymore. I've broken the bonds of my father's servitude. You were my example. You did that a long time ago, didn't you? The other side is still after you, but I see it all so clearly now. You aren't theirs to command either. Good for you. I admire that fortitude, striking out on your own path. It's a trait we share I think. And part of me regrets what must be done. If Elizabeth weren't so close to the truth, I might actually spare you the agony of living without her. I'm soft that way. But it's all in motion now. I overheard the whispers that you were back. Ear to the ground, Darcy. Always. Directional microphones sure do come in handy. And inside headquarters, I don't even need to hide them.

Annnnddd...Bingo! Technology wins again. Well, guess I'd better pack my sunglasses and my sunscreen. I am the Master of Disguise; you didn't even know I was there at The Park. No one recognized me. No one. You're going to her in Barbados. Got you, you son-of-a-bitch. And now I'll get her too.

31

SHE HEARD the shot ring out, stopping her heart, trapping air in her chest. She turned her head and saw dead eyes, a lifeless gaze from the man lying beside her. Lights flickered as her own life drained away, and in a desperate attempt at self-preservation, Elizabeth gasped and forced her eyes open. Momentarily frozen, she was surprised at the rampant, almost painful, heartbeat in her chest. Lightning flashed into the absolute dark, followed immediately by another clap of thunder. She sat up and fought back the haze of disorientation. She was not dead; she was breathing. She was not covered in blood; she was clothed in a sweat-soaked tank top and shorts. There was no dead man beside her.

She was most definitely alone.

She hated being cut off from everyone she knew and playing a waiting game of cat and mouse. She would have given anything for some task to occupy her. She'd never experienced the suffocating inactivity she'd endured since leaving Trinidad—this facsimile of imprisonment. She'd tried to distract herself with television and books, but to no avail. Basically, she'd spent long hours walking around the safe house and turning over the last months' events in her mind, trying to make sense of it all.

She spent the months since Fredericksburg, after parting ways with William Darcy, on various translation projects for the State Department. Boring, tedious work, to be sure, but spiced with the occasional dig into Darcy's and his colleagues' pasts. The director agreed to let her meet with Wickham's potential asset, code-named Viceroy, on Tobago.

She couldn't help being curious. The asset's choice of locale, so close to Darcy—was it a coincidence or a plant by the mole to cast more suspicion on the beleaguered station chief? She didn't know, but that piece of serendipity had changed her life: a chance encounter, a whirlwind romance, and two weeks of paradise with a man so changed from the one she'd known for over a year. Still brooding and introspective at times, just enough to be interesting, but he was also attentive, relaxed, kind, tanned, leanly muscled...

She spent a few minutes in dreamy, love-soaked memories before a crash of thunder jerked her thoughts back to the events at hand. Wickham had tried to contact her while she was with Darcy, then showed up on Tobago, dismissed her objectivity—not without cause, she admitted to herself—and had impulsively taken her place at the drop. Now he was dead. She was aware she let Darcy's influence sway her; she expected to eventually find out Wickham was the mole as Darcy predicted. The history between the two of them, the conflict over Jirina, and the financial information she and Charlotte had dug up on George, all painted a damning picture of the man. It was no secret how much he despised Darcy. Plus, Wickham owed big time money to banks, credit card companies, casinos, and to various friends and family, including Wickham's own mother, according to Charlotte's FBI file. In the final analysis, though, he was not a double agent, only a weak and foolish man.

But if the mole was not Wickham, then who?

It was horrifyingly ridiculous. The traitor, whoever it was, thought she was close enough to the truth to try and kill her for it, yet she knew nothing of his true identity.

Elizabeth tossed the covers aside and shuffled into the kitchen to make a cup of tea. She dug around in the pantry and came up with a stale bake from yesterday's trip into town. She covered the biscuit-like bread with butter and washed it down with tea. Not sure whether she should explain her presence to Georgina and the Pemberley staff, Elizabeth had made do on her own, avoiding Pemberley and Mrs. Reynolds' yummy cooking.

She sat as she munched, the claustrophobic feeling of dread creeping over her once again. As a free woman, Elizabeth had loved Barbados, but her present confinement made paradise stifling. While she listened to the heavy rain patter against the windowpane, she brooded. Slowly, the rain slackened off. And that's when she heard the car door slam.

No one had darkened her door since Barrett dropped her off. She dashed into her bedroom for her revolver, and with her back against the wall, she peered through the curtain. Gray sedan, windows up, trunk open. Elizabeth's heartbeat ratcheted up another notch. She cocked her pistol and waited.

The trunk door slammed, and her heart leaped into her throat. Darcy stood with a duffle bag over one shoulder and a plastic tub in his hands, surveying the house with a critical eye.

She yanked open the door and called, "William!" Her voice broke, and she dashed across the porch.

"For Christ's sake, woman, don't shoot me!" he yelled as he ran toward her.

She gently lowered the hammer and placed the gun on the porch swing. She launched herself at him, jumping into his arms from the last two steps. He barely had time to drop the box and brace himself for the onslaught.

Arms and legs wrapped around him, she covered his mouth with hers. He buried one hand in her hair and held her in place with the other across her rear.

"You're here!" She was breathless when he put her down.

"Elizabeth." His arms tightened around her. "Let me look at you. Are you all right, darling?"

She nodded and pulled back. He ran his hands over her hair, her shoulders, her face.

"What were you thinking...*kidnapping* me?" She pushed at his chest, remembering the days of enforced solitude. "You arrogant ass! Leaving me here twiddling my thumbs for days! I thought I'd lose my damn mind! How dare you...*handle* me like some throwaway asset? You... What's so damn funny?"

He was grinning like a mad man. "God, I've missed you, Bennet." Then he fastened his lips on hers with a feverish intensity that had her blood humming. Her knees buckled.

"I might forgive you. If your story is a good one. And if you kiss me like that again. What took you so long?"

"Information gathering," he answered between kisses. "I went to Washington straightaway, as soon as I could leave Port of Spain. Took a leave of absence." He put her away from him. Raindrops ran off his hair and dripped off his lashes. "Let's get inside."

"What's in the box?"

"I'll show you. Later." As thunder rolled overhead, he hurried up the steps and tossed the box on the table, rattling her breakfast dishes. She covered his face with kisses. Laughing, he turned and gathered her in, lips roaming her face and neck while she pushed up his shirt, running her hands over the lean, warm torso.

"I can't stop thinking about you," he panted. "I should wait, should wait until—"

"Oh, hell no! We're not gonna wait!" She pulled him to the bed, the sheets still rumpled from her thrashing through her nightmare.

He pulled his shirt off and let her take care of the pants. Turning him around, she pushed him to the bed and straddled him. Arms crossed, she grabbed the hem of her tank top and flung it to the far side of the room. Wrapping her arms around him, she clasped him to her as his mouth fastened on her breast.

Her fingers combed through the dark waves of his hair. "You cut your hair while you were away."

"Let me," he demanded, scooping her ass by delving into the waistband of her running shorts.

"No." She leaped back. "This time, you let me."

She drew down her shorts. "First things first."

"You're killing me here."

"I'll make sure you die a happy man then."

***

LATER, thunder rumbled softly in the distance as they lay tangled in the sheets, entwined with her leg across his and his arms around her. He gentled them both by putting his forehead against hers and closing his eyes.

"My dearest, loveliest Elizabeth." His voice was reverent, full of emotion.

"Sometimes I wondered if I'd ever see you—or anybody, for that matter—ever again."

"I wish I could have stayed with you. I wanted to."

"Why didn't you?"

"I had calls to make, things to do."

"Vague and mysterious. Meanwhile, I'm in the worst sort of limbo."

"I can empathize. You don't like a cage."

"No. Even if it's as beautiful as this one."

"I'm sorry, darling."

"If only I could do something to find this person..."

He smiled and indicated the box in the other room with a nod of his head. "Go ahead. Look inside."

She wrapped the sheet around her and stepped out into the great room. "Darcy?" Puzzled, she lifted the box top. Her gaze shot up to his in wonder. "My files!"

"Yep." He pulled on his khakis, leaving them unbuttoned as he crossed over to her.

"How did you ever?"

"Spy craft, with a little help from technology and good, old-fashioned B and E. I broke into your apartment."

"You what?"

"Well, yes. I had to break the code numbers in the files. Good thinking, by the way, keeping that at home."

"I learned from the best."

"Then you don't mind the burglary?"

"Absolutely not!"

"I also read through and photographed some of your office files with this." He pulled a contraption that looked like a pen and pencil set out of the box. "Ina's invention—some kind of computerized camera. I had the images developed, although that probably isn't the right term, by a man in Alexandria just beginning to dabble in the technology. That's why it took me so long to get here. I didn't want to come to you empty-handed, and flowers just didn't seem to fit the bill."

"I'd rather have my papers than flowers any day." She grinned and threw herself at him. "You're my hero!"

He embraced her again, but then he pulled away, his expression turning solemn. "Elizabeth, I do have some bad news from DC as well."

"Bad news?"

"A woman named Charlotte Lucas was found unconscious day before yesterday down by the Potomac."

Elizabeth paled and sat down on the couch, suddenly nauseous and dizzy. Darcy sat down and took her hands in his.

"She's your friend, isn't she? I put two and two together—your phone call to the FBI and Charles's information about your office files. She was helping you?"

"Oh, god! Charlotte! Is she...?" She looked straight at him, shocked, but dry-eyed, ready to face whatever he told her.

"She's alive, but the FBI is keeping that on the down-low, for her own safety. She was beaten to make it look like she was mugged. Whoever did this left her for dead, and it's a miracle she isn't. He must have been interrupted before he could finish the job."

"How do they know it wasn't some random mugging?"

"Her apartment's been searched."

"So our mole's a sloppy bastard."

"Seems to be getting progressively sloppier."

"I asked Charlotte to run some financials a while back, get background on some...people."

"Including me. I found my information in your stash."

"Yes, you were the nexus of all the trouble until the shooting on Tobago. We looked at others connected to you: George Wickham, for one, and other officers and assets—in Prague, Budapest, East Berlin."

"Was there intel stored at her place? Like you had in yours?"

"Just the key to the code numbers. We each kept one, in case..."

"More smart thinking."

"Any leads on who ransacked her apartment?"

"Not yet. No prints—looks professional."

"My office. My apartment. My files." She took a fortifying breath. "Jesus H. Christ. He'll come after me next because he thinks I can make him." Terrifying certainty flooded through her. "That's what the set-up in Tobago was all about—getting to me because of those files. He wasn't a bona fide asset; he was a dangle." She looked at Darcy, wide-eyed. "I can't pinpoint him, Darcy. I don't know who he is."

"Correction—you don't know yet. That's why I'm here with your papers. The mole thinks the answer is in here somewhere, so I'll bet it is. Together we'll find it."

"If he searched Charlotte's apartment, why not search mine?"

"I don't know. Perhaps I got there first."

"I wish I could see her."

"She's in a coma."

"I want to sit with her, do something."

"You can't."

"This is my fault. Wickham, Charlotte, all of it."

He turned her shoulders so she faced him, tilted her chin up. The old Darcy scowl was back. "You are *not* to blame! This is the job, Elizabeth. You know it; you've dealt with it before. Everyone in this business knows the risks."

"Espionage is gruesome except when it's boring," she whispered and swallowed the lump in her throat.

"What?"

"Something Charlotte used to say."

"Well, she's right. Sometimes our job is dangerous. Sometimes it's deadly."

"But it's for the greater good? Isn't that Spy Rule Number Three?"

He turned to the box and began lifting out files. "I no longer live by rules." He glanced up and brushed her cheek with a finger. "I live by moments, thanks to you."

"All my life, I believed what the agency did was for the greater good. Sometimes, though, I wonder."

"Wonder all you want. I have—many times. Walk away if you want after this is over. But until you find this son-of-a-bitch, you'll have no peace of mind, no safe place to run. So let's settle it, Elizabeth, and then if you decide to walk, you can walk away a free woman."

32

"It could be anyone, Darcy. We're not any closer to finding him." Elizabeth closed her eyes, rubbing her fingers over them to dispel the eyestrain. They had returned to Pemberley that afternoon because Darcy was waiting for a phone call from Port of Spain. Huddled over the small conference table in his office, they combed through files and papers spread out like fingers from the center. The eerie whine of tree frogs overlaid the peaceful hum of ocean and cicadas with an unsettling urgency. Elizabeth stepped over and closed the window.

"Charlotte and I had two dozen people on a watch list, including you, George Wickham, Charles, and Cara. Even Bill Collins, for Pete's sake. And the mole might be someone we haven't even thought of."

"I understand Wickham, Georgina, Fitz, Anneliese—even Charles and Cara—but why would you put Collins on the list?"

"We drew maps around you with connections based on who you worked with, who you were seen with over the last five years. Bill was on that list. He's worked with you on every assignment since 1979, at least for part of the time."

"Hmmph. I didn't realize."

"Yes."

"He blends in."

"Unlike George Wickham: Mr. Slick, handsome and flashy."

"George Wickham is not a good man." A soft voice peeped up from behind them.

Darcy closed his eyes and sighed. "Ina, sweetheart."

"Are you working with George Wickham again, William? You should not trust him. He is not the person he seems."

Elizabeth and Darcy exchanged looks. After careful consideration, they had decided not to tell Georgina of Wickham's demise, at least not yet.

"No, we aren't working with him any longer. You don't need to worry about him ever again. Not ever."

"That's"—she paused to find the English phrase—"a relief."

Darcy covered up the chart in front of him. "Why are you up? It's two in the morning."

"I might ask the same of you. And you, Elizabeth. Why are you up at two in the morning? And if you're up, why aren't you upstairs together?" She gave them a saucy grin.

"Georgina!" Darcy was embarrassed, and Elizabeth fought an urge to giggle.

"You are working late in the night. I see that. You asked me to use my camera. I remember. I know you are hiding Elizabeth—like you hide me." She came forward and brushed a lock of hair from Elizabeth's face. "Are you well, *švagrová*? Did they find you too?" The ethereal way she slipped in and out of the past was as unnerving as the tree frog sounds outside.

Elizabeth squirmed at being called "sister-in-law." "I'm well. No one got to me. It's all right."

Georgina took Elizabeth's hands in hers. "You're safe here. William won't let anyone hurt you. Neither will I."

She stepped to the table and looked over the documents collected there. "Maybe I can help you."

Darcy reached over to close a file. "I appreciate it, but aside from Wickham, these are all people you don't know."

Georgina moved the papers aside and studied the chart of pictures. "You are wrong. I know him."

"Who? What?"

She pointed. "I know him."

Elizabeth looked down at the photo under Georgina's finger. "You know Bill Collins?"

"I don't know his name, and he didn't wear glasses, but this man I have seen before."

"Where?"

"In Prague."

"Are you sure you didn't just see him in the embassy? He worked there."

"I only saw George Wickham in the embassy. But this man I know from somewhere else. He attended some Charter 77 meetings. He never said a word, so I didn't know he was American, but a lot of people didn't say anything in those meetings, lest anyone know too much about them."

"Collins was in Prague when I was COS there, but he was a flunky, a minion. If he had that level of clearance, to work those meetings under cover, I sure didn't know it." He glanced in Elizabeth's direction. "But then, there was a lot of intrigue I wasn't aware of."

"Bill always seemed to be underfoot. Are you sure you didn't just overlook him?"

Darcy frowned at her. "Elizabeth, I knew what level of clearance my staff had. No way Collins would have been cleared to attend one of those Prague meetings."

"So why was he there?"

"I don't know."

She concentrated, rewinding her memories of the assignments she'd shared with Bill. He always was...lurking, now that she thought about it. Coming into her office in Budapest several times a day, attending the same meetings she did at Langley. They weren't in East Berlin at the same time, but he had helped Darcy set up before he was called back to the US. And when she worked at Langley, she saw him more days than not. She'd been vain enough to think he might be interested in her.

"He was nervous that day in the safe room."

"What did you say?"

"I met him one day, leaving the embassy safe room in Budapest. He almost ran me over while I tried to open the door."

"The safe room on the second floor?"

"Yes. Why?"

"When was this?"

"Right before I left for Lake Balaton."

"Could it have been?" he muttered to himself. He got up and began to pace. "Right under our noses?"

"What are you talking about?"

Darcy fished through a file. "This report is from my debriefing after Budapest." He ran his finger down the page and flipped through three more pages before stopping to rest on a line buried in a long paragraph. "There."

Elizabeth shook her head, smiling in spite of herself. "You and that photographic memory of yours. Must come in handy."

"It does. Look."

"The safe room was bugged?"

He nodded. "After we reached Vienna, they swept the US Embassy in Budapest for listening devices, thinking that was how we were compromised. They found one in that safe room."

"Lots of people had access to that room. Lots of people could have planted a bug there."

"True, but the timing is right. There were no leaks in Hungary until we went to Alsómező, *after* you saw a nervous Collins outside the safe room door. They never found out who did it."

"He was annoying, bumbling, but even given how inept he was, he never really seemed *nervous* except for that day."

"I assumed the bug was how the Hungarian government knew about us moving Johanna out of the country. I had called that mission in to the station chief."

"Bill was the one who brought you the message about state security knowing our plans to take Johanna out of the country." Elizabeth picked up Bill's picture and studied it.

"All the while, he might have been the one who was ratting us out.

The man was pumping me for information, too, the whole time he told me about the intelligence leak."

"So why didn't they take us on the way to Kőszeg?"

"I didn't tell him the details, remember? I left him out of the loop to protect him—the little shit."

"I can't wrap my head around this."

"In East Germany, he was the one who set up the op with you as Anneliese's cut-out. He left an incriminating set of files in my flat. Then he left the country. And now..."

She and Darcy locked gazes. "He's at Langley."

"Or is he?"

"The last time I saw him was..."

"When?" he asked.

"He and George Wickham waltzed into my office on a Friday afternoon, not even a week before I left for Tobago. I didn't think too much about it. He dropped by a lot. There were files scattered all over the office. He picked one up, started looking through it. I snatched it out of his hand. Told him to leave me be—I was on a mole hunt. It was a careless, throwaway comment. I was annoyed at George because he made a derogatory comment about you—"

"Feels good to have a staunch defender for a change," Darcy muttered, his lips twitching in an amused smile.

"And Wickham said something about the real mole being gone. Bill asked, and George said they sent you to Port of Spain. I remember because I didn't think that was common knowledge."

"Bill knew I was on Tobago."

"But we never said you were on Tobago," Elizabeth interrupted. "It's not much of a stretch, but I *know* Wickham said Port of Spain, Trinidad."

"I missed that detail in Bill's and my conversation in your office. I guess my mind was on other things, but I know he said Tobago—yet no one but Henry and Mrs. G knew I left Trinidad."

"Could someone else have told him?"

"No one else knew. The plane met us in Port of Spain, and I hadn't been debriefed yet."

"So the only way he would know is—"

"If he was there," they chorused.

"That day, in your office, when Bill saw your charts he reacted..." Darcy began for her, trying to encourage her memory.

"Strangely, now I think on it. He squinted at my whiteboard. I had my codes for all of you on it with arrows and dates and places. Then I saw this flash of contempt. I'd seen those flashes before, like when we met after Budapest in Charles's office and he sent him away on a wild goose chase. It was more than contempt, though. There was wariness, calculation. At the time, I just assumed he was a career and social climber. You know, same old Collins." She brought herself out of her memory. "Did you ever see calculation in him?"

Darcy smiled grimly. "Never. Not even once. It took your intuition, or perhaps he thought you were too green to see it and let down his guard a bit. Underestimated you."

"He probably thought 'lady agent' and figured I wouldn't know what I was seeing. I always suspected he didn't much like working with me. I thought it was only male ego but maybe not. A few days after that, I left to contact a new asset with information on the mole. Good lord, Darcy..."

"Collins brought you the order."

"He did. Wickham and the director both knew about it though. It was weird; the asset wanted to meet on neutral ground: Tobago. You were close by, and both Wickham and the director thought that was fishy—thought perhaps the informant was someone who worked with you there."

"So, I wasn't really cleared."

"Thing was, I *had* cleared you officially, but there was still all this postulation. It annoyed me—made me think no one believed my report. That's why I volunteered to go."

"The stain of suspicion that's on me since that investigation—well, it never really goes away."

"Perhaps not. I know George still suspected you, even the night before he was killed."

Darcy ran a hand down her hair, a gesture of affection. "You are not to blame for what happened to George, remember?"

"I know. It's just...the serendipity of it all. Everything turns on a minute decision. George walks to the meeting place first instead of me, and it kills him. The randomness of it is terrifying."

He stepped to her and drew her into his embrace. "Ina's right, you know. You're safe here. You're not alone. We're together now, and I'll protect you with my resources, with my connections, with my life if I have to."

She took a minute to draw comfort from those words and strength from the man holding her. Then she pulled away.

"Let's get out his financials. I've never combed through them because he wasn't on my short list before." She divided them and gave half to Darcy. As they worked, only the scratching of pencil on paper could be heard.

"He has brokerage accounts, but they wouldn't let me pull those."

"What about charge cards?"

"Those I have." She ran her pencil down the page. "Looks like ole Bill has been buying some unusual luxury items: a boat, a sports car, antiques, and rugs and jewelry. Nice, but not too nice." She noted the items and the dates.

"And property—he's bought property, too, within the last year or so. Here's a down payment on a house in Northern Virginia."

"Cross-check that with the bank deposits."

"Maybe it isn't payoff cash. Maybe he legitimately came into some money."

"An inheritance? I don't think so. The family history doesn't support it, and he's never been married, so no in-laws."

"The property purchase was made two weeks after a big deposit —just under the ten thousand dollar limit that the bank would have to report. Deposit was made in cash."

"Holy shit." The low volume of her voice couldn't hide the buzz of excitement. "I can't believe I overlooked him! I was so focused on you and then on Wickham..."

"Until Ina recognized his face in that picture and changed our point of view."

"And you brought some more pieces of the puzzle, like the bug found in the Hungarian Embassy. If only I could find that last piece, let it fall into place. We're close, Darcy. I can feel it. Could the mole really be Bill Collins?"

"He's the front runner now. First thing tomorrow, we contact Langley and find out where he is. We need the most recent charge card bills and banking records too."

"And then?" she asked.

"It's time to put together a dossier on one of our own—one the FBI can use to search his place and, hopefully, make an arrest."

"I never get used to it—the icky feeling that comes with suspicion."

Darcy was overcome with a wave of tenderness. "Which makes me think perhaps counterintelligence is where you belong after all, darling. Because you'll never get used to it, and CI needs people like you." He turned to find his sister sprawled on the couch, asleep. Gently, he woke her.

"Come on, Ina."

She startled, but a smile bloomed on her face when she recognized him. "Did you solve the case?"

"Not yet." He looked over her head at Elizabeth. "But maybe we're on the right path at last."

33

The fastest way to get official information from Langley was through established channels, so Darcy made a pilgrimage to Port of Spain a couple of days later. He left Elizabeth sleeping and drove down to the landing strip where Barrett had his plane ready. He wasn't piloting today; he wanted to read on the way back to Barbados. By 9:00 a.m., he was at his desk in the capital city on Trinidad.

Darcy gestured for Henry to enter as he stayed on the phone with the FBI. "Yes, sir. I'm sending you enough circumstantial evidence for the task force to search his apartment and nab him. Search for physical evidence: a note of where he's meeting his handler, procedures for leaving information, even a journal of some type—if he was stupid enough to write things down." There was a pause while the voice on the other line went on. "Yep. You can reach me through Bingley's office. When you've got him, let me know. I'll bring the investigating officer and her documentation to Washington after he's in custody." He paused again. "You got it. Good luck."

Henry sat down in the chair facing Darcy's desk. "I got stuff for you. From DC."

"Thank you." He took the sealed envelope from Henry's hand. "I appreciate your willingness to step in for a few weeks while I sort this out."

Henry shrugged. "It's no big deal. Not much goes on around here."

"Still, I appreciate it."

"Wish you'd let me in on what that's all about." He nodded toward the envelope.

"Can't, my friend. It's..."

"Compartmentalized Top Secret Information," Henry intoned with him. He sighed. "Ah, well. You heading out?"

"After a while. I'm waiting on another phone call."

"Where are you off to?"

"Sorry, Henry. Call Mrs. G if you need to reach me after I leave."

Henry stood. "I'm out for the afternoon then. There's rumbling coming out of Grenada. Somebody's gotta do the intelligence work around here."

"See ya 'round."

Darcy slid a knife along the edge of the thick envelope and opened the file inside labeled: William Collins.

Inside was a picture of a younger Collins along with some demographic information. He was only a year younger than Darcy himself, born in Maryland to Mary and John, who was employed as a—

Darcy sat up straight and stared:

CIA officer since 1953. Father was part of the team who trained rebels in Guatemala and Nicaragua for Operation Zapata. Collins was stationed with the late Thomas Bennet (killed 17 April 1961 in the aftermath when the Derby, *a supply ship owned by Darcy Shipping, was run aground on Playa Girón during the invasion). Officer Bennet's remains not recovered until several months later with the help of Darcy Shipping president, George F. Darcy. Honor and Merit Awards Board submitted Thomas Bennet for inclusion on the Memorial Wall when it was first created in 1974. Bennet was survived by his wife, Frances, and daughter, Elizabeth, now residents of Charleston, West Virginia.*

So, Elizabeth was this Thomas Bennet's daughter. Not a huge surprise; she told him her father was on the Memorial Wall, but Bennet's connection to Darcy Shipping—and to John Collins—was unnerving. He thumbed back to a report on the elder Collins.

After the investigation into the failed Bay of Pigs invasion, John Collins was terminated when the CIA cleaned house. He died in a single-vehicle automobile accident in 1968, the result of driving under the influence. Collins was survived by his wife, Mary, and son, William.

"April 1961—and the paternal gang's all here, enmeshed in the Cuban mess," Darcy said to himself. Elizabeth's father on the *Derby*, owned by Darcy's own father's company, and Collins, a colleague of Bennet's as they trained rebel troops together. Darcy leaned back, the hair prickling on the back of his neck. Who knew there was a connection among the three of them so far back?

He returned to Bill's personnel file.

Interview with recruit Collins: "After my father left the agency, he drank a lot. I didn't see him much because he and my mother separated in 1965. He left me nothing except a love for my country." Psychological report indicates abandonment issues but otherwise reasonably healthy adjustment. Passed polygraph. Recommend approving security clearance.

The phone rang.

"William Darcy."

"This is Bridget with Deputy Director Bingley's office. We received the passport information you requested on Bill Collins."

"Yes?"

"He did leave the country in the time frame you specified and went through customs in Trinidad."

"Gotcha, you son-of-a-bitch."

"Excuse me?"

"Um...sorry. Obviously, that wasn't meant for you. Thank you, Bridget."

"You're welcome, but there's more."

"I'm listening."

"Bill Collins is not currently working at Langley. Calls to his house are unanswered. And the passport was used within the last forty-eight hours."

"Destination?"

"Barbados."

ELIZABETH STARED FORLORNLY out the window onto the dock and beach below. Gray clouds rolled offshore, threatening a stormy afternoon. Her answering machine, the one Darcy brought from her apartment, sat in her lap. Leaning over, she plugged it into the wall and pressed play.

"Ms. Bennet, this is Capitol Cleaners letting you know your dry cleaning has been here for over thirty days. You can stop and pick it up anytime. Thanks!"

Beep.

"Hey, it's Charlotte. I presented our information to my supervisor. He thinks we have enough to start some surveillance on a couple of these on your list, maybe leading to a search warrant. Call me."

Elizabeth sniffed.

Beep.

"Lizzy, it's your mother. I'm starting to get very worried now. I've tried to get a hold of you for over three weeks. Please, for the love of god, give me a call and let me know you're alive. It's just like when that John Collins came and whisked your father away. He never came home."

Elizabeth could hear sobs over the line.

She replayed the last message three times, incredulous at the coincidence of her mother mentioning a colleague of Thomas Bennet's named Collins. "Serendipity strikes again," she murmured. *Or maybe not serendipity at all. I'm starting to believe there are no coincidences.*

She crossed to Darcy's desk and picked up a phone with a secured line. She should call her mother—let her know she was all right. She cradled the handset between her shoulder and her ear while she put the answering machine in a drawer.

The line was dead.

"Odd," she commented, tapping the phone cradle several times. She picked up her .38 Special and put on her ankle holster. It was common to lose phone service and power when there was a storm, but the clouds were still offshore.

"Is there a problem?"

"Hi, Mrs. Reynolds. Did you know the phone lines were down?"

"No. When did that happen?"

"Not sure. I just discovered it when I tried to make a call to the States."

"Odd. The storm isn't even here yet."

"That's what I thought."

"I'll go into town and report the outage. Maybe they can fix ours first before the storm hits."

"I'll take a look around here. It might be something simple."

"Be careful, dear."

Elizabeth tapped her holster. "Always."

She wandered around the house but couldn't find anything that looked like a phone box. The grey storm clouds gathering off shore drew her attention, so she walked down to the water, listening to waves splash against the rocks, the wind whipping her hair back and forth.

"Hello, Ms. Bennet."

She reached for her revolver but stopped when she felt the barrel of a gun in her back.

"I wouldn't do that if I were you." He reached into her holster, drew out the gun, and slid it up her leg before tossing it away.

"Bill, is that you?"

"Indeed, it is. You can't hide from me anymore."

Elizabeth tried to calm her pounding heart and think. "Why don't we just sit down and talk about this. It doesn't have to be this way."

He put his arm around her neck, forcing her to arch against the pistol. "You know, I wish that were true. I really do, but you've left me no choice now. If it makes you feel any better, it was never supposed to be you who died. Hell, this whole situation was never supposed to be the death of anybody. I was only supposed to turn Darcy."

"Darcy?"

"Typical, isn't it? The KGB tried for him once—no, twice—before, but they were unsuccessful. That second miss was what sealed his fate. He killed my Anneliese."

"She shot him, Collins."

"She wasn't trying to kill him!" Collins's voice broke with anguish. "She had her orders. If he'd just gone along quietly..."

"Bill." Elizabeth tried softening her voice. "You must know he couldn't let that happen." She tried to face him, but he poked the pistol barrel tighter against her ribs.

"Thing is, really, they didn't need Darcy. They didn't. I could have done the job just as well. Here I was, working for them voluntarily, and all my handler could talk about was getting to the elusive London Fog."

"So the plan was to frame him? Why do that?"

"Oh, we didn't want enough evidence to fall into CI hands to convict him, just throw enough suspicion to tank his career for a while. He was too rich to be bribed in the traditional ways. The plan was to make him miserable and angry enough to consider turning, then throw Anneliese in his way."

"But why Darcy?"

"According to my handler, Darcy had enough knowledge, enough access to find most anything the KGB wanted. He knew almost every asset in place in Eastern Europe by the time he went to Prague. That was what they valued."

"You couldn't get that for them?"

"Not all the names. Could never get the clearance, no matter how many boots I licked or stellar reports I wrote. Then he killed Anneliese in cold blood."

"I'm sorry you lost her."

"No, you're not!"

"I *am* sorry, Bill. It was a waste, a shame. But you've been giving the KGB intel for years, long before Anneliese. Why? What made you turn in the first place?" Elizabeth's mind was racing like a squirrel on a wheel. Keeping him talking was giving her time. "Don't you love your country?"

"I do love my country. I just hate the damn CIA—and I wonder why you don't hate it too."

"Why would I?"

"We have the same reasons, you and I. We're two of a kind. Two orphans left swinging in the wind. The CIA took our fathers."

"My father died in the service of his country."

"Is that what they told you? Have you even read the reports?"

"I know he died on Playa Girón during the Cuban invasion. Your father was there too, wasn't he? I just began to suspect that today after a message from my mother."

"Dad wasn't there actually. If he had been, he might have died too. Quick and easy. Not the long, drawn-out misery of drinking himself into oblivion every night and day until my mother threw him out. Not the agony of watching his career implode because he was just following orders. Your father had it easy compared to mine."

He began to move her along the shore toward the dock.

"You won't get away with this, Bill. Not now. Too many people know."

"My spying days are over, true enough, but I've got cash put away. I can hide out somewhere warm and sunny for a long time."

"Where would that be?"

"Nuh-uh-uh. Not telling. But nice try. You and Darcy have that in common. You both think you're so clever. Speaking of Darcy, did you know it was old man Darcy who found out what happened to your father?"

"No."

"True story. He brought Bennet's remains home. Charred beyond recognition."

Elizabeth shuddered. "How did they know who it was then?"

"Dental records, I guess."

"Does William know this?"

"I have no idea. I doubt it. That whole family is full of secrets. You should read Darcy's KGB dossier. I doubt the old man ever told him anything. All that secrecy is unhealthy if you ask me. My father told me everything."

"That must have been difficult. You were just a little boy."

He pushed the barrel of the gun against her spine, tighter still. "Life is one 'tough shit' after another. My father didn't hide that from me. He wasn't a secret keeper like Darcy's old man."

"No, in the throes of alcoholism, he told a child more than he should have," she said.

Collins laughed. Elizabeth had never heard him even snicker before; it was an unholy sound, completely devoid of joy.

"I've always admired your wit, Ms. Bennet. Always. Now, let's get in the boat over there. We're going to take a little ride, and I'm going to feed you to the fish." He nudged her toward the stairs of the dock. Both of them froze when they heard the feral scream.

Elizabeth went limp and hit the sand as the gun went off. Her arm exploded in pain. She covered her head and turned to prepare herself for the onslaught.

Her breath caught in her throat.

Georgina came flying through the air, leaping onto Collins's back from the boulders nestled beside the dock stairs.

Elizabeth watched his gun spin and tumble end over end to land on the ground some ten feet away. Georgina reared back, tightening her forearm against his neck, and wild-eyed and crazed, she plunged the knife into his chest. It skittered off a rib and out of her hand.

Collins reached back over his shoulders and flipped her over his head. They struggled as she clawed at his face and bit like a wild animal. He was no strongman, but Collins had a good fifty pounds on her and managed to pin her down before he threw a punch and rendered her unconscious.

Elizabeth and Collins locked gazes. At the same moment, both lunged for his gun, lying on the sand. They reached it at the same time, knocking it into the surf. Elizabeth pulled up first, but Collins got a hand on her ankle, yanking her face down on the ground. She fought as he pushed her face into the wet, filling her mouth with sand.

"Why couldn't you mind your own business—you and that bitch from the FBI?"

She howled with indignant fury for herself, Wickham, Charlotte, and every officer and asset Collins had already sent into Death's arms. She managed to get her torso off the ground, but he flipped her on her back. Straddled her. Put his hands on her throat. And shook her as he began to squeeze life from her.

Her vision darkened, a red miasma descending over the world as she gasped and fought, flailing against the sand. Somewhere in the distance, she heard the roar of a lion. Then, air rushed into her bruised windpipe, burning as it went in and came out, expelled in a violent fit of coughing. She sat up, saw the two figures grappling in the water and the pistol washed up a few yards away. Grabbing the gun and with trembling hands, Elizabeth tried to take aim. Fear consumed her as she recognized Collins's attacker.

"I can't get a clear shot! Move, goddamn it, move!"

She heard the roar again but never saw the knife complete its fatal mission. Darcy held it high, covered in blood. As the ocean water turned red around Collins's twitching body, Darcy plunged Georgina's kitchen knife into the ground beside him and slumped over.

She dropped the gun and raced toward him as he crawled away from Collins. They collided, searching each other's bodies for wounds, then stumbled toward Georgina's, still lying on the sand by the stairs.

"She's breathing," Elizabeth gasped, her throat still on fire.

Darcy sat on the sand. As he watched Elizabeth bring Georgina back to consciousness, the sky opened, and the tears he wept in relief were hidden by the rain.

34

Langley, Virginia

THE THREE OF THEM, Darcy, Elizabeth, and Georgina, sat around the director's mahogany conference table on the seventh floor.

"This is over. Collins is dead," Elizabeth insisted.

"It's not over, not by a long shot."

"You don't have any leads on who he worked for. There's no other place for this investigation to go."

"Ah, but there you're wrong." The director handed them a report. "From the FBI's search of Collins's apartment, based in part on your colleague Charlotte's casework. How is she doing by the way?"

Elizabeth smiled in spite of the seriousness of the conversation. "On the mend. Her head injuries, thankfully, won't have long-term effects. She lost a lot of blood, but they were able to bring her out of the coma after a couple of days."

"I'm glad to hear it."

Darcy spoke up. "It says here Collins's pocket litter indicated the KGB handler was his father's colleague from Cuba. Are we looking for one of the former Cuban rebels?"

"We don't know yet. But perhaps we can find this man."

"How?"

"We have received preliminary information from the FBI. They have begun debriefing Ms. Lucas. Details are still forthcoming, but it appears she was attacked while following Collins to his drop location. Now that we know that location, we simply make a drop and see if we get a nibble. It's a long shot but worth a try."

"Director..." Darcy locked gazes with Elizabeth for courage. "I think perhaps I should be the person to do that."

"Why?"

"Collins told Elizabeth his mission was to turn me." Elizabeth squeezed his hand under the table. "I have a story to tell you." Darcy took a breath and began his tale. "For a long time I didn't think it mattered, but these things have a way of bubbling to the surface. I should know that, but if you coexist with secrecy long enough, it can start to seem like a normal way of life. Many times you don't see the danger of it until it's almost too late."

"Okay, you've got my attention."

"I was approached several years ago, indirectly, about providing classified CIA information to the other side. I have reason to suspect that Collins's handler was the same man who was behind that overture."

"Sounds like an interesting story."

"It begins with a discussion I had when I first joined the agency."

DARCY FORCED himself to remember that long-ago conversation with his father—one that forged an irreparable wedge between father and son and divided them forever.

"I need your help, son. I've left something...valuable behind in Czecho-slovakia. Something I can't retrieve without assistance."

"I'm just starting at the agency. I don't think I have the connections to help you."

"Perhaps not on your own, but I know someone...an old colleague, a friend, from the Cuban invasion. He says he knows people who can help me

retrieve my...valuables, but he needs information. Information you can provide."

"Hold it, Dad. Let me see if I've got this straight. You have a friend, a colleague—"

"Former colleague."

"Former colleague, who wants information only I can provide on..."

"Just information. On spies, traitors to their country. Whoever you run across in Britain, France, anyone anywhere that might be helping the US."

Darcy stared at his father in shock. "You've got to be shitting me. What you're asking...good god, Dad. It's treason! What could possibly be so important that you'd be tempted to risk everything—your life—hell, my life for it?"

"It's very valuable. I can't explain right now. I'm working on legal channels to extract it, but as a backup, if you could just meet with him...talk to him. It might be enough to get what I need out of Prague. And then you're free and clear. You don't ever need to talk to him again, if you don't want."

"You're insane. I'm not risking my life for some property you left behind on a business trip. I ought to turn you in right now."

"For what? I hadn't seen this man for years until I contacted him a few months ago. I'm not any part of what he's doing. I'm just telling you the cost of his assistance. So, you should think carefully before you say anything to your agency. That would kill your career before it's even begun.

"William, it's not just 'some property.' I know what I'm asking. It's not as if I'm proud of it. You don't need to tell this man anything substantial right now. Just talk to him. He'll pay handsomely just for a meeting with you."

"You think I'd do this—for money? It's treason, and you can go straight to Hell!"

There was a long silence as the two men stared at each other, one with fury in his eyes, the other with desperation. Finally, George Darcy looked away.

"You're right. I shouldn't have asked you. Forget I mentioned it. I don't know what I was thinking."

DARCY FINISHED HIS STORY, taking in the director's wide-eyed incredulity. "But I couldn't really forget, and he knew it. It was the last time we ever spoke."

"Why is this the first time we've heard about this situation, Darcy?"

"I don't know. Mostly because, within four months of that conversation, the old man was dead of a heart attack, and it no longer seemed to matter. To my knowledge, he never pursued the contact, and I certainly didn't participate. I was off in Europe on assignment."

"If it didn't matter, why not report it?"

"My own pride, I suppose. Embarrassment. Fear. And I didn't understand his desperation then. Once I found out what the 'thing of great value' was"—Darcy glanced at his sister—"my anger toward the old man softened. I could empathize more with a frantic man who had a child trapped behind an iron curtain.

"However, it was a mistake on my part not to report it. The fact remains that I knew there was a man somewhere who was in a position to recruit a CIA officer. I knew because he tried for me that one time through my father and, according to Collins, one time through Anneliese Vandenburg. Now that we know Collins's history, I assume this man succeeded in turning him."

"As far as you knew at the time, that discussion with your father was the end of it?"

"It was. I knew nothing about this recruiter, nothing—no name, no location, nothing, except that he was male and about my father's age. Look, everyone knows these recruiters are out there, that they exist. And I think we all know that, regardless of my innocence, with my history of being investigated by counterintelligence, this situation is a career-killer for me. If I stay with the agency, I'll never be free of the stigma."

"It would be troubling to any department, I have to admit."

"I want to stress that I've done nothing wrong. Except be born to a philandering, mercenary shipping magnate. Sins of the fathers, indeed." He covered Georgina's hand with his own. "There was good that came from it—good that's sitting here with us today. But I think

Ina could also say she suffered for our father's mistakes—much more than I."

Two weeks later, after cutting his own deal with the CIA brass, Darcy loaded the drop described by Charlotte Lucas.

Darcy waited at the Chinese Pavilion inside the National Arboretum, perched on a park bench. Precisely at 3:12 p.m., a man in an ivy cap, checked shirt, and khaki trousers sat beside him and opened a paper. He wore sunglasses and a mustache.

"Good afternoon, William. I have to say, you're the spitting image of your father."

"You knew my father?"

"Quite well actually. Back in the old days before the Bay of Pigs. And some after. He patched me up, sent me home."

"Are you the man he wanted me to talk to when I first joined the agency?"

"Let's just say I've been waiting a long time to meet you, William. A very long time."

"You handled Collins."

"While he could be handled, I did. Then he derailed, and I couldn't control him anymore. He was the spitting image of his father too. Self-destructive."

"You knew John Collins from his work with Operation Zapata?"

"Yes, indeed."

"I have to know, what made you do this? You're an American. What made you turn on your country?"

"See now, you're talking like a damn patriot. A Company Man. I'll have to bleed that out of you somehow."

"It's a reasonable question."

The man chuckled. "I suppose it is. What made me turn on my country? The short answer is: the same thing that will make you turn on yours. In essence, my country turned on me. Left me there to die with the others betrayed on Playa Girón. Second and third degree burns on my back and legs. Once I finally made it back home, it made me sick to hear the whole country idolize Kennedy. He let his intelligence officers and the Cuban rebels dive into a secret war. Then he washed his hands of them all. Pulled back all the air support. We called and called until we could call no more, and no help came.

"Then, after it all blew to hell, the CIA shoved aside the officers involved, tossed them out like bad apples. Bill Collins knew all about that. His father lost his career, lost everything, tried to drown his misery in a bottle—but the bottle drowned him instead. Well, I wasn't going down that road. My career at the CIA was over." He beamed a smile over his newspaper. "So I re-invented myself. Made a new career, a new life—one where I was wellpaid for a change."

"I understand, I guess. A little bit. The CIA shunned me after Prague, and my career was dead in the water after that. Just took me a while to see it. I don't want to end up like Collins, either one of them."

"John Collins had an unstable streak. Unfortunately, he passed that instability down to his son. Young Bill could have just taken the KGB's money and run, but the money wasn't enough after a while. He wanted *respect* or some such nonsense. Then he developed that obsession with the East German girl. A man who can't be controlled by money—well, he can't be controlled at all. He drives his own boat, so to speak, for good or for ill."

"My father didn't fit that mold."

"No. George Darcy was a man of substance. He didn't let the Bay of Pigs ruin him or his shipping business. He had the financial means and the psychological fortitude to weather the storm. He even helped a few of us out along the way. Helped me 're-enter civilian life' better than any VA man because he helped me set up my own business."

"Did he know what your 'business' was?"

"I think he was smart enough to figure out what was under the surface. And then he was smart enough to turn a blind eye. We avoided each other for the most part."

"Until I joined the agency."

"The man was tough until he found that by-blow daughter of his. Then he crumbled like a stale cookie. He came blubbering to me—after years without a word from him—to ask me for my help."

"You owed him. He brought you home."

"No." The old man's voice sharpened. "He owed me. I almost died getting his cargo to Cuba. It's not my fault it never reached its destination."

"You used my father—or tried to."

"I did. But no more than I've used many others over the years. You've done the same. We use people all the time. Use them up and spit them out."

They were silent for a minute. Finally, the older man went on.

"Just so we're clear, you and I. I know that Collins is gone. Most likely he's dead. I've been in this business long enough to know that chances are better than even that this overture of yours is a trap. That you are less than sincere, shall we say, in your offer."

"I told you: Collins gave you up. I thought you might be my father's former contact, so I searched Collins's place first before the FBI got there. That's how I found the drop location."

"How did you know about the search?"

"I have...a contact. She said..."

"She?"

"Yeah, so?"

"Interesting."

"If you think this is a trap, why are you here talking to me?" The older man shrugged. "It's worth the risk. You're the coup de grace, young man. The finishing touch on an almost twenty-year run. I'm an old man. I've served my handlers and my own interests well. And I'm willing to take the chance that you are a bona fide asset. I know I haven't been successful so far, but who knows? Perhaps the third time's the charm. What you could do for the KGB is astounding. So, are you interested at all in what they can offer you?"

"I suppose that depends on what they can offer me."

"Money?"

"I don't need money, but I would take money—as a symbol of their respect. How much *respect* could I command?"

"You cough up the names of CIA assets overseas? You could command a lot."

"In cash, correct? I don't want to leave a paper trail."

"Definitely. We'll set up some procedures and a new drop location at our next meeting. I'm too old to sit on these infernal park benches for long."

"Suit yourself. You're the boss."

"I like you, William. I always have."

"Since all of ten minutes ago?" The man chuckled. "We've met before perhaps. You're not the only one who's a master of disguise."

"What should I call you?"

"How about—Pops?" He stood and stretched, his hands on his lower back. "Check our current drop in a month for instructions."

He ambled slowly up the path, a slight limp in his step.

Darcy sat for several minutes, staring without seeing at the trees and flowers, certain that this would be his last CIA mission.

He was going to despise it.

35

The Park Coffee Shop, Washington, DC
February 1984

"TABLE FOR ONE?"

"You think?"

"Don't get smart with me, young man. It isn't in your best interests, and I'm not particularly happy with you right now."

Darcy followed the older man to a table in the corner.

"Cuppa joe?"

"Sure."

"I'll bring it right out."

Darcy shuffled in his seat, staring out at the cold sunlit winter morning.

"Here you go. Milk, no sugar, right?"

He nodded.

"I brought two cups. It's early, and the cafe is empty, so I thought I'd join you." The blue eyes twinkled with amusement. "Sorry to get you out of a warm bed."

"And out of the warm woman in it?"

Amusement turned icy cold. "I think that remark is a bit inappropriate."

"Not sure why you'd care about the remark...or the woman."

"I do care about her after a fashion. She's yours, after all, and I look out for my assets. I did have to deal with that business with Collins. He sure went after her when his back was up against the wall."

"And you had no responsibility in that?"

"I helped make the monster perhaps, but I couldn't let him harm her. It was a real dilemma for me." The old man shook his head.

"The universe plays cruel tricks on everyone."

"So it does, you included. Thank goodness, you took care of my problem for me. I feel guilty about that, but I'll get over it—and probably sooner than I should. But moving forward."

"What do you want now?"

"I'm becoming impatient. Your intel has been lackluster so far. My comrades at the Soviet Embassy say they're having trouble verifying the information you gave me at our last meeting. It's time to cough up some assets, William. I think we now have...shall we say...the proper motivation to convince you."

"I'm still not sure about this. It's a big step, giving up real people instead of information. What happens if I say no?"

"You won't want to do that. You have...so much more to lose now. Your career or maybe even your life is at stake. No longer something you can throw away. Think of your new wife and your unborn child."

"How do you know about Elizabeth's pregnancy?"

"I keep my eye on her."

Darcy tried his best to bluff. "I could leave her in half a second and never look back."

"I don't think so."

"You have no idea what I'm capable of."

"Oh, I think I do. I received an interesting letter several months ago. As the letter principally concerned yourself, perhaps you deserve to know its contents."

"I don't know what you mean."

"No?" The older man pulled out a letter and peered down his nose at it. "You'll be shocked to know the source of my information. This letter is from the late, great Comrade Collins."

"Your golden boy."

"At least until he panicked after your sister was rescued from Czechoslovakia. Who knew that his attendance at an unimportant dissident's meeting in Prague would have such far-reaching effects—for all of us? After that, he went down a road the KGB couldn't navigate for him anymore. He went rogue, as they say. So then, he simply had to go away. But that's a story you already know. Interestingly enough, he was the one who provided the means of your downfall—with this letter." The older man waved the paper in the air.

Darcy cast a surreptitious look around the cafe.

"Don't worry, son. No one's watching or listening in. We're not even open for business yet, but I think we're about to be, you and I." The warm, engaging smile was familiar enough to send a shiver down Darcy's back.

Mr. Baker opened an old, creased envelope. "Would you like me to read it? The decoded version of course. So you know the entire story?"

"Suit yourself. You're the boss."

"'*Comrade:*

I offer congratulations on the capture and execution of the traitor known to the CIA as Top Coat. I know that my source was invaluable in the success of that mission, and she has assured me of her continued support, even though she is currently working undercover in East Berlin.'

"He goes on to talk up his own meager contributions to that op, but I won't sport with your impatience by reading the rest of that obsequious drivel. Collins always put way too much unnecessary information in his communiqués. Now, here is the part that pertains to you:

"'*I have news that may interest you. I know in the past, you expressed some interest in another possible recruit inside the CIA. In accordance with your plan, a team of officers is now investigating this man. The lead on that assignment is GW, but he's being assisted by EB, who is undercover. (GW has real possibilities for us. He has the weaknesses we can capitalize upon, particularly financial obligations he can't fulfill. He's impulsive; however, that may end up being a fatal flaw.)'"*

The older man stopped, took a sip of his coffee. "You know, most people saw Collins as a numb-nuts, but he could ferret out a man's weaknesses in the blink of an eye. Had a real talent for it. Maybe because he was such as weak man himself."

"Still not sure what any of this has to do with me."

"Have patience, my young friend, I'm getting to it...

"'Your interest in the London Fog has always baffled me because I projected he would be a difficult nut to crack and not worth the effort. But recent observations in Budapest, East Berlin, and here at Langley have led me to believe that, although money won't work on him because he has no need of it, something else—or rather someone else—will. He's developed a tendre for another agent, this EB—his interpreter from Budapest, a woman whose assignment dictated she follow him to East Berlin. He tries to hide the attraction, and the woman herself seems oblivious, but it's apparent to anyone with trained observational skills that he's obsessed with her. I believe I can manipulate GW into sending her into his arms, as it were, while he's in the agency's bizarre exile down in the Caribbean. It's perfect—he's been ostracized, separated from his powerful friends like CB, and appears to have lost his lady to the demands of her career. She's certainly been hard at work and a little too close for my comfort since her return from East Germany.'

"Imagine my shock when I learned that this young woman and the field officer investigating you were the very same person!

"It was only later after he disposed of Wickham that I realized Collins was out of control and his days were numbered. His panic-based decision-making on a Tobago beach sealed his fate. He was a lost cause, but perhaps he served his purpose with this nugget of information. It gave way to a previously unknown path leading to you. A viable honey trap! Impoverished Americans think with their wallets, but the wealthy ones? They always think with their libidos. I just had the wrong honey. I had tried to get to you before with poor Anneliese and failed.

"But let's go on, shall we?

"'My reason for cautioning you is this: this young woman has no obvious weaknesses we can capitalize on. Her life up to this point has been her job. If she were smart, she would jump at this chance; the London Fog is rich and powerful—and could boost her career immeasurably—but I'm not sure she has either the sagacity or cynicism to see it that way.'

"Personally, I think he underestimated her. Of course, he had no idea that I had another connection to Elizabeth." The older man smiled brilliantly. "But you know, don't you?"

"I suspected, based on a discussion she and I had once."

"So you kept your ear to the ground and went into the agency archives." He nodded thoughtfully. "Very smart. You are a very smart man, Darcy. Like your father."

"I should have turned you both in when he approached me about you."

"Perhaps you should have, given the way things have turned out. Why didn't you?"

"I never thought it would matter. I never understood the hook you had in him. Then he was gone, and it seemed to be over."

"Until you found out about Jirina. Yes, he wanted my help to get her out. The diplomatic channels were deteriorating, and he thought he was running out of time. He was—just not in the way he anticipated. His little daughter trapped in limbo, and him unable to help or guide her. No wonder he came to me for help. Although we had parted ways years before, he knew I would...empathize with his predicament."

Darcy laughed. "There's not a drop of empathy in you, you cold-hearted son-of-a-bitch."

"You misjudge me, my son. May I call you 'my son'? It has a nice ring to it. I always wanted a son."

Darcy ignored that topic. "In the end, Jirina didn't need either of you."

"Well, that's debatable but a moot point now. Your father's untimely death forced her to take her fate in her own hands. She may not have needed us, but she managed a world of trouble that made her need a whole lot more than I could deliver. However, you, the dutiful brother, provided—a little late, but you've been making up for lost time."

"She's been moved from Barbados now. You'll never find her. You can't use her to get to me. Not now."

"But Elizabeth? She's a different matter. What will the CIA's little darling do once she finds out what you really are?"

"And what am I exactly? I'm the latest victim of 'sins of the father being visited on the son.' As for Elizabeth..."

"Yes?"

"You underestimate her. Plain and simple."

"Ah, how sweet. Love hopes all things, endures all things, does it not?"

"You know, the world is evolving. Far-reaching changes that will leave you and your kind with nothing. I don't know when that will happen, but I've been behind the Iron Curtain, and I've heard the rumblings of the people. Communism is a façade that will crumble, maybe in just a few short years. When that happens, you'll all be extinct, like dinosaurs." Darcy stood up. "I've made up my mind. I'm done here, and I'm done with you."

"You've come too far to go back now, William. Go on home to your young, beautiful wife and tell her...well, never mind. I'll tell her myself. It will be a shock no doubt, but then a girl likes to be crossed in love now and again. Who knows, Darcy? I might try for her next."

"She rose from your ashes, Tom. She's four times the intelligence officer and ten times the human being you'll ever be."

"I hope she's the forgiving sort, for your sake, but don't count on it. She is my daughter after all. I'm so proud of her."

The National Mall, Washington, DC
June 1984

NESTLED IN A GROVE OF TREES, Darcy sat on a bench within view of the Vietnam Veterans Memorial, holding his wife's hand in silence. They watched the tourists amble by the wall in a subdued, reverent procession belied by the bright vacation T-shirts, sun visors, and cameras around their necks. A few stopped to lay a sheet of paper against a name and rub over it with a piece of charcoal or chalk, imprinting the name as a memento of a friend or loved one who now belonged to the ages.

Elizabeth looked up at him and smiled her reassurance while they waited for their friend. "You know, I think this memorial is my favorite."

"How so, darling?"

"It never fails to move me. It starts out small, a scattering of names at your feet. You hear the chatter of people around you. On a day like this, you see the sunshine, feel the breeze on your face, but while you walk alongside the wall, the names grow—and you gradually sink deeper and deeper into the ground. Suddenly, you realize that the wall's enormity has dimmed the sunlight and muted the sounds of life. All you see is the tragedy of a lost war, but then as you continue through the memorial, a quiet reverence takes over. If you keep walking, the despair dissipates little by little. At the wall's end, you return to the present, level with the grass again and back in the world of the living, but you realize the quiet stays with you. You're forever changed by that walk alongside the names of the fallen. Yet you know you will move on."

He leaned over, kissed her mouth, and wiped the little tears that sprang from her eyes. "Are you all right, sweetheart?"

She nodded. "Emotional. Pregnancy hormones, most likely."

"That's all?"

"Maybe not all. But we're doing the right thing."

"He's your father. For many years he was your hero."

"That was all an illusion."

"An illusion that helped shape who you are. Losing him as an emotional anchor is a great loss and a heavy burden to carry."

She held his hand against her cheek. "It is."

"They will charge him with treason. He'll most likely die in prison."

"I idolized Tom Bennet for years, or I idolized the man I thought he was, but now I realize he was just a sperm donor. Jim's really my father because he raised me. Tom's influence was like the first steps of the Memorial Wall—it was the beginning, but it was only a small part of my story. It was what—and who—came into my life as I walked along that had the most influence on making me the person I am."

"And you yourself had the greatest impact of all—by the choices you made."

Charles Bingley approached their bench, hands in the pockets of his khaki dress pants. Darcy stood, and the two shook hands. Bingley leaned down and kissed Elizabeth's cheek.

"How are you doing, Mrs. Darcy?"

"I'm well, Deputy Director. How are you?"

"I'm fine, just fine."

"How's Johanna?"

He beamed. "Also well. She sent in her application for naturalization last month."

"Charles! Wow, that's wonderful news!"

"She wants to be a citizen before we tie the knot. Think I can pull some strings to make that happen a little faster?" He laughed.

"If anyone can, it's you." She gave him a fierce hug. "I'm happy for you both."

"Congratulations, Charles." Darcy clapped him on the shoulder.

"I hear we have some sad business to take care of. Do you have it?"

"I do." Darcy pulled a tiny cassette tape from his shirt pocket.

"Is it over?" Elizabeth asked.

"They're standing by to pick him up as soon as I verify I have the last information. He didn't suspect you were wired?"

"I wasn't. At least not in the traditional way."

"Then how?"

"One of Ina's newfangled listening devices. Elizabeth operated it from the alleyway."

"Very clever. Can we get our hands on one of those?"

"You should ask her; it's her prototype."

Bingley looked down as he dug a little trough in the gravel with his shoe. "Are you at peace with this situation, my friend?"

Darcy nodded. "After Elizabeth, Ina, and I put our heads together, this seemed like the best solution. Not the easiest, not without consequences, but the best. A solution that would give us a real future."

"Are the rumors I hear true? You're leaving the agency?"

"It's a condition of my deal. In exchange for giving them Tom Bennet, the agency will treat me as if I were a triple-agent. I'm not blameless. I couldn't identify Tom Bennet—or Baker, as he was known at The Park Café all those years. But I knew such a man existed, and I wasn't forthcoming. I deluded myself into thinking that, when my father died, it would all go away—that Tom had no one left to handle. I thought the disguise was over."

"I could talk to some people. We could still make a place for you in the agency."

"No. Thanks, but it isn't where I should be. Too much has happened, and there will always be suspicion in some circles about my actions, my motives."

"The London Fog is a legend around the agency water coolers. You'll be missed."

Darcy laughed. "I highly doubt that." He draped an arm around Elizabeth's shoulders. "Besides, I'll still get to see my real friends there from time to time, now that my wife is heading up her team in counterintelligence."

"What will you do?"

"I'm going to assume the blissfully mundane position of president of my family's company in Baltimore. When the director sent me off to Trinidad, it was one of the options I entertained: running the family business and settling down with a modern-day Southern belle. So I guess I did it after all in a convoluted fashion."

"Best of luck to you both." Bingley stood, offered his hand and a one-armed hug to Darcy and another kiss to Elizabeth. Then he walked away.

The Darcys sat on the bench for several more minutes. They heard the shrill call of a police siren, and Elizabeth wondered if that might be the sound signaling the end of Tom Bennet. But no, he would most likely be taken quietly without fanfare or noise, never to be seen or heard from again. She rose and pulled her husband to his feet.

"Let's go home."

He kissed her hand like a gallant gentleman in a Regency romance, and they turned from the sadness of the Vietnam Memorial Wall, taking with them the lessons learned from tragedy and the quiet acceptance that follows in their wake.

Finis

Dearest Reader:

Thank you for letting me tell you a story! If you enjoyed *Undeceived*, please consider leaving a review on your blog, an ebook distributor, social media, or your favorite reader site. Reviews help other readers decide if they, too, would like a book.

So reach out :)

Website: www.karenmcox.com

If you would like to read some more of my stories and get tidbits of authorly goodness in your inbox from time to time (updates, sales, book recommendations, etc.), I want to invite you to receive my News & Muse Letter. It comes with 3 free short stories you can download. (You can access the News & Muse Letter from my website.)

I love to hear from readers, so don't be shy. You can contact me through social media, my website, or on-line stores.

Happy Reading!

BOOK GROUP QUESTIONS

For use in book group discussions, tea times, or happy hour conversations—

Q: *Undeceived* is clearly inspired by Jane Austen's *Pride and Prejudice*. How do Elizabeth Bennet and William Darcy in *Undeceived* compare to Austen's?

Karen's Answer: In Austen's story, both Elizabeth and Darcy learn to see their own mistakes in judgment, and we love them because they discover their faults and gain humility but never lose their dignity or integrity. We also love that they learn these lessons from each other. In *Undeceived*, Elizabeth begins as a naïve young officer who is so swept up in the excitement of her new career that she doesn't realize she's setting out with a whole set of dubious beliefs and expectations. Like Austen's Darcy, my Darcy believes he's the smartest person in the room, but he learns wisdom over the course of the book, and sort of reintegrates humility back into his life.

Q: How did the modern setting and the mystery dynamic compare to the original?

Karen's Answer: The modern setting dictates that the characters (particularly the women) have more freedom. Actually, the mystery and the espionage dynamics were useful plot devices in that they restricted characters' behavior in ways parallel to Austen but still believable in modern times. For example, after the attempt on Elizabeth's life, she is left waiting and wondering in a way that mirrors the way Austen's Elizabeth was forced to await her fate after Lydia runs off with Wickham. Unless there are special circumstances involved, modern women have a lot more control over their lives than those in Regency times.

Q: In this modern mystery, most of the characters translate easily and are readily identified with Austen's counterpart characters. Was any character a surprise?

Karen's Answer: One example of a character I tweaked from Austen's interpretation is Anneliese Vandenburg (her name is a clue to her Austen counterpart.) She is the woman who everyone pulling the strings thinks Darcy should fall for, but he doesn't. However, she doesn't act like her Austen character much at all, so at first it's hard to see the parallel.

Q: So, how does the Bill Collins in *Undeceived* compare to Austen's Mr. Collins?

Karen's Answer: There are a lot of similarities to Austen's Collins: social/career climbing, ingratiating, annoying. But I think he will surprise readers in the end.

Q: And how about this George Wickham compared to Austen's Wickham?

Karen's Answer: Wickham is easy to write into a modern story: a handsome flirt, a self-made "victim" with a gift for smooth, persuasive talk. Who doesn't know at least one person like that in our modern era?

Q: It's highly unusual in *Pride and Prejudice* variations to depict Mr. Bennet as he was written in *Undeceived*. What do you think inspired his creation?

Karen's Answer: I think the Mr. Bennet in *Undeceived* mirrors Austen's in that he's a big influence on Elizabeth (albeit sometimes to her detriment), but he's unavailable to truly guide her. He, like the original Mr. Bennet, leaves his daughter to figure life out on her own.

Q: At the heart of this mystery is a love story. When do you think Elizabeth fell in love with Darcy and why?

Karen's Answer: Elizabeth always is attracted to Darcy, even from the first minute, because, as she discusses with Charlotte, "Let's face it, he's hot." But like Austen's Elizabeth, she really falls for him after she sees Pemberley. In *Undeceived,* Pemberley (located in Barbados) is beautiful but not the overwhelming estate it is in *Pride and Prejudice.* But it serves its purpose in that it is the backdrop against which she sees another side of Darcy—a glimmer of the real man, someone who cares about her and will treat her well. Plus, he really is hot.

Q: The sisters in *Pride and Prejudice* are a big part of that story. How do Elizabeth's relationships with the women in *Undeceived* compare?

Karen's Answer: Being an intelligence officer on assignment abroad sort of negated the influence of sisters on the story, but each "sister" is mentioned in at least a minor way: a fellow recruit, a friend in Budapest, Wickham's girlfriend in West Germany. Jane (as in the original story) plays the biggest role in the form of Johanna.

Q: What inspired do you think inspired the author to set the story at the end of the Cold War? Is it a good choice for a *Pride and Prejudice* variation?

Karen's Answer: In the Acknowledgments, I blame my husband (tongue in cheek) and his idea to mash up the movie *No Way Out* and *Pride and Prejudice.* That was where the idea started, but as I researched and read, it took on a fascination of its own. The 1980s were an interesting time in the CIA: Angleton's "molehunt" was over, but the agency was still disrupted by the aftereffects of it, Casey was using officers with "non-official cover" more often, and then there was the case of the real double agent, Aldrich Ames. Just a few years later, in 1989, the Berlin Wall came down, and a cascade of sweeping political changes followed in Europe. Also, the 1980s seemed to me a time of transitions, sort of like walking on a beach the morning after a wild party—feeling a little discombobulated, an old, tired kind of quiet, trash strewn about. How does one pick up and move to the new day, the next thing? In a way, *Undeceived* is all about leaving the familiar behind, taking what can be salvaged from it, and forging ahead into a future that's different and hopefully better than what you had imagined.

GLOSSARY

.38 Special: the nickname for a revolver with a rimmed, centerfire cartridge designed by Smith & Wesson

Asset: a person within an organization or country who provides information for an outsider or spy

B and E: Breaking and Entering, e.g., burglarizing a locked home or office

CIA: Central Intelligence Agency, a US federal agency that coordinates government intelligence activities outside the United States

COS: Chief of Station, the top U.S. Central Intelligence Agency official stationed in a foreign country

Cardan Grille: a method of writing hidden messages in which a rigid paper or thin piece of metal with rectangular cutouts exposes a secret message when placed over ordinary-looking text

Cover: An operative has "official" cover when employed in an organization with diplomatic ties to his or her government, e.g., working in an embassy or consulate. Official cover gives the intelligence officer diplomatic immunity and protects him or her from severe punishments typically given to captured spies. See below: NOC

Cut-Out: a courier used to pass information in a foreign or hostile place

Dead drop: a designated place for receiving instructions or money

FBI: Federal Bureau of Investigation, a US agency that carries out investigations for the Attorney General and is charged with safeguarding national security

FUBAR: military slang for a completely messed up situation

GDR: the German Democratic Republic, commonly referred to as "East Germany"

Handler: the intelligence officer responsible for an information source (asset), also called a case officer

KGB: the intelligence and internal-security agency of the former Soviet Union

Langley: metonym/nickname for the headquarters of the Central Intelligence Agency

MI6: the Secret Intelligence Service of the United Kingdom that works overseas, analogous to the US CIA

MIA: Missing in Action, also used colloquially to describe someone who is not where he is expected to be

Mole: a spy who is part of and works within the ranks of an enemy's government or intelligence agency, a double agent

NOC: Non-official cover—a "NOC" officer has a covert identity and cover story, and as such, does not have the same safety net of diplomatic immunity as an officer with official cover, if he or she is caught spying

SIP: Standard Introduction Procedures—established procedures for meeting an unknown officer

Stasi: the secret police in the former GDR (East Germany)

State Department: a common name for the US Department of State, which sets forth and maintains the foreign policy of the US

The Farm: nickname for Camp Peary, a CIA training facility near Williamsburg, VA

USBER: an acronym that referred to the State Department's presence in West Berlin, which was not an official embassy, also called US Mission Berlin

ACKNOWLEDGMENTS

Undeceived was a mighty undertaking: over two years of research, reading, postulating, writing, and editing that was by turns exhilarating and challenging. Sometimes this novel pushed me to my limits, and the process was fraught with frustration and uncertainty. As with most of life's mighty undertakings, a laundry list developed of people whose help was crucial at various points along the path.

I know it is customary for authors to say that a book wouldn't exist without their spouse's support, but for *Undeceived*, that statement is quite literally the truth. My husband pushed for the story concept, listened to the manuscript, asked key questions, and answered a few as well. He championed *Undeceived* from the get-go, so he gets the first thank you.

Second, I want to thank those who provided me invaluable feedback. My editor, Christina Boyd, delivered no-nonsense critiques that took a cloudy nugget of a story and clarified and polished it—all accompanied by an unflagging enthusiasm for the project that kept me believing in it. She went the extra mile, made the novel twenty times better, and I'm extremely grateful for her expertise.

I received wonderful input from Ágnes Nógrádi, who helped with Hungarian vocabulary and diacritical marks, and gave me valuable insights into Hungarian culture that improved those chapters immensely. Lynnette Berry provided assistance with the East German sections, giving me suggestions for wording and tidbits of information from that time before reunification. Thanks, ladies!

I also wish to thank the staff at Meryton Press for publishing the first edition of *Undeceived*.

Additionally, I want to extend thanks to the readers of this book. What you hold in your hands is fiction but in many places, it is a delicate dance between history and my imagination. Sometimes I took necessary artistic license with events, locations and organizations, and I appreciate your willingness to suspend disbelief and immerse yourself in the imaginary world of the story. In the years since I became a published author, no encouragement has meant more to me than the words of a happy reader. Whether it's a comment by email, a recommendation on a readers' site, a line on social media or my author blog, or a review—I always appreciate hearing from you.

And finally, I want to express my gratitude for Jane Austen: a writer, a lady, a wit, a genius, and an inspiration. She was a true original, and the mold was broken after she left the world.

ABOUT THE AUTHOR

Karen M Cox is an award-winning author of five novels accented with history and romance: *1932, Find Wonder in All Things, Undeceived, I Could Write a Book,* and *Son of a Preacher Man,* and a novella, *The Journey Home,* a companion piece to *1932.* She also loves writing short stories and has contributed to four Austen-inspired anthologies: "Northanger Revisited 2015" appears in *Sun-Kissed: Effusions of Summer,* "I, Darcy" in *The Darcy Monologues,* "An Honest Man" in *Dangerous to Know: Jane Austen's Rakes and Gentleman Rogues,* and "A Nominal Mistress" in *Rational Creatures.*

Karen was born in Everett WA, which was the result of coming into the world as the daughter of a United States Air Force Officer. She had a nomadic childhood, with stints in North Dakota, Tennessee, and New York State before settling in her family's home state of Kentucky at the age of eleven. She lives in a quiet little town with her husband, where she works as a pediatric speech pathologist, encourages her children, and spoils her granddaughter.

Channeling Jane Austen's Emma, Karen has let a plethora of interests lead her to begin many hobbies and projects she doesn't quite finish, but she aspires to be a great reader and an excellent walker—like Elizabeth Bennet.

Made in the USA
Las Vegas, NV
05 September 2022